Life's Complicated

The Life Series, Volume 2

Sarah Catherine Knights

Published by Sarah Catherine Knights, 2023.

This is a work of fiction. Similarities to real people, places, or events are entirely coincidental.

LIFE'S COMPLICATED

First edition. April 19, 2023.

Copyright © 2023 Sarah Catherine Knights.

Written by Sarah Catherine Knights.

Table of Contents

Life's Complicated (The Life Series, #2) 1
Chapter 1 3
Chapter 2 15
Chapter 3 22
Chapter 4 38
Chapter 5 47
Chapter 6 60
Chapter 7 66
Chapter 8 80
Chapter 9 89
Chapter 10 96
Chapter 11 106
Chapter 12 116
Chapter 13 126
Chapter 14 141
Chapter 15 153
Chapter 16 180
Chapter 17 199
Chapter 18 219
Chapter 19 236
The Epilogue 254
Also by Sarah Catherine Knights 263

This book is dedicated to anyone whose life hasn't turned out as expected - which must be just about everyone.

Previously ... in 'Life Happens'

RACHEL, JEN AND GRACE have been friends since university where they formed a bond that has lasted into their early fifties.

They are all married: Rachel to ZACH, an airline pilot and they have two sons, GEORGE and HARRY. Jen is married to MIKE, whom she met at uni and who is now a property developer with a failing company; they have an only child, AMBER. Grace is married to LEO, a highly successful barrister, the son of one of the few black judges in the country. They have no children.

They arrange a holiday in Cyprus for the six of them in 2019. They rent a beautiful, old village house with a pool and courtyard. With its oppressive heat, beauty and culture, Cyprus acts as a stunning backdrop to love, hate and betrayal. They make friends with two Cypriots, ANDREAS and DEMETRIS, the latter being a young, good looking man who is attracted to Rachel.

Zach was an RAF Tornado pilot and visited Cyprus on two detachments. His friend, LIZ, still lives on the camp, having divorced her husband.

Rachel married Zach on the rebound and has not had a happy marriage. His controlling and jealous behaviour comes to a head in Cyprus and they split up over his affair with Liz. Rachel has always been in love with Mike. They slept together twice, once before his marriage and once after. Rachel is convinced that her first child is Mike's but has never told a soul.

Amber comes out to join her parents, unexpectedly. She reveals that she is pregnant and that she and Leo are in love. She has been working with Leo in his chambers and their friendship flourished, despite the age difference. Grace and Leo's marriage was over many years ago after several failed IVF attempts. A year before the holiday, Grace met and fell in love with ANNA, a fellow musician. They are having a baby together by sperm donor.

Amber's revelation has a devastating effect on the group but her parents must face up to the reality of their love. Jen worries about the lump she has found and Mike has to learn to live with both his own and Leo's betrayal. Grace and Amber look forward to their babies' arrival.

Rachel must move on from her marriage to Zach and her love of Mike; perhaps she can see a future with Demetris? The group dynamic is changed forever.

Chapter 1

Brighton, in August 2019, was rainy and windy – the sun and blue skies of their holiday were a distant memory. Rachel wished she could remember the warmth on her skin, but it was all gone now.

Jen had said she'd call that night and Rachel kept looking at her mobile to see if she'd missed her. She was so worried about Jen but didn't want to call her; she was dreading it being bad news.

She hadn't had any contact with Zach; the last time she'd seen him was when she'd left him at the villa and gone out with the others. He'd collected his stuff while she was out and she presumed he'd gone to Liz. He'd disappeared from her life that day; she could still remember the relief she felt when she got back to the villa and he wasn't there.

She'd also been relieved when the seat beside her on the flight home remained vacant; sitting next to him for four and half hours would have been awful. Part of her wondered where he was – had he delayed coming back to the UK? She doubted it, as he had to go to work, but if he *was* here, where was he living? He hadn't rung or texted; he was just proving how little he cared about her by his complete radio silence.

She could be dead for all he knew.

It had been strange coming back to their home, alone. Nothing had changed but at the same time, everything was completely different.

She'd felt vulnerable, but the house had silently wrapped its arms around her. She'd grown to love its rooms over the years; its garden and its outlook were beautiful and as she'd walked around it on that first day back, she'd felt at peace. She wanted to stay here, whatever happened. She'd sacrificed so many years at the altar of Zach's career and now it was *her* turn to be where she wanted to be. She was determined that the house would be part of the divorce settlement.

The location suited her too. Her business was near, she'd made a good circle of friends and she could be swimming in the sea within five minutes of leaving her front door. It was perfect. George and Harry weren't too far away either: they could hop on a train and be in Brighton in an hour.

She hadn't told either of them yet about their father. They'd rung her when she got back but she'd managed to divert the conversation away from him. She'd told them about Amber and Leo and that had been quite enough for them to take in. Neither of them could believe it; they asked lots of questions about Grace and Anna and the two babies that were expected at the end of the year.

She'd said goodbye to Demetris that night in Cyprus with a heavy heart. He'd kissed her on the cheek, saying "I will come to London soon." She wasn't sure he'd meant it but she'd hoped he did. Since she'd got back, she'd thought of him often. She'd see his face when she closed her eyes at night and remember him singing in the moonlight. She realised she was in danger of behaving like a love-struck teenager and would give herself a serious talking to.

You're only feeling like this because your husband has gone off with someone else. You can't have Mike, so you're idolising a random guy who showed a bit of interest in you. Stop being so pathetic.

Maybe she was just hanging onto the memory as a way of lessening the reality of her situation.

Her mobile suddenly came to life and the familiar ring chimed out. She'd been dreading this call; she'd had a bad feeling about what Jen was going to say. When they'd said goodbye at the airport, they'd hugged and Rachel had said, "It'll all be okay, you see. The surgery probably just want to confirm things with you," but even as she said it, she didn't believe her own words. They'd clung to each other and Jen, with tears in her eyes had said, "I'll be fine. I'll let you know."

As she'd hugged Mike goodbye, Rachel'd said, "Try to accept this new situation, Mike. No good will come of you pushing Amber and Leo away. You're going to be a grandad ... just think about that for a minute. It's such great news. And," she'd added quietly, "... you look after Jen for me, okay?"

"Jen's far more accepting of the situation than me. She's a much kinder person," he'd said. He, of course, didn't know the reason why she'd said *Look after Jen*. How could he? It was a secret between the three women.

She saw the name *Jen* on her phone and hesitated before pressing the green button.

"Hi, Jen ... I've been waiting to hear from you. Any news?" It seemed such a lame thing to say.

There was a gap before she replied. "Hi, Rachel. I'm sorry I haven't been in touch earlier, I'm sure you've been lonely in the house, there on your own."

This was so typical of Jen, thinking of others, before herself.

"Don't be daft. I've been fine. Now, tell me. What did they say?"

She knew before Jen even said anything, that it wasn't good news. There was something about the tone of her voice, the hesitations. Rachel sat down and noticed the clock said 19.05.

"Well ... it's what I thought ... I'd convinced myself that the lump was cancerous and it seems that I was right to think that way."

"Oh God, Jen. I'm *so* sorry. What did they say *exactly*? Surely they don't know what's going on, just from a mammogram?"

"No, they don't ... but they've advised a ... biopsy. And soon. I'm going in next week. So they must be worried."

Rachel stared at the vase full of yellow roses she'd bought back for herself from the shop; she lent forward and sniffed the perfume. She could hear the fear in Jen's voice. She tried to sound positive when she spoke.

"Well, that's brilliant that they're acting so quickly. If it's bad news, they'll be able to get it early, then."

There was a long silence that felt palpable.

"Yes, I suppose so."

"Have you told Mike?"

"Yes, I *had* to, as I'll be going into hospital. I told him this morning."

"How did he take it? Is he okay?"

"No ... not really. It's shaken him terribly. He had no idea, of course. I've had a couple of weeks to prepare myself, I suppose.

He's been dealing with problems at work and trying to come to terms with Amber's news. It just seems as if *everything's* going wrong at once."

Rachel hesitated; she was aware that she didn't want to say the wrong thing. "Look, Jen, Amber's news is *good* news and Mike's just got to get a grip. At the moment, you don't quite know what's going on with you, so until you know for sure, try to stay positive."

"Can you tell Grace for me? I don't think I can face having another conversation about it. Tell her not to ring me. It sounds strange, but I just don't want to talk to anyone at the moment."

"Okay, of course. Does Amber know?"

"No, I'm not going to say anything to her, unless I have to. She's in such a bubble of happiness at the moment, I don't want to spoil it for her."

"Oh, right. Don't you think she'd *want* to know?"

"Maybe ... but I'm going to wait until the results of the biopsy. Please don't tell her, Rachel."

"No, of course I won't. So, Mike's business ... what's happening?"

"He's talking to the bank ... but it's not looking very hopeful. It's hard to get loans these days and unless he does, the business ..."

"Look, Jen ... do you want me to come over? I can, easily. Millie did really well with the shop when I was away; it's all ticking along nicely. I could pop over any time."

"Rachel, that's so sweet of you ... but there's nothing you can do, honestly. You've got enough on your plate. Just knowing I can talk to you on the phone is good enough. But I promise I'll tell you if I need more support. Anyway, enough about me, have you heard from Zach?"

"Not a *thing*. I find it incredible that he can just walk away from the villa in Cyprus like that and not contact me at all. He's behaving very strangely. I think he must have come back by now but I've heard *nothing* from him. I'm expecting him to walk in the house any time. He's got a key, of course, and I keep imagining I hear the front door open. God knows what'll happen if he does come round."

"Long term, what do you want to happen?"

"It's got to be a divorce, Jen. There's no other way."

"Have you spoken to the boys yet?"

"Well, yes, I've *spoken* to them but I haven't told them what happened on holiday. I managed to avoid that but I know I've got to have a conversation. They never ring their Dad and he never rings them, so …"

"Do you think they'll be shocked?"

"I don't know, to be honest. They know we haven't been getting on for years, but you always think your parents will somehow stay together and be your parents forever, don't you? We're not real people as parents, are we? Harry's always been closer to his Dad than George; I think he might be quite upset … but thank God they've got their own lives now. George's job is very full on and Harry's just started at some fancy restaurant and his hours are ridiculous, so I don't want to bother them really, but they're both planning to come down next weekend, so I'll have to tell them then. Harry's not sure he can get the time off yet."

"I hope they *do both* come, Rach. You need to talk to them."

"I do. I can't say I'm looking forward to it, though."

"So ... I'm going to go now, Rach. I'm tired. I'll let you know what happens."

"Okay ... lots of love to you."

THE 'TODAY' PROGRAMME on Radio Four was blaring out of the speaker on the worktop in the kitchen the next morning. Rachel's mind was whirling round and round, thinking about all the orders she had to get ready that morning and the planning she needed to do for the wedding coming up. She was eating toast and drinking coffee as she thought about what the bride wanted: little posies at the end of all the pews, two altar pieces, four bridesmaids' flowers and the bride's bouquet, not to mention the men's button holes. It was going to be a big job and she needed to sit down today and make sure everything was in place.

Apart from the droning of the radio in the background, the house was quiet. These days, she felt more and more alone and was pleased to know that she had a busy day ahead.

Suddenly, she heard the familiar turn of the front door key. Her stomach flipped as she realised that it could only be one person. In the past, Zach might have called out and said 'hi', but there was nothing now and she heard the door close. Her heart was racing; she didn't know how she was going to react or what she was going to do. She stood up and went quickly to the sink, so that her back was to the door when he entered.

"Hello Rachel," he said. His voice was even, not angry; it was as if nothing had happened and he was coming home from work as usual. Her whole body felt 'on edge' and she was aware of a weakness in her legs that radiated all the way down to her feet.

What are earth am I going to say to him?

"Hello Rachel," he said again, a little louder, as if she was deaf.

"Yes, I heard you the first time, Zach, but to be honest, I was wondering how to respond."

She turned around and there he was, tanned and relaxed.

"Good of you to let me know you were coming," she said. "Am I meant to be pleased that you've now just walked back into the house? I had no idea where you were, you didn't ring me, you didn't text me. I could've been dead for all you cared."

"Rachel, don't be so dramatic. You knew exactly where I was."

"Did I?"

"Yes, of course you did. I was in Cyprus with Liz, after you chucked me out of the villa so kindly. I stayed on for a couple more days after the flight I was meant to catch and then I had to go straight to work when I got back, so I've been living in a B&B in Gatwick. I thought I'd come and see you today to work out what we're going to do. "

"Well, that's pretty straightforward as far as I'm concerned. I want to divorce. I want this house for me and the boys to live in. What you do, is up to you. I don't care anymore."

"So you want to carry on living in this house without me? How do you propose to fund that, then?"

Rachel walked away from the sink and sat down at the kitchen table, took a swig of coffee and stared at him. "I think it's the least you could do, under the circumstances. I love this house and I want to stay here. None of this is my fault. You're the one who's ruined everything. I followed you around so that you could pursue your career for years. Now it's *my* time to live where

I want to live. I'm sure we can work something out. I've got a successful business and I expect, with some financial advice, I can buy you out or something. Have you and your new girlfriend decided what you're going to do or was it just a fling because you were bored with my company?"

"It's too early to know what we're going to do. It wasn't just a fling, we've known each other for years. We get on and who knows, maybe I'm going to move to Cyprus? I haven't worked it out yet ... but in the meantime, I need somewhere to live and I intend to move in here."

"I don't think so," replied Rachel. "That's definitely not what I want and surely I have some say in it? You've made your decision. You left me to fend for myself in Cyprus and now I'd like you to leave me alone."

"I'm afraid that's not possible, Rachel. This is *my* house. If you remember rightly, I'm paying the mortgage and I have every right to live in my own house."

"But that'll be impossible, Zach. We can't be near each other without arguing. Oh my God. How did it ever come to this?"

She put her head on her hands and started crying. Crying had always annoyed Zach, he'd never been sympathetic in the past. It seemed to anger him; he was incapable of dealing with a woman's emotions.

"Oh, for Christ's sake, Rachel, tears aren't going to persuade me to live somewhere else, so you may as well stop right now."

She stood up, pushing her chair back roughly, so that it fell over backwards and she left the room. She walked to the stairs, ran up them as quickly as she could and crashed into the bathroom, slamming the door behind her.

She stared in the mirror; the make up that she'd put on earlier was smudged, there were black marks under her eyes. She got some cotton wool out of the cupboard and some cleanser and started scraping it all off her face. She'd always liked her reflection as a young woman but now all she saw was someone defeated, someone old and in her eyes, pathetic.

She put her face close to the mirror, pinched her cheeks, opened her eyes as wide as they'd go and then grabbing some loo roll, blew her nose and said out loud, "Come on, girl, get a fucking grip."

She wasn't going to let Zach get to her like this. She realised that he was right and that she probably had no right to stop him living in the house before any legal discussions had taken place so, before she could change your mind, she decided to let him stay, on condition he slept in a different room from her.

She redid her make up, took a deep breath, pulled the door open and went downstairs again.

Zach was calmly making himself a coffee; he didn't turn around as she entered the room.

"So... I've decided you can stay, on one condition and that is ... that you sleep in the spare room. We don't eat together and we avoid each other as much as possible. I will go to a solicitor tomorrow and start the ball rolling for a divorce. We need to tell George and Harry what's going on, I haven't told them yet and they need to know. They're coming down this weekend and I think we should tell them together."

"Well, it's good of you to let me stay," he laughed, "considering it's my house. I'll go and move my things into the spare room, I know when I'm not wanted. Maybe you can move Mike in instead of me?"

"What *are* you talking about? Don't bring Mike into this. He's got so much to contend with at the moment; you don't know the half of it."

"I'm sure I don't. The two of you made me sick, to be honest, on holiday. He was always defending you, he was always there, in the background, like your knight in shining bloody armour. If you're talking about me and Liz, what about you and him? You're far too close to him. Poor Jen, innocent Jen, has no idea you two lust after each other all the time."

"Don't be so ridiculous, Zach. What on earth are you talking about? We don't lust after each other. He's been my friend since uni. He's my best friend's husband. Of course, we're close."

"If you say so ... but I wasn't the only one who noticed on holiday, you know. I saw Grace looking at you two."

"Shut up Zach. I can't sit here any longer listening to you talking such crap. You think what you want to think. It's not me that ruined the holiday and broke this family up, so stop trying to put the blame on me. I'm going to work now, and when I get home, I really don't want to see you."

"That's fine by me. And how did your Greek lover boy react when you left, by the way? Did he declare undying love? You're so in demand at the moment. A young, greasy waiter, or a washed-up, overweight so-called friend. What a great choice."

"If you don't stop, Zach, I swear I might ..."

"You might do what?"

"I can't even bear to look at you."

She walked out of the kitchen, trying to look powerful and confident but feeling neither.

Had Mike and she let others see? She tried so hard to hide her feelings but maybe it was obvious to people who were looking closely. Grace had never said anything to her about it and she really didn't want to go there, talking to her.

She was going to have to put up with Zach's constant jibes and innuendos. Knowing what she did about Mike's business, Jen's illness and forthcoming hospital visit, she felt so guilty. She loved them both.

Grabbing her coat, she opened the front door and walked out into the windy Brighton streets. She breathed in deeply, taking the salty air down into her lungs, trying to dispel all thoughts of what Zach had said.

Breathe in for three ... and out, for four ... and repeat. She needed to calm herself in order to face the day.

She walked to the shop as quickly as possible. He'd made her late and upset but she decided to focus on the day ahead.

She couldn't prevent Zach from invading her space so she would simply have to enjoy the time when she was away from him.

Chapter 2

George woke up and gazed at Beth in the half-light; she was facing him, her breaths, rhythmical and soft. She looked so beautiful, her dark hair spread out on the white pillows. He didn't want to wake her; she was very late back last night from the hospital. Her job as a midwife was so unpredictable – he often wondered how she did it; he knew he certainly wouldn't be able to deal with terrible hours *and* life and death situations.

He sat up as gently as he could, so that the bed didn't groan and then stood up slowly. He glanced down at her but her breathing rhythm hadn't changed. He walked to the bathroom, trying to avoid the creaky, wooden plank near the door.

Standing under the shower, the hot water cascading around him, he slowly felt himself coming to life. He lowered the temperature and reached for the shower gel. Squirting some onto his hands, he rubbed himself vigorously all over, until he was covered in bubbles. He was using some of Beth's gel and the smell made him think of her. He was so lucky to have her; he'd known her now for a year and although they'd only lived together for a few months, he knew she was 'the one'. He was going to find the right moment to propose to her; he had no idea whether she'd say yes or not, but he hoped she would. She was always so tired and they got so little time together that it was almost impossible to find time for a romantic meal or weekend away. Maybe he'd try to persuade her to take a few days off so that they could go to Paris or somewhere equally romantic.

He rinsed himself, making sure all the soap was gone and turned off the tap. The bathroom was full of steam and was warm and cosy; he was reluctant to dry himself and head out into the cold of the rest of the flat. Still, he had to get to work, and he had to face the day. Having done his teeth, combed his wet hair and quickly shaved, he tiptoed into the bedroom and got dressed. Beth hadn't moved, except to bury herself a little further into the duvet.

Checking himself in the mirror, making sure there wasn't a fleck of toothpaste on his face, he went and put the kettle on. He was regretting having said to his mother that he'd go down to Brighton this weekend. He knew that Beth wouldn't be able to come with him, as she'd said she was on duty. He could have done with a quiet time in London, simply trying to get on top of everything that was happening at work. Working for a huge drinks company in the digital marketing department, wasn't the most exciting job in the world but, for some reason which he couldn't fathom, he enjoyed it. He had huge ambitions for himself and he was always looking for the next step up.

His father had always expressed his disapproval of his career choice. Zach had hoped George would go into the military, like he had; he'd always gone on and on about how wonderful the life was. But George had never felt that the military was for him. He didn't want a job where you were basically being trained to kill someone. Harry felt very much the same as him, so they were both a disappointment to their father. As a consequence, Zach never really asked any questions about his job or showed any interest in it at all. It didn't bother George anymore, he'd got used to having a distant relationship with his father.

It was very different with his mother; she was always asking him everything about his job (perhaps she asked a few too many questions) but at least she showed some interest. His job was really quite difficult to explain to people and so he'd answer her questions as generally as was possible.

Having grabbed a coffee and a couple of slices of toast, he rushed out, remembering to close the front door quietly.

He was lucky to live near Kings Cross; the tube was only a three minute walk. He hadn't got an Oyster card, he couldn't see the point. As he used his contactless card at the turnstile, he looked at his watch and realised that he would only just make the early morning meeting he'd planned.

As he was going down the escalator, he texted Beth:

On my way to work. I didn't want to wake you. I forgot to tell you that I'll be going to Brighton on Friday but I know you're working so I hope that's okay. I love you. You look gorgeous when you're asleep. XX

As he got to the platform, his tube was just approaching and he jumped on with hundreds of other people, everyone pushing and shoving, trying to get a seat. He ended up standing, holding onto the loops above him, next to some smelly old bloke. God, how I love London sometimes, he thought to himself. He only had three stops to go until he had to get off to change trains. This was his daily commute; often he wished he lived in the country and could work in a shed at the bottom of his garden. But to get on in his line of work, you had to be in London.

The next train wasn't quite as crowded and he got a seat. He decided to text Harry to ask if he was coming to Brighton too.

Hi Hazza, How are you doing, mate? How's the job? I must bring Beth to the restaurant one evening. Any chance of a discount? Ha ha! Anyway, are you coming to Mum's this weekend? If you are, shall we travel down together? I'm sure it must be hard to get away but maybe you could come just for the day? Let me know. G.

George couldn't think of anything worse than cooking all day, but Harry had always wanted to be a chef. He hadn't wanted to go to university (much to their father's disgust). He'd gone to college to do some nutrition and hygiene courses and then gone straight into being a very lowly and poorly-paid kitchen assistant in a busy hotel restaurant. He hated the hours and the pay but he loved the buzz of the kitchen and the camaraderie.

He'd gone through several jobs; the latest was at a slightly higher level. He was a sous chef, working for some famous chef George had never heard of, who Harry said was amazing. George wondered how Harry would get away at the weekend, because surely weekends are the busiest time?

His train drew into the station, he filed along all the windy corridors with everyone else, grabbing a coffee from Costa in passing when he emerged into the main atrium. I wonder how much money I spend on coffee, he thought, as he tapped his contactless card yet again. If I really want to save money, I should bring a flask and a sandwich to work but that would be crazy – no one does that. Life in London is one long round of takeaway coffees, takeaway meals from Pret, quick pints in pubs, Ubers and expensive meals in overpriced restaurants. Not forgetting the astronomical rents... still he loved the London vibe and he couldn't imagine living anywhere else.

As he entered the revolving door at the entrance of his building, his boss was just coming out of a door near him.

"What time do you call this?" she laughed, glancing at her watch.

Although she said it as a joke, he felt that perhaps she was making a point. He knew he was cutting it fine, but he wasn't late. He was just about to say something about his journey or a late night, in mitigation, when she said, "Don't worry, George, I'm only pulling your leg. Can you get everybody into room 42 and I'll be up in a sec."

"Okay, see you up there," he said, wishing he'd arrived a few minutes earlier. She was one of those bosses who always seemed to catch him out and made him feel guilty, when really there was nothing to feel guilty about. Maybe one day he would start his own company, be his own boss and not have to answer to anyone.

Unfortunately, he couldn't see that happening any time soon.

BETH WOKE UP WITH A start. She couldn't think where she was. She must've had a bad dream. She couldn't remember what it was about; all she knew was that her heart was beating fast and she felt hot and sweaty. She vaguely remembered being stuck in something and not being able to get out.

Sitting up slowly, she looked at her mobile which was on the bedside table and saw it was 11 o'clock. For a moment, she wondered how come she was still in bed so late in the morning, but then a wash of relief cascaded through her, as she realised she had the day off. She still wasn't used to a midwife's hours. She found it difficult to work all night and sleep during the day. Her shift yesterday meant that she'd left the hospital at one o'clock and didn't get home until two am.

Her body felt exhausted but she looked back on last night's birth with so much joy. Twins born to a first time mother, healthy and already feeding well. Her poor sleep was certainly compensated by these wonderful events that happened on most of her shifts. She'd had her fair share of difficult births and even a baby death, which at the time, made her want to give her career up, but her friends and colleagues rallied round and persuaded her to stay and move forward.

She reached for a cigarette from a packet that was also on the bedside table and lit one guiltily, knowing how much George hated her smoking (and particularly inside the flat). He couldn't understand why she didn't give it up. He made the point that if you worked for the NHS, you really ought to set a good example – which was easy for him to say, as he'd never smoked in his life.

She lay back against the pillows, drawing the smoke into her lungs, enjoying the process and trying to forget the consequences.

She read the text from George, which made her start thinking about eventually having to meet his family. He'd rarely ever mentioned Zach, which she found strange, but he was obviously very close to his mother.

She was pleased that she was working this weekend and had a good excuse not to go with him. She couldn't work out *why* she persistently found reasons not to go but she thought it was because for some reason, it made their relationship more 'committed' if she met his family. She was happy with the situation as it was, with them just living together with no pressure. She knew that his parents would start talking about marriage and babies and she had no intention of doing either of those things at the moment. She loved George, but didn't feel ready for marriage and certainly not for babies. People assumed that, because she was a midwife, that automatically made her an earth mother, someone who would want to fill her life with numerous children – but this was far from the case. She wasn't even sure she ever wanted her own. Although living with someone was a kind of commitment, marriage was a step too far for her. She actually felt sick at the thought of it.

She shook her head, to try to get the picture out of her mind and got out of bed. She went into the shower to wash her body and cleanse her mind. She was sure that Rachel and Zach were nice people but she had no desire to meet them. She didn't want to be part of his family; she'd never been close to her own family and didn't want to get involved in someone else's.

When she got out of the shower she decided she ought to text him back, so she wrote:

Hi George – how's work going? I've only just woken up and I'm going to the shops this afternoon. That's fine about the weekend. See you later xx

A bit matter of fact, she realised, but she wasn't the effusive sort.

She got herself dressed and grabbed a yoghurt and coffee before heading out. She passed a young girl struggling with a pushchair and a toddler on the way to the shops.

That's not the life I want, she thought, and went on her consciously single way.

Chapter 3

George caught the train to Brighton at 7:30, after work. He hadn't been able to get away earlier than that; he'd had to text his Mum to say he'd be late.

The train was packed and noisy, full of people drinking and eating on their way for a night out in 'London-by-the-Sea' that would be very different from his own. They were clearly on a mission to get as drunk as possible before getting to the clubs. He put his AirPods in and tried to knock out the sound of stupid laughter and conversation. Harry had texted to say that he wouldn't be able to get there until Sunday, which was expected, as Saturday nights are so busy in the restaurant. He'd managed to wangle the Sunday lunchtime shift off, as he'd been working for six days on the trot.

As the train approached the station he, along with all the other travellers, stood up in anticipation of getting off. People were grabbing their bags from the overhead locker and pushing forward, to try and retrieve the bags from the luggage boxes near the door. A group of twenty year olds had been drinking pretty solidly all the way and were right now even louder and more annoying than they were before. One of them managed to knock over a bottle of red wine, which sent the contents flowing all over the table and onto the floor. They didn't seem to care about the mess and found it hilarious.

They made him feel as if he had grown up without realising it.

When the train eventually came to a halt and someone opened the doors to get out, everyone spilled out onto the platform like ants along a tree trunk and made their way to the barriers. Rachel had offered to come and collect him but he'd told her that he didn't know what time he'd get there, so he'd catch a bus.

He was able to catch a bus almost immediately, right outside the station which took him within five minutes' walk of his parent's house.

He always felt the same when he was in Brighton – a feeling that he had come *home*. He loved watching all the characters walking past, as he sat on the bus looking at all the familiar places of his childhood. While walking the last five minutes of his journey, he could smell the sea on the wind; part of him wished he could still live here.

Maybe one day, he thought.

"Hi there!" he called, as he let himself in with the key that he'd never given up. Rachel came out of the kitchen, threw her arms around him and squeezed him hard.

"Oh George, it's so lovely to see you. It feels like ages since I saw you last."

"Well, it hasn't been that long," he laughed, trying to extricate himself from her arms. "I saw you a week before you went to Cyprus. Is Dad here?"

"No, he isn't," Rachel said, wanting to steer well clear of all questions about Zach."He's working. I don't think we'll see him until Sunday ... I gather Harry can't come till Sunday either, so it's going to be just you and me. I don't often get you all to myself." She squeezed him again.

George couldn't help thinking that there was something not quite right about her. He couldn't put his finger on it but she seemed different, as if she was holding back in some way. Although she still had a healthy glow to her skin from the holiday, there was a pallor about her eyes. He would have to try and cheer her up and maybe find out what was troubling her.

"I've made your favourite for supper – Spag Bol; as it's just us, I thought I'd do something simple. I hope that's okay?" she said, taking his jacket from him and chucking it on a large pine chair in the hall.

"Yeah, fine by me. Can we have it on our knees in front of the telly? I'm absolutely shattered," he said, reverting, as always, to being a child again.

"Yes, let's. That sounds perfect. *Have I got News for You* is on in a minute."

They went into the kitchen where the mince was bubbling happily on top of the cooker; the spaghetti was already cooked and waiting on plates to be reheated. Rachel put the plates in the microwave for a couple of minutes and then piled the mince on top and grated some cheddar over everything.

They took their plates into the sitting room and sat companionably in front of the television, laughing at the jokes about the politics of the day. They didn't feel the need to make conversation. They simply enjoyed each other's company.

Part of him wished Beth was with them, but another part of him was perfectly content to be alone with his mother.

GEORGE DIDN'T WAKE up until 10 o'clock. Rachel always let him sleep in when he came home, as if he was a teenager.

They spent the day walking by the sea, visiting her shop, looking at the latest gifts she was offering and then pottering in the Lanes. They decided to go to the cinema in the evening where once again, he felt like a child as she bought 'pick and mix' and popcorn. The film wasn't great but he always enjoyed the experience of sitting in a dark room full of strangers, with the large screen and loud stereo sound. You could lose yourself in the experience and forget about life on the outside.

As they walked back to the house, she asked a lot of questions about Beth and said how much she was looking forward to meeting her. When they got home George tried to FaceTime her so that Rachel could at least chat to her virtually, but she didn't pick up. They watched the Ten o'clock news together, kissed each other goodnight and went to bed.

It seemed odd to George that his mother didn't mention his father at all and appeared to avoid talking about him. As he lay in bed, he stared at a picture that was on his bedside table of his parents. They looked so young, their faces were in profile, looking at each other, laughing. His father, handsome in his RAF uniform, his mother, beautiful with her hair flowing down her back, her eyes sparkling, with what looked like love.

It struck him that Beth looked like his Mum. He'd never seen it before and found it odd that he'd been attracted to someone so like his own mother.

Harry, at the age he is now, looks so like Dad, he thought, but how different they were in personality and attitude to life. His father had been away so much when they were growing up, but when he was at home he was always strict with them, serious and distant.

Harry, on the other hand, never took life too seriously, was fun to be around and you got the feeling that when he became a father himself, he'd enjoy his children and let them lead a life free of restraint. George often resented the way his father had been with them both.

He undressed and got into bed and in the darkness, he texted Beth.

Hope you're okay? Tried to ring earlier so you could talk to Mum on the phone but you didn't pick up? Going to bed now. Miss you and love you always xx

He was woken in the morning by his brother launching himself through the door, shouting, "Get up, you lazy bastard! What are you doing still in bed at 11 o'clock? I've caught a bus, a train and another bus and all you've done is lie in bed. Here, take this, I've brought you a cup of coffee. Well, Mum *asked* me to bring it up to you, ha ha."

"God, why am I so tired all the time? I can't believe I've slept this long. How's it going, mate? Good journey down? Is Dad home yet?" said George, slowly sitting up and reaching for the hot cup.

"Mum says he'll be here in time for Sunday lunch. Yeah, the train was quiet and I managed to read a lot of the Sunday Times. So ... quite relaxing ... a relief after the shifts I've done this week."

"Enjoying the new job?"

"Yeah, really good," he said, sitting on the edge of the bed. "I'm learning a hell of a lot and the team are great. The boss can be tricky as hell sometimes but you have to live with that. He knows his stuff and expects a crazy high standard from everybody. If you're not prepared to work hard, you're out. So, I just try to keep my head down and say 'Yes, Chef!' as often as I can."

"God, I'm not sure I could cope being in such a stressful environment with an over-bearing boss and all those artistic temperaments floating around. Food's weird, isn't it? It's such an essential part of survival and its preparation is so practical, but us humans have complicated it by making it an artistic endeavour at the same time."

"Very philosophical, bro. I *love* that side of it. Making a plate a work of art is amazing ... they say you eat with your eyes. I wonder where I get it from? Certainly not from Dad. He wouldn't know a work of art if it hit him in the face," he laughed.

"Well, Mum's always had an artistic streak with her flower paintings and photography. She's kind of melded the two sides of her personality with her flower shop, too; the beauty of flowers and the practicality of selling them."

"Wow, I'd never thought of it like that, you clever man. You're *right*. Anyway," said Harry, standing up, "enough of this. I'm going for a run before lunch. Do you want to come or are you going to laze?"

"Give me ten minutes and I'll come. I'm not running as much as I did but I fancy a jog by the sea. We'll get a good appetite up for lunch. You'll have to slow down a bit for me, though."

Before he got dressed, he reached for his mobile. A quick text from Beth.

Sorry, I was asleep. See you later xx

Short and to the point, he thought.

When they got back from their run, their father's car was in the drive and the smell of roast beef was wafting from the kitchen.

"Where's the old man then, I wonder?" said George, as they crashed through the front door. He put his head into the kitchen. Rachel had her back to him.

"I see Dad's back. Where is he?"

"Not sure. Maybe in the study. Lunch'll be in fifteen minutes, so go up and get showered, can you?"

"Okay, will do. Harry's already up there."

His mother's voice was flat. There's definitely something wrong, he thought.

They came downstairs together and Harry laid the table. George considered going to find his father but decided to get Mum a drink instead and stay with her. Surely he could make the effort to come down and say hi to his sons?

Rachel called his name from the door and said that lunch was ready; they heard the door to his study open.

George went out into the hall and said, "Hi, Dad," and held out his hand. They shook hands briefly, George wishing that they could somehow get past this ridiculous farce of formality. Why couldn't they just hug each other, like normal people?

"Hey, George. How's it going?"

"Yea, good," he answered. "You okay?"

Zach didn't answer and they dropped hands; he moved past him to repeat the process with Harry.

"You look well, Dad," said Harry, "you've still got the remains of a tan, I see."

"Yes, it's hanging in there."

George could feel the tension in the air. It was almost tangible; he noticed his mother had deliberately kept her back to them.

She said, still not facing them, "Right, sit down, it's all ready. Zach, you carve. Harry, you take these dishes to the table please and you, George, do the drinks."

The meal progressed with what can only be described as polite conversation. George tried to talk about his job but gave up, as no one seemed interested. Rachel asked Harry about the menu at his restaurant and Harry asked Zach about his latest work trip, but there was no flow, no laughter, no banter at all.

Rachel cleared the plates and when she came back to the table, she looked at Zach, hesitated and said, "Okay, boys ... we've got something important to tell you."

Her eyes flashed with anger towards Zach, who did a half-smile. It was impossible to know what was going on; George looked from one to the other.

"Shall I tell them, then?" she said.

"Yes ... go on ... you're the one who's insisting ..."

"What?" said Harry, his normal sunny smile, gone. George caught his eye and felt protective of his younger brother. He could still see Harry's little boy's face in his grown-up body.

"You're worrying us, Mum ..." said George.

"Okay ... so ... your Dad and I have decided to get divorced."

The word reverberated around the room, falling like a stone into the prolonged silence.

Rachel was still standing at the end of the table, the boys were each side, facing each other and Zach was at the other end. He scraped back his chair and stood up, holding his wine glass and said, "Cheers to us all! Your mother's idea, not mine. I've already been banned from the marital bed."

Both boys stared first at Rachel and then at Zach. Zach was taking a large swig of red wine; he finished the glass in one and sat down again.

"Get me another one, George, will you?" he said. "I'm going to need it."

George got up, poured Zach's wine and filled up his own and Harry's. Rachel put her hand over her glass.

"Would you like to explain why I want a divorce, Zach?"

"Not particularly, no. Why don't *you* do the honours?"

The boys looked at each other, neither of them knowing how to react or what to say.

Rachel sat down. "So, the holiday wasn't what you would call a 'success'. It had all the ingredients to be wonderful: a beautiful villa, wall to wall sunshine, friends, great food but ... your father met up with an old Air Force friend ... a lady friend. It turns out ... they've been having an affair, on and off, for years. She was good at putting on a show of being friendly to us all and kept wanting to meet up and take us out on her speed boat. I was taken in for a few days but then, I caught them together and confronted them. He went off with her and never came back to the villa. I flew home alone. So, maybe now you can see why ..."

She looked at the three of them and shrugged her shoulders.

The boys were dumbstruck.

"You chucked me out, if I remember correctly and told me not to come on the plane ..."

"So, let me get this straight," interrupted George, "you left Mum in Cyprus and she had to fly back on her own? How could you *do* that, Dad? What the hell ..."

"Who is this woman, anyway?" said Harry, his voice wavering. "I can't believe this. After all these years together, you're going to throw it all away …"

"Look boys, we haven't been happy for years and this was the final straw," said Rachel. "I've always tried to put on a united front for you both but it's been going wrong for a long time …"

"Well, that's news to me. You seemed perfectly happy swanning around Brighton …" said Zach. "You don't know how lucky you are … big house by the sea, your own business; most women would kill for a life …"

"It's not all about money and possessions, Zach! You KNOW we haven't got on for years. Maybe Liz did us a favour? She gave us the excuse we'd been looking for. I notice you haven't denied anything I've said, have you?"

"No. Guilty as charged. I'm a terrible person and it's all my fault … of course," said Zach, shrugging his shoulders.

"So, what's going to happen?" said George, feeling a mounting panic.

He'd never imagined them leaving each other but … maybe he'd ignored what he hadn't wanted to see. They hadn't seemed like a close couple for years, he realised … but this … this was a shock. He looked at Harry and he could see a sheen of tears glistening in his eyes. He got up and took his chair to sit next to him. He'd always wanted to protect him … and now, he realised, he couldn't.

"I'm going to see a solicitor next week. Your father is considering going to live in Cyprus, I think, aren't you, Zach?"

"Why? Does this 'Liz' live there or something?" said Harry.

"Look, boys, it's very early days but ... yes, Liz has asked me to join her out there and I'm considering it. It's a brilliant lifestyle. I'll have to see how I can do it, work-wise."

"Oh, I'm glad about that," said Harry. "I'm glad you're lifestyle will improve. Have you considered what it will be like for Mum, being here on her own? We're not here any more, you know. You'll be okay with your new-found love, but poor Mum ..."

"Don't worry boys, I'll be fine. I've told your Dad that I want to stay on in this house."

"I don't know about that ..." said Zach.

"It's the *least* you can do, Zach. The boys will be able to come here whenever they want – it's their *home*. Anyway, that's the situation, boys. I'm sorry we've sprung this on you but you've both got your own lives now, so hopefully it won't affect either of you. We've just got to get on with life and move forward. All of us."

"You're right, you've certainly sprung this on us," said Harry. "It's not every day your parents split up." His face had lost all its sparkle. "I don't know what to say."

George put his arm around his shoulders.

"There's nothing TO say, Harry," said Zach, looking at the boys with a certain amount of disdain. "It's *life*. Two people have decided to go their separate ways. It happens all the time. You'll be able to have lots of cheap holidays in Cyprus. Look at it that way!"

"Thanks Dad, that makes me a feel a whole lot better," said Harry. "That's quite an offer."

"Yea," said George, taking a large swig of wine. "We can't wait to spend time with Liz, who we don't even know."

"You'll like her when you get to know her. Actually, you *have* met her but when you were a lot younger. Anyway, it wasn't just me who behaved badly on holiday. Ask your mother about her Greek waiter."

"Zach, for God's sake. Boys, NOTHING happened. We were all friendly with Demetris and Andreas ..."

"You were *particularly* friendly with Demetris ..."

"I was friendly with BOTH of them. My friendship with Demetris hardly compares to your affair with Liz. Don't listen boys, he's just ..."

Zach laughed. "Uncle Mike will always stick up for you, anyway. Ever the gentleman, helping your mother with every little problem."

"What's *that* meant to mean?" said Harry.

"Ask your mother ..."

"Look, Zach. Stop trying to blame other people. I don't know what I'd have done without the others' support. Mike and Jen helped me deal with a very difficult situation, so don't start making snide comments. Let's all just stop talking about it now. *Nothing* is going to change my decision. The sooner we can sort this out, the better."

Silence fell around the table; nobody wanted to speak, not even Zach.

George wondered if he knew either of his parents at all.

He stood up and started clearing the table. They hadn't had dessert but their appetites had somehow waned. Harry stood up and started helping too.

Zach left the room, without saying another word.

George put his arms around Rachel when she came into the kitchen.

"I'm *so* sorry, Mum. What a nightmare. Why didn't you tell me? What can I do?"

"Nothing, George. Don't worry about me, honestly. I'll be fine."

"I *do* worry about you, though."

"So do I," said Harry, also coming up and putting his arms around her; the three of them forming a group hug.

"I'll be okay, boys," she said, extricating herself from them and beginning to load the dishwasher. "Honestly, I've got my business, my friends ... you've got your own lives to lead. Dad and I will sort it out, promise. He's being all confident and smug at the moment, but when reality hits, he'll maybe realise what he's done. The truth is, your father and I have been drifting apart for years. I never really fitted in with military life, but I made the best of it and when we moved down here to Brighton, I felt as if I'd been given a second chance at life. We began to realise we didn't have much in common, your Dad was unhappy having left the Air Force and things went downhill. I'm sorry you've had to find out now, but at least you had a happy childhood without divorce. You *did* have a happy childhood, didn't you?"

"Yes, of course we did, Mum," said George, "didn't we, Harry?"

"Yes, we did. I'm just sorry that we didn't know what was going on."

"I, for one, am really pleased you *didn't* know," said Rachel. "So, what are your plans? What time are you both heading back?" she smiled, trying to give the impression that all was now put to bed.

"Um, I want to get back to London at around 8. How about you, Harry?"

"Yea, that's good for me too. We'll get an Uber to the station around 6.30?"

"Don't be daft, I'll take you," said Rachel.

No more was said about anything of importance. The three of them headed out for a post lunch meander along the shore, ending in a seafront café for a cup of tea. By mutual, silent agreement, they didn't discuss the Cyprus holiday or the imminent separation, they just enjoyed the wonderful feeling of being together and being a unit. Zach had never really been part of this close-knit group, so he wasn't missed.

When it was time to go, both George and Harry went upstairs to say goodbye to their father but found the study empty. His car was in the drive; they could only conclude that he'd gone out when they were on their walk and hadn't returned. It seemed odd to leave without seeing him again; they felt even more disconnected from him than usual.

"I wonder when we'll see him again?" asked George when they were in the car.

"Who knows?" said Rachel.

"It's sad ... I feel he's abandoning us, even though we're perfectly old enough to be independent ... I can't forgive him," said Harry.

"Neither can I," said George. "I wonder if it will last with this Liz?"

"He's not the easiest of people to live with ... but they were both in the Air Force, so they've got a shared past."

"Well, so have you and him, Mum ..."

"That doesn't count, apparently," said Rachel, looking in the rear-view mirror, smiling at George in the back.

Even on a Sunday evening, the Brighton traffic was bumper to bumper along the main coast road. They passed the pier, George reflecting on the hours they spent on it as teenagers. There had always been a feeling of adventure and excitement, no matter how many times they went.

"How long have we got? This traffic is crazy, today," said Rachel.

"It's okay, Mum. Don't panic. We should be there in good time. There'll always be another train, anyway," said Harry, not wanting to cause his mother any more stress.

A motorbike, at that moment, weaved in and out of the traffic, causing Rachel to brake suddenly. "Goodness, no wonder so many bikers are killed. What an idiot. Don't ever buy a motorbike, boys. They're not safe."

"Well, they're not when they're driven like that," said Harry.

"Don't worry, Mum. I don't think Beth would let me buy one, anyway," said George.

"She sounds as if she's the boss already," said Harry. "Why are you keeping her under wraps, bro?"

"I'm not! It just hasn't worked you all meeting her yet. She does such awful shifts, we don't seem to get much time off together. But, I'm hoping to take her out for special meal soon to your place, so you'll meet her then."

The car was just pulling up to the back of the station, where they had to fight their way to a temporary parking slot. "Jump out boys, there's CCTV here and I've been done loads of times …"

"Okay, Mum, chill," said Harry. "Give us a sec."

They both leaped out and grabbed their bags from the boot. Rachel wound down her window and each of them bent down to kiss her cheek.

"Look after yourself, Mum," said George. "I'll come down again as soon as I can."

"Keep us up to date ... after you've seen the solicitor," said Harry.

"Okay, you two. Don't worry, I'll be fine," she said, trying to reassure them (and herself). "Now, go on ... run, or you'll miss it."

They started jogging down the entrance that ran parallel to the lines, both turning once to wave, but Rachel had already moved off.

George was glad he was with his brother for the journey.

He suddenly felt rather alone.

Chapter 4

It was now 15th September and Jen's alarm rang out at 6.30 am.

The day of the biopsy.

She reached across to the bedside table to switch it off but managed to knock the clock off and it landed on the floor with a clutter.

"Oh, for heaven's sake," she said, glancing across at Mike, who was still snoring. Nothing ever woke him up. She reached down to pick up the clock, her mind cleared and her appointment came into her mind with a thump. That's why the alarm had been set so early, she realised. The hospital had said to be there by 8.30 am.

"Mike?"

"Mmm ... what?"

"Mike, we've got to get up ... come on, wake up," she said, getting annoyed at his ability to sleep, whatever was going on. She reached across and pushed him, maybe a little harder than she needed to.

"Ok, ok ..."

"We've only got an hour till we leave. We mustn't be late."

He rolled over onto his back, opened his eyes and hauled himself up a little. Poor Mike, he was beginning to look his age.

His hair was sticking up and Jen could tell he could hardly keep his eyes open; they slowly closed again.

"I'm just going to lie here for ten more minutes," he said.

She flicked back the duvet and stumbled over to the en-suite bathroom. She didn't need a shower as she had had a bath last night but decided to have one simply to wake herself up.

As she stood under the strong jets, she tried not to think about the day ahead. She wasn't so much scared of the biopsy but more scared of the potential result although, she had to admit, she wasn't looking forward to the procedure. But it had to be done, so she had to put it from her mind.

She thought about the phone call she'd had with Amber two days ago. She'd decided she *had* to tell her in the end – Rachel was right, as always; it wasn't fair on her, not to. She'd hated having to impinge on her happiness, though. Amber radiated contentment and love; ever since the revelation in Cyprus, she'd seemed to be floating on air.

"Amber, I need to tell you something but I don't want you to panic, ok?"

"What, Mum? I *am* panicking ..."

"Well, I've got to go into hospital in a couple of days for a very small op ... they are just investigating a small lump, but there's nothing to worry about."

"Oh my God," said Amber. Jen could hear the fear in her voice. "What do you mean, a lump? And where is it?"

"It's just a small lump in my breast, Amber. It could be nothing."

"Yes, it might be nothing ... how long have you known? When did you find the lump?"

"I found it before the holiday ..."

"You've known all this time ... and you haven't told me? You should have told me."

"Well, there was nothing to tell ..."

"But you knew all the time you were in Cyprus? Did anyone else know?"

"Just Grace and Rachel ..."

"Not Dad?"

"No, I didn't want to worry him until I'd had the results of the mammogram."

"So, what does this mean, this op, then?"

"It means that they're unsure what the lump is from the mammogram and they want to take a little bit of tissue and analyse it. Often you don't have to stay in hospital for such a small op but they're keeping me in overnight."

"Oh Mum, I wish I'd known. There I was, messing about, having fun, and I had no idea you were going through this."

"You've got other things to think about at the moment. How are you feeling? Everything okay with the pregnancy?"

"Yes, yes, I'm fine. I'm loving Leo's house, so much roomier than my flat. Grace pops over now and again to collect stuff. We all get on fine, although it does seem a bit weird. We talk babies and domestic bliss."

"That's good. Anyway, Amber, I just thought you ought to know. I'll let you know when I'm home again."

"Okay, Mum. I love you. Give my love to Dad. I'll be thinking of you."

Jen had tried to make light of it all to Amber and she hoped she'd succeeded. She'd also tried not to make a big deal of it to Mike. He hadn't taken it well; when she'd seen his face this morning, she felt the news had really taken its toll on him.

When she got out of the shower, she stood and looked at her naked body in the misted up mirror. How could a small thing, a small lump, wreak such havoc in a person's life? You couldn't even see it, for goodness sake. She peered close, felt her breast and there it was, as plain as a pimple on a face, to the touch. She gently rubbed it, willing it to be nothing more than a collection of benign cells, not some rogue invasion of cancer.

Mike was still in bed when she went back in the bedroom. He was looking at his phone with a blank expression on his face. She didn't want to nag him but at this rate, they *were* going to be late. Instead of going on about time, she asked questions about the rest of his day; he was dropping her off and then coming back in the evening. He had an important meeting with a financial advisor and then another meeting with the bank; he seemed to lurch from one crisis meeting to the next, at the moment. She felt guilty, this was the last thing he needed to have to deal with.

He eventually rolled out of bed and limped towards the bathroom, closing the door behind him.

Jen packed a few bits into a small overnight bag, making sure she had her Kindle, her phone and clean underwear, all essentials for a trip to a hospital, she thought. She looked in her purse to see if she had some cash; she rarely had any with her these days but thought that it might come in handy in hospital, for drinks machines and the like.

She went downstairs and put on the coffee. She'd been told not to eat or drink anything after 7 am, so she made a cup for only Mike. She put on some toast for him and took the plate and the cup upstairs, so he could grab something while getting dressed.

He was sitting on the bed, reaching down to put his socks on. When he sat up, he said, "Why's life so unfair?"

"What do you mean?"

"Well, we've both worked so hard to get this far and suddenly everything seems to be falling apart. You ... Amber ... our finances ... why are we being punished?"

It was unlike Mike to be so defeated; Jen was shocked. His face looked drawn and pale.

"Look, we don't know what this biopsy will find, so don't let's get ahead of ourselves. Our finances will be okay ... you'll always be able to find work, Mike. You're a talented architect ... if the business goes under, it doesn't matter. You'll get a job, I know you will ... and we'll still have each other. Amber is happy news, Mike. She's having a baby ... there are so many worse things that could happen to a child. She could be on drugs ... or be with someone we hate ... or have mental health issues. She's going to be fine. She's with one of our best friends, who's going to care for her and who loves her. Please try to see the bright side."

"Yea, I'm sorry, Jen. I'm just finding it hard to see things positively at the moment. I'm just being selfish ... and stupid. You're the one I should be focussing on."

He stood up, accepted the coffee and toast she was offering, kissed her forehead and said, "Thanks, my love. Let's get you to this hospital."

Jen felt sorry for him; he was trying so hard to look okay but she knew he wasn't.

"Yea, come on, the sooner we get there, the sooner I'll be home again," she said.

Life *was* unfair but there were millions of people worse off than her in the world. You just had to be grateful for what you had: she had a loving husband, a beautiful daughter and good friends she could rely on.

What else did she need?

MIKE HAD DELIVERED her to the hospital, got her settled in and then left with a heavy heart. Jen knew exactly what he'd be going through – he was such a big, strong-looking man but beneath it all, he was a typical 'gentle giant', a complete softy, with so much empathy, sympathy and love. He was always trying to fix other people's troubles and if he couldn't, he took it as a personal slight. He hated to leave Jen alone in the hospital bed – he couldn't 'fix' her and he felt helpless.

While Amber was growing up, he was so protective of her that if another child or teacher was 'mean' to her, it was all Jen could do to stop him from going round to confront them. This was why he'd taken her falling for Leo so hard: it was something he couldn't control. Amber was effectively handing herself over into the care of another father-figure.

This trait had also caused a myriad of problems for him in the distant past: he was always trying to 'fix' Rachel in her unhappy, student days: rescuing her from that awful man in the nightclub, the night they'd first met; trying to cheer her up when she was down; stopping her drinking too much at parties. This mission of his had eventually led to the night at the RAF camp, when he'd sensed her isolation and loneliness and again tried to fix her, but all it had done was to make the situation so much worse.

The undeniable fact was that he'd always loved her, right from the start. He'd had to accept it was possible to love two women at the same time. Jen was his wife, but Rachel was his first true love. The way time and circumstance had intervened to weave all their lives together, was more than cruel, but it was something he'd learned to live with ... eventually.

If he could have taken the lump out of Jen's breast and placed it in his own body, he would have done. He couldn't bear to see her suffering. When he left the hospital, he kept picturing her, sitting on the bed in that awful gown, looking so vulnerable.

Why had this happened to someone so kind, so loving, so innocent of everything?

He went to his meetings which only served to make his mood even blacker. He was running out of money, the business was rapidly becoming less and less viable. He was tempted to just throw in the towel but at his age, would he be able to get a job? His CV didn't look too appealing; he could just hear the sarcastic interviewers:

"So, what have you been doing in this large gap here?" or "Can you explain why your business failed?"

He'd enjoyed being his own boss but perhaps he just hadn't got the resilience and confidence needed to persevere during hard times. He certainly didn't want to burden Jen with it all; maybe he would only tell her how bad things were when he'd finally got a job and some money was coming in.

Before he went back into the hospital, he went home and started scouring the internet to see what was out there. Most of the jobs he could find were for young, inexperienced architects, straight out of university. Jobs that were suitable for him were in London and he really didn't want to commute, but maybe he was going to have to. It was possible; he knew plenty of people who did it, but the thought of becoming one of those poor sods who stand on a platform at 6.45 am on a cold winter's morning and then get back into Kemble at 7.30 pm, to then drive home by 8 pm, only to start it all again the next morning, absolutely appalled him.

That wasn't a life and that wasn't why he lived in the Cotswolds either.

There must be another way?

Banging the laptop lid down with a loud sigh, he dragged himself to the car and drove the short distance to the hospital. He found Jen asleep, her face rested, but pale.

He sat down next to the bed and read a newspaper he'd bought in for her. A nurse poked her head in and asked if everything was okay and as they exchanged pleasantries, Jen roused and smiled when she saw him.

"Hi, Jen Darling ... how are you feeling?" he said, reaching for her hand. He picked it up in both of his and kissed it.

"Fine ... fine. I just dropped off."

"Yes, I saw. You looked very peaceful. And beautiful, I might add."

"Hardly! Nice of you to say, though," and they smiled at each other. "How did it go today? Your meetings okay?"

"Yea, good thanks," said Mike, wanting to gloss over his failures. "So have you had any feedback yet?"

"No ... it won't be for a while. They say I can go home after lunch. How are you fixed? Can you come and get me?"

"No ... you'll have to get the bus," he laughed. "Of course, I'm coming to get you, you old fool. By the way, Amber rang to find out how you were."

"She's a good girl, isn't she? Have you heard from anyone else?"

"Well, Rachel wants to come up and see you but I tried to put her off for now. I think you should rest of a bit."

"I'll be fine in a couple of days, Mike. It just rather depends on what they've found."

He showed her what he'd brought in – anyone would think she was staying for a week the amount of reading material, sweets and snacks he'd brought with him.

They arranged for him to come back in the next day at 2.30 and he went back home, happier to have seen her but worried about what might have been revealed.

What if it *was* cancerous?

The thought gave him the shivers.

Chapter 5

George was determined to propose to Beth as soon as possible. He knew he loved her and wanted to spend the rest of his life with her, so why on earth wait? She was the sweetest, kindest, most beautiful girl he'd ever met. He couldn't believe his luck.

So one wintry day in late October, he went out of the office for lunch (he didn't do this normally, often opting to go to the canteen) and was on a mission to find a ring. He'd been looking on the internet and studying rings in shop windows for what felt like weeks. He'd noticed one in passing in a shop around the corner and he was pretty sure that it was the style Beth would like: a sapphire with diamonds around it. He'd noticed she had a pendant with what looked like a sapphire (but might well have been an imitation), which suited her colouring and she wore it a lot.

He walked round to the shop and it was still there in the window. He couldn't see the price tag, which was never a good sign, but there was no harm in going in and finding out, was there?

There was a young guy, about his age, behind the counter in the shop and no other customers. He realised he felt embarrassed but ploughed on anyway.

"I'm interested in a ring in your window ... the one with the sapphire and diamonds around it."

"I know the one, sir, excellent choice. Let me just get it for you ..." and with that, he went to unlock the sliding glass door of the display cabinet. Reaching forward and delicately picking it up, he re-locked the door and placed the ring on the counter top with such reverence, it was as if it was part of the crown jewels collection itself.

George stared at it. At close quarters, he was even more impressed. He could visualise it on her finger, could see her smile, as he slid it on.

"May I pick it up?"

"Of course, sir," and with that, he placed the ring in George's hand. It felt heavy and looked sophisticated ... the blue of the sapphire was stunning.

"What if it doesn't fit?" said George, thinking more practically.

"That's not a problem ... we'll alter it for you."

The price had still not been mentioned but in his mind, George had already bought it; he could see it nestled in its box, deep in his pocket, to be brought out.

"How much it it, please?" he asked. There was no point unless he could afford it.

"£2,560, sir."

George's heart started beating fast. He *could* afford it, couldn't he? Nothing was too good for Beth. He started to do calculations in his head. If he paid by credit card, he could pay it off ...

But the more serious side of him said,

Have you gone completely mad? That's a huge sum ... it's just a ring. You could find something much cheaper.

The shop assistant could sense him wavering.

"I'm sure your future wife will absolutely love it. We could keep it aside for a day while you think about it, if that helps?"

George stared at it. It was perfect and he convinced himself Beth would not only love it ... but cherish it forever. He didn't earn a huge amount ... but he could afford this.

With a dry mouth, he said, "I'll take it."

He felt light-headed as he reached into his pocket for his wallet. Should he discuss this with someone first? But who? Harry would just make jokes about it and his mother would start questioning him about his finances and worrying. He decided it was one thing he wanted to do without any input from anyone else.

The assistant placed the ring reverently back in the box and then presented him with the credit card terminal. He slipped the card in, put in his code and the deal was done.

"Thank you, sir, that's all gone through."

He took his card and receipt, thanked the guy for his help, picked up the ring and walked out of the shop. A thought came into his head which he tried to dismiss.

Had he gone temporarily mad?

No, he hadn't. It was now a reality.

He was going to ask her.

"SO, LOOK, HARRY ... I thought it would be really nice to bring Beth to your place for a special meal," he said into his phone, as he walked back home from the tube. He'd been on a high all afternoon, since he'd bought the ring. He'd had to attend two particularly boring meetings but he'd got through them by just day-dreaming about his plans.

"Ok, bro, that would be cool. I'd get to meet this mystery woman at last. What's the occasion?"

George paused. Should he tell him?

"If I tell you something, please don't tell Mum ..."

"Whaaaat?"

"I'm going to propose ..."

"Bro, that's huge. Are you going to get down on bended knee?" he said with a chuckle.

"Well, yes ... I thought I'd do the whole thing properly, you know. I love her. I want to show her how much."

"This I've got to see! Do you want me to tell the restaurant ... to do something?"

"Yea, it might be an idea, but can I just think about it first? I've got to pin her down as to when we can come first. She's got a couple of nights off next week, so maybe then."

"Okay, mate. I'm on a quick break at the mo. Must go. Give me a ring when you've booked. Chow."

And he was gone. Talking to Harry was usually like that - he was always in a hurry. Maybe he could get the restaurant to lay on something special, though?

He walked on, lost in his plans. Maybe he could lay on a musician or ... the ring could be in the bottom of a dessert or something ... or hidden in a bread roll? The options were endless.

How long should they be engaged? As far as he was concerned, why wait? He just wanted to get on with it and get married, settle down, build their love nest together. But he'd have to respect Beth's wishes; she may want to wait a while.

When he reached his flat, he felt even more certain that this was what he wanted. It always felt right as he stepped through into their home. Beth was the perfect fit for him. He knew he was an old romantic. She was more down to earth, more practical. But they complemented each other.

They were soul mates.

GEORGE HAD ASKED HER to be ready by six. He didn't say why, but he said to wear something smart as they were going somewhere special.

To be honest, it was the last thing she wanted to do. She'd rather have had a bath, get some fish and chips and have an early night, but they so rarely went out together these days that she felt she ought to make the effort.

She went into the shower and turning on the water, stood underneath the jet, hoping to give herself a new lease of life. She used her favourite lemon-scented shower gel and washed her hair with her expensive shampoo, which promised to 'enrich her hair with natural oils.'

Having dried, she went to her cupboard to see what to wear. She picked out a slinky red dress, which she always felt sexy in. Before putting it on, she blow-dried her hair and tied it back in a sophisticated knot. She could hear George in the kitchen, singing to his favourite band on the radio. Why was he so full of beans tonight? He'd told her that his day had been tough ... but he had a swagger about him.

She put the dress on, reaching behind her to do the zip up. It felt tighter than normal. The trouble was, when you worked in a hospital, people were always offering you snacks. The nurses were renowned for always having packets of crisps and sweets behind the desk and after hours on her feet and an early start, she could never resist eating them. Still, she stood in front of the mirror and was relatively pleased with her appearance, as long as she held her stomach in. She put on some earrings, her blue pendant and a little make up; she liked the natural look.

"I'm ready," she called. "What time are we leaving? Did you say seven?"

"Yes, I'm just going to change and then I'll get an Uber."

"Where are we going? It must be somewhere very posh for all this palaver."

"We're going to Harry's new restaurant. It *is* very posh but I thought we deserved it. Harry says the food is magnificent and he's told them we're coming, so I'm hoping it's going to be extra special tonight."

In the Uber, George held Beth's hand. He knew he was doing the right thing but he was nervous. Was she going to be impressed by this demonstration of his love?

"Why did you choose tonight?" asked Beth.

"Well, we don't exactly get many nights off together and the restaurant's always fully booked, so I grabbed these two available places. You don't mind, do you?"

"No, it's fine, but I don't want to be too late. I'm so tired after today." This was the trouble with her job; it was always in the background. He was able to forget his, pretty much, when he wasn't there. He sometimes did extra work in the evenings and weekends but the routine of his hours suited him. Her hours really took their toll.

George felt in his pocket with his other hand and his fingers wrapped around the ring box. When he got there, he was going to ask to speak to Harry and see if all the arrangements were in place. The booking was for 7.30 and they worked out that he would do the proposal at 9 pm. Harry had said they have a quiet medley of songs playing all night and at the given moment, they'd been primed to play, *I Will Always Love You*. It was a song that meant a lot to them both and Beth particularly loved it. Whether it was the sentiment or the quality of Whitney's voice that Beth loved, he wasn't sure, but it would be his signal to start the proposal. He'd decided against putting it in a dessert or a cake. He was worried that it would get dirty and sticky and he liked the idea of producing it from his pocket. It was traditional.

The taxi pulled up outside the restaurant which was called *Love of Food*, all very understated and classy. They were greeted at the door, a girl took their coats and they were shown to what they were told was the 'best table in the house'. They ordered some wine and when it arrived and was poured into their two glasses, George made an excuse to leave the table and said he had to nip to the boys' room. When he was out of sight, he asked the barmen to get his brother.

Harry came out, grinning from ear to ear, doing a big thumbs up.

"Okay, Georgie boy? Ready for it?"

"Yeah, I am ... I think. Is everything okay at your end? Why don't I pretend I just bumped into you and you come over and meet Beth? It would seem strange to her if you didn't come out, I think."

"Okay, I'll come with you now, briefly," he said and the two brothers walked back across to the table.

"So, this is my long lost brother, Harry, Beth," said George, stepping back, so that Harry could greet her. In typical Harry fashion, he hugged her like a sister and gave her two enormous kisses on each cheek.

"At last," he said. "Why've I never seen your beautiful face before?"

Beth looked a little taken aback by his effusiveness, but stood up and returned his hug, smiling.

"So lovely to meet you. I've heard a lot about you. Will *you* be cooking our meal tonight?"

"Not all bad, I hope? Well, not *me* doing the cooking exactly, but I'll be certain to add some touches and make it a special night," he said, grinning at his brother. George raised his eyebrows and smiled, trying to get his brother to shut up.

"Anyway, must go. Things to do, people to see. Don't leave without saying goodbye," and he rushed off, making his way through a group of diners who had just arrived.

After a lot of discussion, they chose their starters and main courses, which all sounded delicious, but George secretly wondered if the portions would be tiny – they usually were in places like this; all exquisite presentation and no substance. The menu was so complicated – he struggled to understand some of it and was worried that he had made the right choice, but he felt that he was killing two birds with one stone by coming here. It had two Michelin stars and he wanted to support his brother.

The food turned out to be amazing and surprisingly filling. There were lots of delicate sources which were rich. He'd chosen a steak for his main meal, and it really was melt in the mouth stuff. Beth had chosen sea bream; when it came, she took pictures of it and posted it on her Insta page. She kept saying 'mmm' and 'ahhh' every time she took a mouthful.

George was getting nervous now and he glanced at his watch. It was 8.45. He realised that the waiter knew what was going to happen as whenever he came to the table, he smiled encouragingly at George.

He'd arranged with Harry that at 8.55, if all was well and good, he'd text him to say that he was ready.

Taking his phone and pretending he had to text his mother about something, he did just that. He kept looking round nervously, wondering when the music would change to the song.

There was a short pause when the music stopped playing and as George glanced towards the bar area, he could see a few people emerging from the kitchen, his brother at the front, holding a bottle of bubbly, as planned.

This is it, he thought to himself and stood up.

The song started playing and he walked round the table so that he could be next to Beth. She was blissfully unaware of anything. She looked up at him, wondering why he'd got up from his seat.

"Beth, you know I love you ..."

"Of course, I know you love me," she said, looking at him strangely, "why are you standing ..."

"Can you hear the song? It's one of your favourites: *I will Always Love you*," he said.

As George nervously reached into his pocket, Beth's face started to take on a somewhat startled (and embarrassed) look.

Lifting the ring out and opening the box, he slowly got down on one knee and looking into her eyes, said, "Beth ... would you ... do me the *honour* ... of marrying me?"

By this time, all the diners were aware of what was going on and were watching with interest and encouragement. Harry and his workmates started clapping.

Beth jumped up, as if her chair had given her an electric shock, now with a truly horrified look on her face and said, "George, what on earth are you doing? How *could* you?"

The music continued but the clapping slowly petered out and the smiles on the other diners' faces turned to sympathy; many people looked away, not wanting to witness this man's utter humiliation.

"But, Beth ... I thought you ..." whispered George, as he tried to stand up with some dignity, but fell against her chair.

"This is so *not* what I want, George ... why did you ever *imagine* this would be something ... I have to leave now." Her face was red with anger, embarrassment and shock, her eyes steely and blazing.

She looked for her coat, gave up and walked to the door. She flung it open and in a second, was gone.

George was left standing, still holding the ring. He stared at the door, his mind in turmoil. He had no idea what to do. He felt as if he'd been stripped naked in public and whipped.

Harry was now by his side, his arm around his brother. "God, bro, that was harsh. I'm so sorry. Do you think you ought to go after her?"

It was as if he was speaking to an automaton. George stared at him.

"George," said Harry, more loudly, "go after her, man. You must go ..."

"Should I?"

"Yes, of course. Go now. Don't worry about the bill or anything, we'll sort it."

George came to his senses. Looking around, seeing all the other diners studiously *not* looking at him, he rushed to the door and was on the street before he even realised what he was doing.

It was a busy road: buses were driving in both directions; taxis and cars were vying for position; groups of people were walking past him – the noise of traffic and chatter overwhelmed him.

He looked left and right, scanning the crowds for her familiar face or outline but … nothing. He went to the edge of the pavement, stepped out and nearly got knocked over by a cyclist, who swerved and shouted at him.

"Fucking idiot … look where you're sodding going, mate!"

"Sorry …" muttered George, as he stepped back onto the pavement, his legs now weak and shaking. He scanned the other side of the road, between passing traffic, but it was hopeless.

He stood there, with the miasma of movement around him, lost and almost crying. He put his hands to his face; he could feel the tears springing from his eyes.

God, what an absolute fucking mess.

"Come back inside, bro," said Harry, who had appeared beside him.

"No, I can't … how embarrassing … everyone will look at me."

"Sod everyone else … come in and I'll take you to the staff room. Come on," and he dragged him back inside. George had lost all strength and confidence and let himself be led. They walked straight through the dining area and into a door at the back.

"Sit down. I'll get you a coffee," said Harry and promptly left the room. George just stared in front of him, numb.

"Here you are, mate. I've put some sugar in it. Well, that didn't go quite as planned, did it?"

"No, not quite."

"What are you going to do?"

"I've no idea ..." he said, as he sipped the coffee. "Where do you think she's gone?"

"How would I know, bro? I only met her an hour ago ... where do *you* think she'd go?"

"Maybe home ... but I doubt it. I've never seen her so angry. She'll probably want nothing to do with me ... shall I phone her?"

"You could, but do you think she'll answer?"

George got his phone out and pressed her name. "It's gone straight to voicemail, I reckon she rejected it."

He stared at the phone as if it was the phone's fault.

"Look, I think you should go home and get some sleep, mate. I would say 'don't worry about the bill' but I'm not in a position to do that. Give me your card and I'll go and settle up."

George handed over his card and Harry left.

God, this is a fucking disaster. I've completely blown it with her now.

Harry came back in the room with his card and a receipt. "Sorry you've spent this much, mate. I tried for a discount but management weren't having it ..."

"It's my own fault, don't worry about it."

They hugged; Harry held onto his brother longer than usual, feeling he could do with a bit of support. He slapped him on the back and said, "You're an old romantic, you really are, bro."

"Don't mention a thing to Mum, Harry. I don't want *anyone* to know about this."

"No, of course. No one will know, except the whole restaurant," he laughed, trying to lighten the mood, slapping his back again.

"Yea, thanks,"

"You'll look back at this evening in the future and laugh, you really will," said Harry. "Honestly."

"Maybe, but I'm not laughing now," George said. "I'm off. Thanks for everything, Haz. I'll be in touch," and with that he let himself out of the room and walked across the restaurant.

No one even noticed this time. He collected his and Beth's coats and went out into the night.

Chapter 6

When Beth walked out, she had no idea where she was going or what she was going to do. Her mind was in turmoil.

She simply turned left and kept walking, as fast as she could. She didn't want George to find her; she couldn't trust herself right now not to dump him on the spot. She felt so *mad* at him ... why on earth did he think she would like that sort of public display? It was literally her worst nightmare ... surely he knew her better than that? She hated being the centre of attention for a start and hadn't she even said in the past, that sort of thing made her want to vomit? She was sure she remembered watching some football match with him when a proposal came up on the big screen: a couple in the crowd were there for everyone to see and didn't she say *then* how she thought that it was cringy? Was it him she was with? She was beginning to doubt herself now.

Anyway, forget the restaurant proposal, surely he'd got the hint that she didn't want to get married yet, or indeed maybe ever? She'd avoided meeting his family, avoided any sort of commitment ...

She looked back and couldn't see George.

Thank God, he's taken the hint, this time.

All around her were people out for the evening: couples hand in hand; groups of lads on the pull; girls laughing done up to the nines off, no doubt, to a club for the night. She felt invisible, as they all streamed past her.

She wanted to sit in a café and blend into the background after that humiliating experience. She dived into the next one, a Costa, and joined the queue. She ordered an Americano, black, and went to sit in the corner, as far away from everyone as possible.

The coffee was soothing; she wished the smoking ban didn't exist so that she could light up. She could also do with a stiff drink.

She got out her phone and saw a missed call from George. Should she ring him back? Knowing him, he'd be worried, not knowing where she was.

But no, she wasn't going to ring him back. She couldn't face talking to him right now and wondered how they were *ever* going to get over this.

She went onto Google and searched for a hotel in the area. She booked herself into a Premier Inn that was just round the corner; she certainly wasn't going home.

Home ... was it *home* now?

She was on duty tomorrow. She'd sleep at the hotel and then go back to get her work clothes after George had gone to work. She'd do her shift and then work out what she'd do next.

Did she regret doing what she did?

Not one little bit.

Just then, her mobile vibrated. George's name was displayed on the screen.

She opened the message app.

I'm so sorry, Beth. Where are you? Come home. xxx

She went to the side of the phone and turned it off.

She couldn't face talking to anyone, never mind George. He could worry about her all night as far as she was concerned.

PART OF GEORGE WAS hoping Beth would be at home when he got back, but the other part *knew* she wouldn't be there.

He was such an idiot. What had possessed him? He'd got carried away with the romance of it all and hadn't considered whether Beth would like such a public proposal. But was it *that* she'd run away from ... or was it from *him*? Perhaps he'd read it all wrong and she just wasn't ready. Or maybe she didn't even love him? She said she did, but it's easy to say *I love you.* Did she ever say it without him saying it first? Did he force her into saying it? Maybe doing what she just did *proved* she didn't love him.

He looked at his watch, it was 10.35 and he'd heard nothing from her. He texted her, hoping for an instant reply but he waited for ten minutes, staring at the phone and nothing came.

Was he trying for the 'happy ending' after the awful news of his parents' breakup? Had that upset him more than he'd realised and he was hoping to secure his own future in light of his parents' divorce? He didn't want to put too much psychology into it but maybe there was an element of truth in it?

He wanted to talk to his mother ... she'd know what to do. He looked at his phone again (still no text). Was it too late to ring Mum? She was a nightbird and never went to bed before 11 pm. He knew he'd told Harry not to tell her but out of all the people in the world, he knew she was the one he wanted to talk to.

He pressed her number; he hadn't meant to do a video call but he didn't realise he'd pressed 'video' until it was too late, when she answered and her face appeared on the screen.

"Hi, stranger ... haven't heard from you for a while ... George ... is everything okay?"

"Hi, Mum. Sorry to ring you rather late but ..."

Rachel's face was now full of concern and she said quickly, "What's the matter, George? Has something happened?"

He looked away from the screen; he felt hot and flustered and tears came to his eyes.

"George?"

"Yes, Mum ... sorry ... I ... I've done something so stupid and I don't know what to do."

He wiped his eyes.

"Oh, George ... I wish I was there to give you a hug. What's happened? Don't cry, George."

Rachel was totally fazed by the look on his face. She hadn't seen him cry for years and her heart beat fast, as she thought of all the things that might have gone wrong. FaceTime was wonderful but seeing him like this and so far away, was awful.

"Mum, I proposed to Beth tonight, in front of everyone, and she ran away. It was terrible. I've been a total idiot." The words came tumbling out, as if he just wanted to get them out of his head.

"Oh ... I see."

Secretly, Rachel was relieved that it wasn't something a lot worse. She'd been imagining all the worst scenarios in her head – he'd hit someone, stolen something, lost his job ... not that this wasn't awful, but ...

"When you say, in front of everyone, what do you mean?"

"We went to Harry's restaurant and I got down on bended knew ... everyone was looking ... the diners, Harry and all the staff ... it was the most ridiculous thing I've ever done."

"Don't be so hard on yourself, George. You were doing a lovely thing ... so romantic. If she didn't like it, she's crazy. Most girls would love ..."

"But she's not *most* girls, Mum. I should have known ... she's a very practical person, she's not showy ... I've completely blown it."

"No, you haven't, I'm sure you haven't," said Rachel, wondering if he had.

"Where is she now?"

"I don't know, Mum. She left the restaurant – I went looking for her but I couldn't find her. She's not answering my calls or texts."

"Well, she's a grown woman, she'll be fine. She's probably gone to a friend's or even to a hotel. Give her time to come to terms with everything, give her some space. She'll come back, you'll see."

"Do you think so, Mum?"

"Yes, of course. She'd be mad not to. You're such a great catch, George."

"She obviously doesn't agree with you."

There was silence at both ends of the phone, with neither of them knowing what to say next.

"Thank you for listening, Mum. Sorry if I woke you."

"No, I was watching crap on the TV. No worries."

"Are *you* okay, Mum? Have you been to the solicitor?"

"Yes, but don't let's talk about that now. You need to go to bed and have a good night's sleep. Everything will seem a bit better in the morning."

"I doubt it."

"It will, I promise."

"Okay, I'm going now, Mum. Bye," and he clicked off the call. He couldn't bear to hear her being so unrelentingly positive any more. He knew she was only doing her best, but he just wasn't in the mood.

He poured himself a large whisky, turned on the TV and slumped down on the sofa.

He woke with a start at 6 am, still on the sofa, with the TV muttering softly.

He jumped up and rushed into the bedroom.

The bed was empty … no Beth.

Chapter 7

It was now the 2nd December and the day had started quite normally. Grace had got to work, as usual, at 8.30.

She and Anna had eaten a leisurely breakfast as they'd got up early. Anna was now huge and was finding it hard to get comfortable in any position, whether it was lying down, sitting or standing. That day, she'd got up complaining of backache and Grace had tried to ease it by giving her a back rub, while she leant against a chair. Anna thanked her and said it had helped but Grace wasn't so sure it had; she had told Anna to go and sit at the table while she made the tea and toast. She was finding being so large difficult to cope with, often feeling breathless and needing to go to the loo every half hour. Grace tried to help her as much as she could, but there were limits as to what she could do.

Anna was by now at home all day; she'd given up work three weeks ago and there was just under a month to go. Although she found life at home on her own lonely and boring, she couldn't even contemplate going to work anymore. Their spending was now restricted but Grace was happy to be the sole breadwinner and do as much as she could in terms of shopping and housework.

Anna spent her days reading and watching daytime television. Sometimes, she ventured out to the shops but only to visit places that sold baby gear nearby. They'd decided they could no longer put off buying baby things – they wanted to be ready when the time came. They'd given the small second bedroom a makeover, Anna using her artistic skills to decorate it. It was now just about ready, except for a few things they'd get at the last minute.

Anna would go into the nursery and simply gaze down at the cot, trying to imagine the baby living inside her, lying on the mattress in front of her. Although the baby made herself known constantly with her sheer weight and kicking, the fact that she was going to be a real person, a real baby, was hard to grasp.

She instinctively knew that Grace would be an amazing mother, she had all the right character traits: patience, kindness and empathy. Whether she herself would prove to be a natural mother or not, she'd soon find out. She hoped so.

The birth itself secretly terrified her. She pretended to Grace that she was calm and relaxed about it; she didn't want her to be anxious, after all the time she'd spent, waiting to be a mother. They both wanted it to be a natural birth; she and Grace had been to NCT classes together and in some ways, she felt well prepared. But were you ever prepared for such a huge event in your life?

That day, after Grace left for work, she took herself back to bed, feeling utterly exhausted. Her backache was temporarily eased when she lay down; she rested on her side with her bump on a pillow and her upper leg on another pillow, as she'd been taught to do and for a while she was able to drop off to sleep. When she woke up, she reached for her mobile to look at the time and realised she'd been asleep for only half an hour. The pain in her back had intensified and she reached round with her hands to try to massage her own back.

Although Grace had said *never* to have a bath without her, she decided that maybe a warm bath might help. Heaving herself out of bed, she stumbled to the bathroom, the pain radiating down her legs.

Leaning against the basin, she tried to catch a breath; she then turned her attention to the bath. Bending over to reach the taps felt virtually impossible but she managed it after two attempts. Having carefully undressed, she placed one leg into the water and then lifted the other leg over the edge of the bath, gripping the cold porcelain. She sat down with great care and tentatively lay back. She had deliberately made the water lukewarm, knowing that hot water would probably make her feel weaker.

When she looked at herself, prone and vulnerable, huge yet beautiful, she couldn't believe the transformation that a human body could go through. It was such a miracle. The baby wasn't moving as much as she used to; she supposed there really wasn't much room anymore. But now, it was as if she was trying to make more room by pushing her limbs against her watery walls. It was mesmerising to watch a passing elbow or knee glide across her bump.

To start with, the water helped to distract her from the pain that never seemed to go away but as the water cooled, the pain rushed back in. She made a pathetic attempt to wash herself and then, gripping the sides of the bath, she slowly raised herself until she was standing. She was so aware that she could slip – she could hear Grace's voice in her head, telling her to be careful.

At that moment, she felt helpless and wished that she had taken Grace's advice.

Very gingerly, she extricated herself from the bath, wrapped herself in a towel, and stared at herself in the steamy mirror above the basin.

It comes to something when taking a bath is such a big deal.

The effort involved had made her feel even more fatigued than she did before and now she had to find the energy to get dressed. She put on some trousers that could be very loosely tied around her; she couldn't bear anything touching her stomach. A sloppy jumper that had absolutely no shape was the finishing touch. No bra. No knickers.

While she was on maternity leave, she'd been trying to write some songs, as a way to fill her time and to make her days seem more meaningful. She went to her computer and opened one song she'd been working on the day before. It was all about new beginnings and hope and as the melody floated around her, she could visualise the perfect person waiting to live her life, curled up inside her. She felt a surge of joy and turned the volume right up; she didn't care about the neighbours, she just wanted to immerse herself in the song.

The pain and the music now merged into one, a crescendo of agony. She pressed stop and silence once more descended, with the suddenness of an explosion.

She stood up and started walking around the flat. She felt hot; her forehead was burning and perspiration was running down her face – she felt sweat trickling down her bump from her armpits. She caught sight of herself in a mirror. Her face shocked her; she had a wild look about her. Her eyes, normally so bright, were dull and hollow.

What's happening to me? Maybe I'm in labour and this is what it feels like?

But she knew there was something not right and the realisation, made her panic.

Her heart was beating hyper-fast, her legs felt as if they were collapsing beneath her. Thoughts were flashing through her mind – *I must get to hospital and quickly. It's too early, there's still a month to go, this can't be happening. But it is happening and I've got to stay calm. My bag's packed, I know what I've got to do. Everything will be okay. I'll call for an ambulance, right now.*

The pain had crept from the small of her back around to the front as well; she'd read that this was a sign of true labour, so she picked up her mobile and for the first time ever, she dialled 999. It was such a dramatic thing to do but she was alone, there was no alternative. They talked calmly to her, but her voice gave her away. She tried to describe her symptoms so they'd understand that she wasn't just having Braxton Hicks contractions. She was terrified. They said they would be there very soon.

She knew she must phone Grace and let her know. She could barely think straight but she dialled her number and soon heard her voice.

WHEN THE PHONE CALL came in, Grace was in an important meeting with about ten other people. She always kept her phone on these days in case Anna rang, even though the company's policy was 'no phones' in meetings. She had it on silent but she could hear it vibrating loudly in her bag, next to her laptop.

"Sorry," she said, apologetically to the others, "I'll have to take this," and she stood up and rushed to the door.

Her work colleagues didn't know about her home situation. As far as they knew, she was still with Leo. She didn't think it was anyone else's business.

She could tell the moment she heard Anna's voice, that something was wrong.

She tried to keep her voice even when Anna said the ambulance was on its way.

"Right," she said, "I'm leaving now. I'll see you at the hospital as soon as possible. Remember all the breathing you've learned."

She ran back into the meeting, picked up her laptop and bag and without explaining why, said she had to leave immediately. Everyone looked taken aback, as this was so unlike the way Grace usually conducted herself.

"Is everything okay, Grace? Is there anything I can do?" asked her boss.

"No ... nothing," she said abruptly, not looking up. She continued to collect the numerous papers that were on the table.

"I'll see you tomorrow," she muttered, as she fled through the door.

Little did anyone know, including Grace, that she wouldn't come back to her job for a long time.

WHEN SHE REACHED THE street, she grabbed her phone from her bag and quickly went on her Uber app. Five minutes, it said. She watched impatiently as the map showed her taxi making its slow progress towards her. She knew the car's make and registration number and that her driver was called

Mohammed and saw that it was annoyingly stuck in traffic, only a stone's throw away, then suddenly it moved and she saw it approaching. He pulled in and she felt relief flood through her.

She climbed in the back seat, looking at her watch – it was 2.25 p.m. The journey was going to take at least 30 minutes. The traffic was, as always, heavy and the taxi was crawling along at walking speed.

"Can you go a different way? My partner's in labour and I need to get there," she said, sounding ruder than she meant to.

"I'm sorry m'am, this is the best way, I'm afraid. It should speed up in a minute when we get past those lights."

She wanted to get out of the taxi and run but she knew that would be a stupid thing to do and fortunately, he was right: once they'd got through two sets of lights, he sped up and seemed to understand the urgency, as he overtook and swapped lanes. Grace didn't care about his sudden breaking and rather dangerous manoeuvres. She just wanted to get there. She kept checking her watch, willing time to slow down and the taxi to speed up.

She texted Leo: *In taxi on way to hospital. Anna's in labour. Stuck in traffic. I can't believe it's happening. It's too early. G.*

Opening Google maps, she put in the destination and could see their blue dot inching its way towards the destination and after a lifetime, it said 'time to destination, five minutes'. The journey had been interminable; how could time stretch like that? Normally, she'd have made conversation with the driver, but today, she couldn't – there was just too much to think about.

She suddenly thought of Alex and looked hurriedly through her contacts for his phone number. Should she call? He'd always said he was happy to donate his sperm but wanted them to be the 'parents'. But now that it was happening, surely he'd want to know?

She decided to text instead.

Hey Alex, thought you'd want to know that Anna is in labour. G

Her phone buzzed and she saw it was Leo; she hadn't expected him to reply, to be honest, she thought he'd probably be in court.

Oh my God. So exciting. Keep me informed. Be strong for Anna. Love Leo.

At last, they pulled up at the entrance of the hospital. She flung herself out of the taxi, shouting 'thank you' to the driver as she slammed the door. She ran up the steps and asked an official looking person the way to Obstetrics. She marched to the lift and pressed Floor 2. It was full of people and everyone studiously avoided making eye contact; no one spoke.

With a ping, the doors opened and a lot of people exited at Floor 2. Grace followed the arrows and after what felt like a marathon, she arrived at the desk.

"My partner, Annalise Baker ... she came in ... ambulance ... maybe in the last twenty minutes?" she said, breathing heavily.

"Okay. Let me just take a look ..." said the annoyingly slow woman behind the desk.

"Ah, yes ... she's been taken down to Room 3."

"Thank you," cried Grace, as she started heading off down another corridor. She could hear sounds that frightened her, coming from closed doors: someone was wailing, another moaning. Having never given birth herself before, the noises were alien and intimidating.

Room 3 turned out to be about as far away from the desk as was possible. Grace knocked tentatively and pushed the door open.

There was Anna, surrounded by machines. Grace rushed over to her, grabbed her hand and said, "I'm here, I'm here."

Her face was ashen, her eyes dark and tired.

"I can't do this, Grace. I can't do this ... it shouldn't be like this," she murmured.

"Yes, you can. Hold my hand. Squeeze it as hard as you can."

"That's right," said the midwife. "Hold her hand; encourage her ... rub her back. She'll be fine. I'm Anna's midwife, we have a great team here."

Grace looked at her; she was so young. Was she experienced? She looked as if she was just out of university. Was no one else going to help her? Where were the doctors?

"What's the situation?" said Grace. "How many centimetres ... is it going to be long?"

"Baby will come when Baby is ready," said the midwife, smiling tightly. "Annalise is doing very well. We're just going to check for signs of foetal distress."

Putting something on her stomach, the midwife looked at the monitor by her side, which started pulsing. She said, "It's okay at the moment, but we'll keep an eye on this."

She then left the room.

With another contraction, Anna was starting to make the kind of noises Grace had never heard before: wild and loud, like an animal. She was squeezing Grace's hand so hard that she could feel her knuckles being crushed. This is wrong, thought Grace, but then again, what was she to know? She'd never experienced it. The reality was terrifying.

The midwife eventually came back in with a young male doctor. They both bustled over to the machine; they looked at each other and Grace sensed it wasn't good.

"The baby is beginning to show distress. We're going to keep this monitor on now. If things don't improve, we might have to get the baby out. Let's wait and see."

The doctor bustled out, leaving Grace feeling sick.

"What do we do now?" she asked the midwife.

"Nothing for you to worry about. We'll take care of her. We don't want to do a C-section, unless we absolutely have to. I know Anna had plans for a completely natural birth but sometimes that just isn't possible. We'll keep popping back in to check."

Grace looked at Anna; she was so vulnerable and afraid, so unlike her. She went into the toilet and dampened one of the paper towels.

"We can do this, we can," said Grace, wiping her brow. Anna moved her head from side to side, saying, "It's *me*, only *me*. I'm the one ... there's no *we*. Why did I think I could do this?"

The contraction started again, building up so high that Anna was breathing through the gas and air mouthpiece, as if her life literally depended on it.

This sequence went on for an eternity, time slipping by for Grace in mists of panic. She tried to help but it was true, only Anna could do this, only *she* could feel the pain.

The nurse and midwife would bustle in now and again, look at the monitor, and walk out again, leaving Grace to deal with Anna alone. She saw Anna fading fast into a world apart from her, a world beyond anyone's control; she felt utterly helpless and alone.

"Please ... do ... something," Anna pleaded softly, at the end of yet another contraction.

Grace looked at the clock; only an hour had passed since she'd last looked.

No one was in the room, only her and Anna.

Where are they all? Shouldn't someone be with them?

She let go of Anna's hand and went outside into the corridor and shouted, "Can someone come? Is anyone there?"

She crashed back through the door and pushed a button, hoping someone would come; she couldn't stand it any longer. Someone should be in here, with them.

After a minute or so, the midwife came in and went straight to the machine again.

"We need to get this baby out NOW," she said, her serene calmness evaporating.

She pressed another button and then the room was full of people, noise, chaos and confusion. Anna was lifted onto a trolley and before Grace realised what was happening, Anna disappeared through the door. "Can I come ..."

"I'm sorry," said a nurse. "An emergency C-section."

As the midwife was leaving the room, Grace called after her, "Will they both be okay?"

"We just need to get the baby out. Anna will have a general anaesthetic ... we'll do all we can," and with that, she dashed out.

The nurse, a young auburn-haired girl of no more than twenty, smiled wanly at Grace and held the door open. "Come with me."

They walked down the corridor, in silence, the noise of the previous minutes now gone. Grace was in a daze. She couldn't believe what was happening. All their plans, all their natural birth strategies had been for nothing. Poor Anna was now in the hands of strangers and machines and there was nothing she could do about it.

Nothing.

She sat down on a hard chair where the young nurse indicated. "Would you like a cup of tea? There's a machine just down there," she said, pointing down yet another corridor.

"No, thank you." She felt sick, there was no way she wanted anything.

"Just wait here ... I'm sure you'll hear something very soon. Is there anyone who could wait with you?"

"No ..." she said. "There isn't."

"If you need anything, I'll be down there," she said and walked off.

Grace didn't care about anything except Anna and the baby. She stared ahead at the posters on the wall opposite about HIV, breast-feeding and heart disease. She tried to focus on them, but the words meant nothing.

She looked at her watch; only three hours ago, she'd been sitting in a meeting, oblivious of what was in store. If she'd only known ... she could have got to Anna earlier, helped her ... if only, if only. She knew it was pointless thinking this way but she couldn't stop her mind going round in circles.

She thought of telling someone ... the only person she wanted to talk to right now was Leo. She needed him, she really did. She got out her phone.

Leo this is a nightmare. I'm not allowed into the operating room. She's having an emergency C-section. I don't know what to do. I couldn't help her.

He came straight back: *Oh no. Do you want me to come?*

She texted: *No. I'll let you know when it's over.*
He came back with: *OK. I'm thinking of you all. xx*

GRACE HAD BEEN WAITING for over three quarters of an hour now.

Why had no one come out to see her? Surely the operation was over now? They said they were going to get the baby out immediately. Her stomach felt as if it was swirling around inside her, her legs were as weak as a foal's. She kept standing up, then sitting down again. She'd been up to the desk but all they could say was, there was no news. She sat back down, leant forward with her head resting on her knees. She stayed like that for a while and then sat up, still dazed.

At last ... the young doctor and the midwife were walking towards her. Something about their faces alerted Grace. They weren't wearing the faces of good news. They looked serious, embarrassed, unsure.

"Grace?" said the doctor.

"Yes," she said, standing up unsteadily, almost stumbling. The doctor grabbed her arm to steady her.

"Would you like to follow me?" he said, glancing sideways at her. "Just here ..." and he pushed open a door which led into a small room, stood back and let her go in first. The nurse sat next to her.

"What's happened? Can I see them?" she said.

"Grace ... we got the baby out and she is a good weight. She's doing fine. She's a little jaundiced ..."

"Oh, thank god ..." said Grace, tears brimming over. "I thought something awful had happened."

The doctor put his hand on her arm and waited.

The world stopped spinning.

"I'm afraid ... Anna ... suffered ... severe bleeding. We tried everything we could ... but, I'm so *very* sorry, Grace ... Anna ... died ... a few minutes ago."

Grace could hear a loud buzzing noise in her head; she couldn't hear what he was saying ... something about Anna dying ...

"Excuse me ..." she said, her head slipping forward over her lap. She sat up, stared at him, this person sitting opposite her saying this ridiculous thing.

"I don't understand ... where's Anna? Where's the baby? I need to see them ..."

"Grace ... Anna ... is ... dead. I'm so very sorry for your loss. We did everything we could. Sometimes ... there is nothing ... we can do. Do you understand?"

His words meant nothing. It was as if he was speaking a foreign language and that noise ... she couldn't stop the buzzing in her head. She stood up abruptly, saying, "I must go to her, I must go ..." and her legs buckled beneath her and she fainted flat out on the floor.

Chapter 8

Leo was just packing up to go home when the phone call came. He'd been thinking of Grace all afternoon; fortunately, he hadn't been in court. He saw her name on his mobile and felt a surge of relief. He quickly answered the call, but it wasn't her voice.

"Grace?"

"No, this is Nurse Jackson, Leo, calling on behalf of Grace. She asked me to ring you."

"What's happened, where's Grace?"

"I think you should come down to the hospital, if you can, sir. Grace needs you right now."

"Please tell me …"

"Not on the phone, sir. Can I tell her you can come?"

"Yes, yes, of course. I'll be there as soon as I can. Where is she exactly?"

"Just get to Obstetrics and ask at reception."

"Okay, will do," he said, looking at his watch. "It should be in about forty minutes, all being well."

"Thank you," said the distant voice and the phone went dead.

He quickly texted Amber, explaining the situation and said he'd text again when he knew what was going on.

There must be something wrong with the baby, he thought. Very wrong. Why else would Grace need him? Why couldn't she call or text herself? Why couldn't Anna give her the support she needed? It was all so strange.

He had a very bad feeling about it.

He rushed around, collecting his papers he was due to work on in the evening and put his head around the door of one of the busy offices.

"I'm off ..."

"You're early ... everything okay?"

"No, I must run. See you tomorrow," and he was gone, leaving the people in there somewhat confused. It was very unlike Leo to be so curt.

Despite what he was wearing, he jogged to the tube station, about a casual ten minute walk away, dodging in and out of people on the pavement and getting some annoyed looks along the way. He went straight to the barrier, wanting to queue jump all the slow people in front of him. He would normally stand on the escalators and let them take him down into the depths of the station but this time, he walked quickly down them, saying 'excuse me, excuse me' as he went.

He knew the tube map like the back of his hand so there was no need to work out which platform he needed, he just followed the crowd, feeling the rush of warm, stale air forcing its way down the corridor. There were masses of people on the platform but another train was due in three minutes.

How can three minutes feel so long?

At last, the train approached with a shock of noise and movement and he stepped forward. The doors opened, some people got out, but not many, and he pushed his way onto the already crowded train. He had seven stops to endure. He stood by a stainless steel pole, holding onto it as he was shoved around by other passengers and sudden jerks of movement. He'd lived in London for so long and commuted by the tube so much, that he was normally oblivious to those around him; he could block out the discomfort and the incessant loud noises that were part of this form of travel. But today ... he was aware of everything, as if his brain was on high alert.

At last, his stop arrived. He had to wait, while the sheer number of passengers shuffled down the corridor but when he saw the up escalator, he shoved forward and ran up the steps, flying towards the exit. He didn't know this part of London that well and he had to pause in the main atrium, get out his phone, go onto Google maps and work out which exit he needed. He put in his destination and soon, with the miracle of technology, he had the bright blue dot showing him the way. An eight minute walk, apparently. Again, he jogged the distance and by the time he arrived at the Obstetrics desk, he was in a muck sweat.

There were two nurses at the station, who were both staring at a computer.

"I was rung by a Nurse Jackson, regarding Grace ..." he said, hoping one of them might look up.

"Are you Leo? I'm Nurse Jackson," she said and came round the desk. "That was lucky ... come with me, please," and she walked briskly down the corridor, ushering him into a room.

"Please, sit down."

Leo, by this time, was fearing the worst, whatever that was, but nothing prepared him for what the nurse said next.

"I'm afraid I have some terrible news ... Grace's partner, Anna, has ... died, Leo." She let the words fall into the room and waited.

"Can I get you some water?" She peered at him with concern etched on her face. She could see the devastating effect of her words.

"What?" he said, leaning forward with his elbows on his knees, his head in his hands. "How can this happen? How could you LET this happen?" he cried.

"We did everything we could, but Anna suffered what we call a 'postpartum haemorrhage' or severe bleeding, as a result of complications during labour. The baby was showing signs of distress and we had to do an emergency C section. This is a very rare situation, to lose a mother … I'm so sorry."

Leo, having felt hot from his frenzied journey, turned as cold as if he'd jumped into the Thames on a winter's day.

He looked up. "Is the baby …"

"The baby is doing well. As you know, she was early but, all things considered, she's doing well and is an incubator. She has jaundice."

He felt so confused. The birth of a baby should be a happy event but this was shrouded in death and grief.

He said, "Thank God she's alive. Where's Grace?"

"She's lying down, just down the corridor. I wanted to tell you before you went to her. She fainted when she heard the news but she's come round now and beginning to feel a little better but it's been, as you can imagine, a terrible shock for her. Can I ask what relation you are to her?"

"I'm her ex-husband. It's complicated … we were married for years and we're still best friends."

"Of course … I'm so pleased you were able to come. She said you were the only person she wanted to see. Shall I take you to her now?"

He stood up, his legs nearly giving way.

"Yes, please. Has she seen the baby yet?"

"No, not yet. She's not been well enough. Maybe that's something you could do together?"

"Yes, maybe ..." he said, not knowing what would be the right thing to do.

The nurse opened the door and saying, "Follow me," she walked ahead of him. At a door on the right, she stopped and said, "Here we are. I'll leave you ..." and she walked away.

He stood outside the door, hesitating.

GRACE WAS SITTING ON the edge of the bed, her head down. To Leo, she looked like a lost child.

"Grace, I'm here."

She looked up, stared at him as if she wasn't sure who he was, tears running down her cheeks. Her beautiful hair, normally her crowning glory, looked dishevelled; her face was ghost-like.

He walked towards her, she shuffled to her feet and he enveloped her in his arms. He could feel her body shaking and clung to her even harder, holding her up. She now sobbed loudly, the noise getting louder and louder.

"Sh ... sh ... sh ..." he whispered, stroking her hair. "Come on, Grace. Sit down here," and he placed her back down on the bed. He sat beside her, his arm around her shoulders, as her sobs quietened. He was trying to work out what he could possibly say to make the situation better but he decided there were no words ... nothing he could say would make any difference. Talk of what actually happened could wait ... he had to help her right now.

They sat in silence; he felt the best thing for her was to simply be there for her.

The same nurse put her head around the door; Leo looked at her and she disappeared again, not saying anything.

"So, Grace ..." he whispered, "the first thing we must do, I think, is to go, together, to see Theadora. She's doing well ... in an incubator for her jaundice. We must ..."

"I can't, I can't ..."

"Yes, you can, Grace. She needs you ..."

"But ..."

"Grace, you *must* be strong for her. You're her *mother* now."

Grace's head, which had been hanging down, swivelled sharply to look at him, as if reality had hit her forcefully.

"How can you say that? I'm *not* her mother ... I don't know what to do ..."

"Grace, you've wanted to be a mother all your life. You'll *know* what to do. I promise you. It will come naturally to you. I know it will. Come on, we'll go and see her," he said and stood up, pulling on her hand. She stood up reluctantly and he guided her to the door.

He realised he had no idea where to go, so he went down to the nurse's station again and got directions. Grace walked at a slow pace, breathing heavily. She had to lean against the wall on two occasions to catch her breath.

They entered the room, full of little boxes with precious lives in them. A nurse took them to the one in the furthest corner.

They both stood, gazing down at this little scrap of humanity, sleeping peacefully. A mop of black hair adorned her head; her skin, so smooth, did have a yellow tinge but only added to the overall beauty of her. Her eyes were covered and they could see a light shining above the cot.

"Baby is just undergoing some treatment for her jaundice called phototherapy. We need to get her bilirubin levels down; this should only take a day or two. Don't worry, this happens a lot," said the nurse, smiling encouragingly.

"She's so tiny ..." said Grace.

"Actually, she's quite a good weigh for a baby born early ... she's a strong little thing."

"That's good," said Leo, but sharing Grace's concern. She did indeed look so vulnerable, so small.

"You can stay with her for as long as you want. Talk to her ... touch her through here," said the nurse indicating a hole. "She's aware of your voices and your touch. It will help her recover." The nurse went off and collected two chairs for them and they sat either side of her, watching her intently.

"Shall I ..." said Grace, tentatively moving her hand towards the hole.

"Yes, go on ..."

Very gently, Grace put her hand through and with one finger, she stroked the tiny, bird-like arm. Her finger went back and forth, back and forth.

"It's so soft."

They sat like this for at least an hour.

Leo could tell Grace was exhausted and he was trying to work out what to do. There was no way she could go back to the flat, that would be too terrible for her. There was no other alternative but to take her back to the house. Amber wouldn't mind ... not in these circumstances. His mind was in overdrive, thinking about all the people who should be informed of what had happened: Grace's family ... Alex ... Anna's father ... Jen and Rachel ... but how was he going to bring the subject up with her?

It was all just ... so ... cruel.

"I'm just going to make a phone call ... you stay here, and then I think we should go and get you some sleep."

Grace looked at him – her finger still on the baby's arm – and stared blankly as if the words didn't penetrate.

He smiled and went to leave the room. One of the nurses said, "I think your partner should maybe get some rest now ..."

"Yes, I'm just going to make some arrangements," not correcting her assumption.

Once outside in the corridor, he wondered who to call first. He didn't know Alex's number; he would have to wait until he'd broached the subject with Grace.

He called Amber's number and when she picked up, he realised he was going to frighten her with what had happened. She, too, was going to give birth soon; this was not the sort of thing a pregnant woman wanted to hear. He told her as gently as possible and he could hear the shock and fear in her voice.

"Oh My God ... Oh My GOD. Surely this doesn't happen these days?"

"It's very rare ... very rare ... Amber. We mustn't dwell on this now, we have to think practically about what we do. Grace can't possibly go back to the flat ... she desperately needs some sleep. I'm going to bring her back to the house, if that's okay?"

"Of course, of course," she said, distractedly.

"Are you there now?"

"Yes ..."

"Can you make up the spare room for her ..."

"Yes, sure."

"I'm not sure what time we'll be there – we'll get an Uber. I'll text you when we're near."

He ended the call, maybe too quickly but he was so aware of all the other people he should inform.

He rang one of Grace's sisters and asked her to tell the rest of the family. He rang Jen, who was so shocked, she nearly fainted on the phone. Fortunately, Mike was there and he told him too and asked him to phone Rachel. Leo couldn't face making any more calls and he needed to get back to Grace.

He went back along the corridor, wondering how he was going to cope with one of the most difficult things he'd ever had to face.

Chapter 9

Hello Rachel, it is me Demetris, from Cyprus. I coming in London, to visit my cousins. They live in the east part, Walthamstow. I arrive in middle December and I am seeing London a lot. My cousin, Petros, he says Brighton is very fine and says I would like it. I hoping to come to see you and maybe you may show me your city – is ok with you? From your Cypriot friend, Demetris.

Rachel stared at the text. She'd thought a lot about him when she'd got home but as time went by, his memory had faded and she'd decided that it was just a stupid holiday crush. Now, six months on, he'd popped into her phone – how was she going to respond? Did she *want* to see him?

She was sitting by the open fire in the sitting room; the flames were leaping up the chimney, the logs occasionally crackling and spitting. She'd lit a candle and closed the curtains to shut out the cold, damp December day. She'd recently read an article about Danish *hygge* and she was determined to use their ideas during the long winter months. The scent from the candle was heavenly – spicy and orangey.

Cyprus was so far away now.

She shut her eyes, sat back in her chair and tried to imagine lying on those sun-soaked beaches. Her mind meandered to the villa and the village taverna ... could she even see Demetris' face?

She could, but she preferred the memory of Mike touching her hand on the beach.

She hadn't seen much of Mike since Cyprus; she'd popped up to see Jen when she'd had the result of the biopsy. Poor Jen, she'd been so scared at the thought of having a lumpectomy and although Rachel was no expert about these things, she'd gone up there to persuade her it was the right thing to do. She'd been shocked at how bad Mike looked – the worry about Jen and the business had certainly taken its toll.

She opened her eyes, read the text again and decided to reply to Demetris and say 'yes'. She'd like to see him and it was only for a day – what harm would there be? Now that Zach had finally moved out, she had to admit she felt alone and in need of company. Funny how a negative presence can still be felt as another human in the house. She wasn't used to her own company all the time.

It would be fun to show him round – they'd go to the Lanes, the pier, the beach ... he'd love it all, she was sure. So, she picked up her mobile and wrote:

Hey Demetris, How lovely to hear from you. Yes, do come down. Text when you know which day you arrive and I'll come and pick you up from the station. Rachel x

That was non-committal enough, wasn't it? Friendly, but not OTT, she thought. She closed her phone and was just going to turn on the TV when her phone started vibrating; she didn't often have the ring on, she found it too obtrusive.

She snatched it up, hoping it would be one of the boys (she hadn't heard anything from George and she decided she *must* text him) and her mood lifted when she saw it was Mike's name up on the screen. He never rang her, or very rarely; they had a silent agreement that they would keep their distance. His name on her screen filled her with the usual longing. But then she immediately thought that there must be something wrong with Jen. Had he been able to persuade her to have radiation therapy? She was being very stubborn about it. She poked the green button with her forefinger, wanting to hear his voice.

"Hi, Rach ..."

His voice sounded strained and flat. Oh God, there *was* something wrong.

"Mike? Is everything okay? You sound strange ... Is Jen all right?"

"Rach ... it's not Jen. She's doing fine. But ..."

"You're scaring me, Mike. You're not ill, are you? I couldn't bear it ..."

"Rach, I'm fine ... but I do have some truly awful news. There's no easy way of saying this. Anna went ..."

"Anna? What's happened? Is the baby ..."

"Anna went into early labour ... she had to have an emergency C section ... the baby is fine ... but ... Anna ... passed away a few hours ago. I'm so sorry to tell you ... Rachel, are you there?"

Rachel's mind went into shock; she took the phone away from her ear.

She could hear Mike's voice and pressed the speaker button.

"... I'm here, Mike."

"That's all I know at the moment. Leo rang me, he's with Grace. He asked me to ring you. So I have. I'm numb. Jen is in bits. I know we never even met her in the end, but she seemed like part of our group. Poor Grace ... what the hell is she going to do?"

His voice rang out, filling the room.

Of course … Grace would have full responsibility now … how would that work? Did they have a legal document to prove that Grace was her partner?

"Leo says he's going to take her home with him and I can understand why. She can't go back to the place she shared with Anna. It's unbelievable that this could happen these days, isn't it … in this country? Mothers just don't die in childbirth … do they?"

Rachel realised that he was thinking of Amber, due to give birth soon. Poor Mike.

"It's very rare, but it *does* happen, Mike. Anna was an older mother; I think it's more prevalent with people who are considered 'old' to give birth." She paused and then added, softly, "Amber will be fine, Mike. She's young and fit."

There was a long silence as they both were unsure what to say next.

"I wonder whether there was some sort of medical negligence or something?" said Rachel, subconsciously trying to make Mike realise that it couldn't happen to Amber too.

"I don't know anything … just what I told you. I'm sure Leo will be onto any suggestion that the hospital did something wrong."

"What do we do now? Do you think we can help in any way?"

"No … Rach … I think we've just got to sit tight and see how the next couple of days pan out. I must go now … Jen's really not taken this very well. She's finally getting over the operation, thank goodness, but I'm worried this will set her right back."

"What about the radiation therapy? Have you managed to persuade her?"

"No ... God knows what's going on in her head, but she thinks she's been through enough and they say the cancer has been excised completely so what's the point of putting her body through yet more trauma? I've never known her be so stubborn."

"Well, it's her body, maybe we've just got to respect her views?"

"But they're wrong, Rach ... I've told her she's being selfish, which I know sounds awful but she kind of *is* ... she could leave Amber without a mother and me without my wife ..."

He sounded so miserable that Rachel was at a loss as to what to say, so she just said, "Let me know if you hear from Leo. I won't contact him or Grace for a couple of days ... or maybe I'll text Leo just to say I'm thinking of them both."

"Okay, bye, Rach."

It was strange to put Grace and Leo together in a sentence again.

THAT NIGHT, RACHEL sat alone, her mind churning. Mike had rung her an hour ago and she'd been in a daze ever since. She'd never even met Anna but she was devastated for Grace. How was she going to carry on? When she thought about how excited Grace had been, she had to close her mind.

She stared at the TV screen, hardly understanding what she was watching. When a medical drama came on, she turned the channel over. She didn't feel like eating but forced herself to have some toast.

All she could think of was Grace ... and this tiny person who didn't have her birth mother any more.

Should she tell Zach? He'd been, to be fair, part of this friendship unit but ... she decided he'd lost the right to be considered one of 'them' a long time ago. He didn't know Anna and he never got on particularly well with Grace, so would he even be interested?

He was so smug about the prospect of moving to Cyprus, which was looking distinctly possible; he'd found a job flying executive jets to the Middle East and he could base himself with Liz; he just needed to make the final decision of resigning, but he was sure he would. The new job paid far better and was more interesting, he assured her. He'd told Rachel with such excitement, she'd almost felt pleased for him ... but she was still fighting with him over the house, so that feeling dissipated quickly. She'd found herself a brilliant solicitor and she had every confidence in him. If Zach was going to be so much better off, then he could give her his share of the house, couldn't he?

She decided to go to bed but before she did, she thought she must text George. With the upset of Anna, it put things into perspective and she wanted George to get back with Beth. Life was too short. She decided not to tell him about Anna; he'd had enough to deal with at the moment.

Hey – How are you? Just wanted to check in with you, love, Mum xx

She turned off the TV, tidied away the newspaper, straightened and plumped up the cushions and turned off the lights. This was when she felt acutely aware of being alone. When the TV was chattering away in the corner of the room, she could convince herself that she had company, but the silence of the house was all pervasive now. She felt like she had to walk quietly; she didn't want to break the hush.

Having poured herself a glass of water to take upstairs, she checked the back door was locked and then went to the front door too. It was strange, when Zach lived here, it didn't occur to her to do this. She turned off the hall light and made her way upstairs, finally turning off the corridor light outside her bedroom. The house was now in darkness. She quickly turned on her bedroom light and as she closed the door, she slid the lock across – a hangover from when she and Zach were intimate and didn't want the boys barging in. She knew it was ridiculous – a passing rapist or burglar could easily break the lock, but it gave her a small feeling of security.

She was just getting into bed when her phone buzzed. It was a text from George.

Hi Mum – yea, thanks, I'm ok. We haven't talked about the proposal – Beth's had the worst shift at the hospital. She's absolutely devastated. One of her mothers died just after an emergency cesarean. They couldn't stop her bleeding. She's even saying she doesn't want to carry on being a midwife. I'm sorry I haven't been in touch – but you can imagine? Love George x

Rachel couldn't believe what she was reading. It was too much of a coincidence to be anyone other than Anna. She got into bed and flopped back onto the pillow, leaving her mobile on her stomach.

How was she going to break it to George?

Chapter 10

The next day, Rachel decided she *had* to tell him about Anna and how she must have been the mother Beth had to deal with.

He was on a lunch break when she called, as she knew he would be; his routine was predictable.

She started off by saying how sorry she was to hear about Beth's experience at work and casually asked which hospital she works in. The answer was, as she suspected, the same one as Anna's. She then had to tell him, very gently, that the person who had died was Grace's partner.

"Oh My God, Mum, that's terrible. Poor Grace ... I don't know what to say. What on earth do I tell Beth?"

"There's nothing you *can* say, George. I just thought you ought to know. I haven't spoken to Grace yet. Leo is looking after her. Maybe don't tell Beth anything?"

"Leo? I thought they'd split up – what about Amber? Is she okay?"

"I don't know any of the details but I think Leo was the only one Grace asked for."

"But Mum ... this makes it *so* much worse for Beth. This is someone we all have a connection with, someone real, someone ... she's no longer just a 'patient'. I think I'll have to tell her now; if I leave it, it will be so much worse."

"Well, you must do whatever you think's right, George. Unfortunately, Beth will come across very difficult situations in her work – babies dying, disabled babies, Downs Syndrome ... she'll have to get used to dealing with horrible things."

She felt awful being so 'practical' with George but she was trying to make him see the reality.

"Yes, Mum, she knows all that; she's had a baby death and a case of permanent brain damage ... but the death of a mother, relatively young ... it's really affected her."

"I'm sure ..." said Rachel, not knowing what to say.

"I'll tell her tonight. She's got a few days off ... it will give her time to think."

"Okay. I'll phone you again in a couple of days."

"Bye, Mum."

"I love you, George," she said, as the phone went dead. She stared at it, her eyes filling with tears.

HE TOLD BETH ABOUT Anna as gently as he could. He knew he had to tell her and it was better coming from him.

Beth was very shaken by his news, even though she didn't personally know Anna or Grace.

"So ... Grace is your Mum's best friend? Oh My God ... I saw her there, of course. I remember her beautiful red hair from those photos you showed me of the three friends; we had to get her out of the room when it all started going wrong."

"It seems unbelievable ..." said George. He was just about to say something about the fact that Anna died, but stopped himself. Him going on about the rarity of a mother dying as a result of childbirth wouldn't help Beth ... she didn't need to hear his opinion. What could he say that could be of any comfort to her?

"I keep going over the whole labour in my head. It's churning round and round. Could we have done anything differently? Did we miss something?"

"You can't do that to yourself, Beth."

"I know, I know. There'll be an enquiry ... they'll scrutinise everything ... my job might be on the line."

"I'm sure it won't ..."

"How do you know? You don't know anything, George."

He decided not to say anything back – how could he? She was right, he knew nothing about the circumstances, nothing about medicine, nothing about how she was feeling. All he must do is offer her his support.

They hadn't talked about the proposal – it didn't feel right somehow. He wanted to ask her if she still loved him. He wondered if she'd simply come back to the house because she had nowhere else to go.

"Why don't you go and have a long soak in the bath, Beth? Are you hungry?"

"No, I couldn't eat a thing. Okay, I will ... and then I'll go to bed."

He'd already decided that he'd sleep in the spare room. He didn't want her to have to face him with his body in close proximity to hers, when she was already so stressed. They would have to leave that for another day.

THREE DAYS LATER, BETH got up early and went to work. They'd continued to sleep in different rooms and had hardly talked to each other, except for practicalities, like shopping and the dishwasher. George had tried to carry on as normal; he'd decided to stay in the spare room, so as not to put any pressure on her.

It was as if they were flatmates, living their own lives, but with none of the sex, fun or camaraderie. He was going to wait for *her* to come to *him*. It was against all his instincts; he wanted to hold her and kiss her and tell her how sorry he was – about *everything*. But he knew that would be the wrong thing to do.

His phone buzzed as he was walking to the Tube.

Mum.

Could he face talking to her? He decided he should, even though he wasn't in the mood.

"Hey ... how are you?"

"I'm good. I was ringing to find out how *you* are. Have you spoken to Beth?"

"Yes ..."

"How did it go?"

"Well, it made things worse, really. She couldn't believe that I was loosely connected to Anna and that Grace is your best friend. Such an awful coincidence. Have you heard how it's going? When's the funeral?"

"I spoke to Grace for the first time last night. I rang her, not expecting her to pick up to be honest, and she did. It was so strange to talk to her; her voice was totally flat. I tried to steer the conversation to Theadora. She's a very placid baby apparently – sleeps a lot and is contented, so that's good. Let's hope it lasts. I tried to broach the subject of where she's going to live but all she said was she's going to stay with Leo for a while. I've texted him and he seems quite laid back about it, but I do wonder how

Amber's feeling. I think the funeral is in a week. Why don't you give Amber a call? You two always get on well and she could probably do with a friend ..."

"Yea, okay, I will. Good idea. I could do with the distraction ... Beth and I are hardly talking."

"Why? Is she still mad at you?"

"Yes. It's almost like we're strangers living in the same place. She's gone back to work but God knows ..."

"Oh, George ... I'm so sorry. I'm sure it will all sort itself out."

"Anyway, Mum ... I must go ... I'm at the Tube now. Speak soon."

He pressed the end button and put the phone back in his pocket. At that moment, a couple walked past him; the guy had his arm firmly around the girl's shoulders. She was leaning into him, laughing at something he'd just said and then they kissed each other as they walked.

He was jealous of their closeness, the love that shone out of her expression as she turned to him again.

His own life was a disaster. He loved someone intensely but it blatantly wasn't reciprocated.

How had he got himself into this mess

WHEN HE GOT HOME THAT night, as usual, he was on his own. He knew that Beth's shift was till 6 pm that day, so where was she? He texted her but she didn't reply. He tried to be reasonable – she'd probably just gone for a drink with a friend but ... was she trying to avoid him?

He poured himself a glass of wine, sat on the sofa and decided to ring Amber as his Mum had suggested. He couldn't remember when he'd spoken to her last. Since he'd been with Beth, he knew he'd neglected other people.

"Hey, Ams, is this a good time?"

"Yea, hold on," and the line went quiet for a minute or so. "Sorry about that, I thought I'd take it in the bedroom. Let me just get settled ... right ... all good now. God, I'm the size of bloody bus. It's such an effort to get comfortable. I feel like a beached whale most of the time."

"God ... I'd almost forgotten you're pregnant ... well, not really, but I haven't seen you for ages so I can't imagine you with a large stomach. You're always so slim and sporty."

"Ha ha, well, you wouldn't say that now. I waddle everywhere and just about make it across the room without puffing. Gone are the days when you and I would go for a jog for five miles and hardly break into a sweat."

"I haven't been running for months ... I'm so unfit. All I do is walk to the station these days."

"Why's that? Is all the sex with Beth wearing you out?"

"I wish ..." he laughed. "But look, I was talking to Mum this morning and she, of course, has told me all about this awful thing with Grace and I thought I'd give you a ring. It can't be easy for you."

"Yea, too right."

"I suppose you've heard that Beth was the midwife on duty?"

"Yea, Rachel told us ... it's crazy. Poor Beth ... and poor Anna, more's to the point."

"But how are *you* coping? It can't be great having your lover's ex moving in? And especially when she's grieving and a new mum. It must be so difficult."

"Yea ... I feel so sorry for her. What a crap thing to happen. The baby is an absolute sweetheart. But ..."

"What?"

"But ... it's so tricky. I find I'm tiptoeing around her; I don't know what to say to her and Leo is ... Leo is being so kind to her and supportive. It's making me feel like I'm in the way, half the time. They were married for years and would you believe, they're *still* married?"

"Really?"

"Yes! They've just never got round to divorcing and here we all are, the three of us living in their house. They were going to sort it out after the babies were born. They're the older, grown-up pair and they have me ... the stupid young one, who got herself up the duff."

"Don't say that. I'm sure that's not how Leo feels, Amber. He's being torn in two."

"But ... it's the way they *look* at each other. They instinctively know what the other one is thinking. I've got no history with Leo."

"But you're having his child, Amber."

"I know, but they've had years of a relationship – I was probably still in nappies when they met, for God's sake."

"Well, the age difference was always going to be there. Once this current situation is sorted, you'll go back to how you were. You'll see. Have you any idea what's going to happen? Is Grace going to find a place? Is she going to go back to work?"

"I don't know the answer to *anything*. Perhaps Leo is going to set up a harem? Maybe I'm the young, nubile one, Grace is the wife and perhaps he's planning on moving other ones in? I know I'm being ridiculous and it's early days ... I feel so mean being like this, but I liked it when it was just me and him. Everything's different now."

"I'm sure it feels different, Amber, but once the funeral's done and Grace has moved out, it will be back to normality again, whatever that is."

"Anyway, enough of me ... how's your life with the invisible Beth?"

"What do you mean, invisible?"

"Well, no one's met her, have they? Does she even exist?"

"Yes, she very much exists, as you well know. She's reluctant to meet my family ... maybe I should have taken that as a hint."

"What do you mean?"

And then George told her the whole sorry story of the proposal in gory detail. When she started hooting with laughter, he began to see the funny side too.

"So ... let me get this straight ... you were actually on bended knee, in front of the whole restaurant and she just ran out?"

"Yes, that's about it."

"Oh ... my ... God ... I wish I'd been there. It's not funny, I know, but it kind of *is* ..."

He was smiling to himself, but said, "Well, I'm glad I've cheered you up, anyway."

"You must admit, it's a great story. When you're old and grey, you'll be able to tell your grandchildren how *not* to propose!"

"Yes, that's true ... I *can* see the funny side. I must have looked a complete pillock."

"No, not you George, surely? So what's going to happen now? Is she keeping her hands hidden from you, in case you slip 'a ring on it'?" and she burst into Beyoncé's famous song.

"Very amusing, Ams. She's hardly talking to me; we're like ships that pass in the night. I was going to talk to her about it and apologise profusely but then this whole Anna thing happened and it seems inappropriate now."

"Yes, I can see that. What a couple of innocent prats we are," she laughed. "At the mercy of our lovers."

"We must get together before the baby comes," he said, realising that he'd really missed her sense of humour and her wonderful laugh. "It won't be the same when you have a baby in tow. Do you know what you're having, by the way?"

"A *baby*, I think," she guffawed. "No ... we didn't want to know. Whatever happens, it's going to be called Joshua, after Leo's dead brother. If it's a girl, it's just going to be tough for her, a bit like the boy called Sue."

"Ha ha ... Only *you* would have a girl called Joshua!"

"Look, as much as I've loved talking to you, I need to go to the loo now. Joshua is sitting on my bladder and I'm going to wet myself in a minute."

"Oh, nice. Okay – let's meet soon."

"Lovely to talk and don't go proposing to anyone before we meet, will you?"

"Oh, you're so funny, Ams. You really are."

"Byeeee."

And she was gone.

She really was a breath of fresh air in his stale life.

There was still no sign of Beth and no text. He rifled through the fridge and made himself garlic mushrooms on toast. He liked cooking but couldn't be bothered to do anything more adventurous tonight.

He poured himself another glass of wine, scrolled through Netflix and watched some dreadful American drivel. It was just what he needed – totally mindless. He kept looking at his phone but no texts came.

Why should he bother if she couldn't even be bothered to reply?

He took himself off to bed and was asleep in seconds.

Chapter 11

When Leo brought Grace home with him that night, he had no idea how it would all pan out; he was just working on his instinct and his instinct was telling him to help Grace, who was still technically his wife.

They hadn't divorced, which was a crazy situation to be in, being as he was a lawyer and … he was living with his girlfriend, who was soon to give birth to his child. He'd come across many family dramas in his career and if he'd come across his own scenario, not only would he have been rude about how people get themselves into such terrible relationship problems, but would have been skeptical at the possible outcomes.

When his parents heard about it, they warned him to be careful. They'd always adored Grace and were upset when they'd split up, but they'd been supportive of him and when he'd told them about Amber, they'd metaphorically bitten their lips and not said anything. They thought she was 'a gorgeous young girl' with a 'great future in the law' ahead of her. They were excited to be grandparents at last too, but secretly wished it was not in these circumstances.

"We can understand you moving Grace into the house, Leo, we really can," said his father on the phone, "but … it's such a difficult thing for you all to deal with. Grace must only stay until she feels stronger."

"Yea, I know Dad ... but you've no idea how bad this is for her. She's suddenly the only parent left; she's totally unprepared and terrified."

"But that's for *her* to face, not *you*, Leo. You're responsible for Amber now. How will this all impact her and your baby?"

"Sometimes life throws things at you and you just have to react, Dad. Surely you understand? After Josh ... you had to deal with so much."

"I know, I know ... but just be careful, that's all I'm saying."

Grace had been in their spare room for three days now. She'd hardly come out of her room at all except to visit Theadora. Leo had taken food and coffee up to her and each time he'd knocked, she'd been under the duvet, hiding. He'd taken a couple of days off work and had driven her into the hospital but today was the day they were going to collect the baby and bring her 'home'.

Leo had asked Grace for the key to their flat and had gone round to collect all the baby things they'd bought; he'd brought them back to the house and encouraged Grace to help him put up the cot and arrange the clothes and nappies in the drawers in her room.

Amber was understanding, up to a point. The first three days she'd accepted Grace was better off in their house, but when Leo came home with all the gear, she'd freaked out.

"So, what's happening, Leo? Are you setting up a kind of commune here? Am I expected to welcome your ex-wife and baby into our home without batting an eyelid? I know it's an awful situation but ... I think you've got to start seeing it from my perspective? I've got my own pregnancy to worry about and you're bringing a tiny baby into the house and a grieving ex-wife.

What am I meant to do with this?" She knew she was being unreasonable but this was meant to be *her* time.

"Sh ...sh ... Grace will hear you, Amber. Don't be so selfish. It'll only be for a few days, until we can find somewhere for Grace to go. You can't expect her to go back to Anna's flat, surely?"

"No ... I know ... but ..."

"But, nothing, Amber. We've just got to do this. We're leaving here at 3 pm to collect her; we'll be bringing her home, here, and we're all going to help Grace as much as possible, okay? Alex, the sperm donor, has asked to come round at 6.30 pm as he hasn't been able to visit the baby yet. Is that okay?"

"I suppose it'll have to be, won't it?"

Leo and Grace set off together. They had the car seat, some nappies and at Leo's suggestion, some milk already made up, in case she needed feeding.

When they arrived at the hospital, Leo parked and then got out to pay for the ticket. He placed the ticket on the dashboard and looked at Grace. She'd made no attempt to get out of the car. She was sitting, staring ahead.

"Come on, then, Grace. It's time to go and get your baby."

"I can't do it," she said, her voice flat.

"Yes, you can. You *can* do it, Grace. She needs you. She has no one else, does she? Anna would want you to do it, you *know* she would." He walked round to the passenger's side, opened the door and put his hand inside the car. "Come on."

She took it and he pulled her out of the car.

They walked together towards the entrance, Leo's arm around her shoulders.

THEY GOT BACK TO THE house at 5.00. Thea had cried a little in the car but she soon fell asleep, lulled, no doubt, by the engine and movement.

Amber greeted them at the door, her earlier outburst forgotten. She peered into the carrier at the still sleeping Thea and her heart visibly melted.

"Oh my Goodness, she's so gorgeous, Grace." Leo glanced at Amber's face; he was surprised to see tears in her eyes.

"She is, isn't she?" said Grace. "She's been very good in the car."

"Let's get you both inside," said Leo, ushering them through the door.

Grace was carrying the baby seat in the crook of her arm. She looked pale and terrified, yet she couldn't stop looking down at the sweet, innocent human who was now in her care.

She put the car seat down on the floor of the sitting room and all three of them gathered round, staring. Theadora had a white knitted hat on her head and she was tucked in cosily with a white blanket. Her breathing was soft and even.

"So, she slept on the journey home?" whispered Amber.

"She was as good as gold," said Leo, "but I don't think we need to speak quietly, Amber. She needs to get used to noise."

"I think she'll need a feed soon ..." said Grace. "I fed her before we left ... but she'll surely wake soon?"

They continued to stare down at her; she was so peaceful and angelic, it didn't seem possible that soon her voice would be heard throughout the house, demanding to be fed.

"Let me make us all some tea," said Amber. "I think we could do with it."

"Good idea," said Leo. "Grace, you go upstairs and rest. I'll bring your tea up. We'll get you up when she wakes."

Without argument, Grace walked wearily out of the room; Amber and Leo looked at each other when she'd gone.

"I don't know what to say to her," whispered Amber, despite Leo's wish for them to speak normally. She was frightened Grace might hear.

"I think at the moment it's best just to focus on the baby. We'll have to face Anna's death soon ... but not yet. I'll take up her tea; you look after Theadora."

Amber felt so conflicted. Her space had been invaded and selfishly she hated that, but when she looked at Thea, all she wanted to do was to help, to support Grace. She knelt down next to the car seat and gently ran her finger over her rounded, sweet cheek. The baby stirred a little, made a noise and Amber quickly withdrew her finger but she leant in even closer and took a deep breath – that classic baby smell filled her with love.

Thea still hadn't stirred when the door bell rang at just after 6 pm. Amber went to the door as quickly as she could, so that whoever it was, didn't ring it again and wake her up.

When she opened the door, she didn't recognise the tall, handsome man standing there.

"Hi, I'm Alex, you must be Amber?"

She had to wrack her brains; she was obviously meant to know this person ... and then it suddenly dawned.

"Oh, your Thea's dad," she said, without thinking. It was so inappropriate, in so many ways. "Come in," and she wrapped her arms around him.

"Yes, you could say that," he said, taken aback by her effusive greeting.

Amber remembered that he was one of Anna's best friends. "I'm *so* sorry about Anna. What a shock. Let me take your coat."

He handed his coat to her and she thought for a moment he was going to cry. She rushed in with, "Have you met the baby, I mean Theadora, yet?"

"No ... no, I haven't. I didn't feel it was right to interfere at the hospital."

"Well, come in and meet her. She's absolutely gorgeous."

She opened the door to the sitting room and ushered him through. She was wondering why Leo hadn't come downstairs – where was he?

"There she is, still sleeping ... like a baby," she giggled, trying to lighten the mood.

Alex walked slowly towards her and went down on his haunches.

"Oh my goodness," he whispered. "She's so *tiny*."

He gazed at her silently for a minute or so and then he stood up and went and sat on the sofa, bending over his knees, his hands covering his eyes. His whole body began to shake.

Oh God, he *is* crying now, thought Amber.

She went over and sat next to him, rubbing his back. "It's all so upsetting, isn't it? But you've got a beautiful baby daughter and we must all think of *her* now," she said, knowing her words sounded empty.

Leo came into the room and looked askance at the scene in front of him.

"Where've you been, Leo? This is Alex."

"I'm sorry – I was looking at some paperwork upstairs." He went over to Alex, who had now looked up but his face had devastation written all over it.

"Alex, I'm so sorry to hear about Anna ... you must be heart-broken, man." He sat on the sofa arm next to him. "I can't imagine what you're going through right now."

Alex looked at him and said, "When I promised to help Anna have a baby, I never thought it would end like *this*. I feel it's my fault she died; if I hadn't donated my sperm, none of this would have happened. It's crazy ... I didn't realise mothers still *die* in childbirth in this country."

"You can't think like that, man. You did an amazing thing for Anna and Grace. You've got to hang onto that. You can't live thinking about 'what if's'. It's terrible, but it could have happened, however she got pregnant ..."

"I know, I know ..." he was putting the heals of his hands in his eyes, forcing himself to stop crying.

Theadora started to stir and suddenly she let out a long, loud wail.

"Someone wants feeding, I think," said Amber, looking at Leo, relieved to have something else to focus on. "I'll go and get Grace."

Even though any one of them could give Thea her bottle, it was decided by them all that Grace should be the one.

She came in, looking exhausted. Alex got up and went towards her and they stood, arms wrapped around each other for a long time, as Thea's cries got louder.

Grace got her out of the chair and soon peace was restored as Thea drank hungrily from the bottle. The others all simply watched, mesmerised by the baby's natural instinct to survive, despite everything.

"Do you want to hold her, Alex?" said Grace, when the bottle was empty.

"Erm ... I'm not sure. I've never held a baby before."

"You'll be fine," said Grace, standing and gently placing her in Alex's arms. He looked awkward and frightened, but gradually relaxed into it and gently leant back in his seat. Thea began to cry again.

"Maybe she needs to sit more upright ... maybe she has wind?" he said and he managed to shuffle her up onto his shoulder and he patted her back.

"You look as if you've done this before, mate," said Leo.

"No, I haven't ..."

"You're doing really well," said Grace, smiling.

There was a silence that now permeated the small, warm living room. Everyone was looking at Thea and no one knew what to say. It was difficult and painful. Anna's absence floated through all of their thoughts so vividly. They were thinking ... she should be *here*, enjoying this moment with them; *she* should be feeding Thea, holding her, kissing her. But she was gone, gone forever and for the two people in the room who knew her so well, it was the most gut-wrenching feeling, knowing they would never see her again; knowing that Thea would never meet her own mother; knowing that Grace would have to do all this, alone.

Knowing that Anna, their talented, beautiful friend, was no more.

GRACE STAYED FOR SIX, long weeks and it wasn't until late January that she left. Amber couldn't express how glad she was when she and the baby eventually went. Not that she disliked Grace or the baby, but Leo was different when they were around;

he was still loving to her, of course he was, but he seemed to avoid touching her in front of Grace, as if he was embarrassed.

Leo had found her a flat round the corner from their house: near enough for him to visit easily but far enough for Grace to start trying to be independent. She'd moved in four weeks after the funeral, when she'd felt a little stronger.

No one ever likes funerals but this one had been particularly challenging for everyone who attended. The death of a new mother was a cruel manifestation of how close birth and death could be ... and the brevity of our time on earth. The funeral had been a terrible ordeal for Grace and Leo had literally had to hold her up. She'd insisted that she took Thea – how could she leave her behind at her *real mother's* funeral, she'd said?

For everyone in the congregation, Theadora's presence added a poignancy they could have done without. In reality, Grace had been unable to cope with her and her own crippling grief at the same time, so Leo had asked Amber to take over Theadora and she'd done so willingly. She was such a good baby – if hers was half as good, she'd be lucky.

She'd wheeled the pushchair up the path to the church door, she'd jiggled it when she looked like she was going to wake and she'd taken her out into the vestry when she'd started to cry. She'd secretly thought it wasn't a good idea to take her but could understand the logic: she would never know her mother, but at least she could say when she was older that she was *present* at her goodbye, even if she had no knowledge or memory of it.

They'd had tea at a local hotel after the service – Amber hated the forced conversation and dainty sandwiches; she was relieved to be able to use Thea to distance herself. She'd never been to a funeral before and hoped she wouldn't have to go to another one soon.

She'd looked across the room at Grace and had thought she looked as pale as a ghost. All the life had drained from her – the days leading up to the funeral had been bad enough, but now she'd looked defeated, broken. She had Alex on one side of her, Leo on the other, both men looking at her with anxious, quick glances, all three holding china tea cups, as if they were at some Victorian tea party.

The old friends were all there: her Mum and Dad, Rachel, George and Harry. George had made excuses for Beth – he'd said that she thought it was inappropriate to come and Amber'd had to agree, even though she was intrigued to meet the enigmatic Beth.

They'd all rallied round, but Grace had been like a person surrounded by glass, visible but untouchable. She barely spoke and had accepted their hugs and love with glacial distance.

After the enforced social, they had gone back to the house, along with Jen, Mike and Rachel, the boys escaping.

Leo had insisted that Grace go straight up to bed when they got home. Rachel and Jen had helped Amber change Thea's nappy and prepare her bottles; both had sat and cuddled her, cooing and saying how beautiful she was, while looking anxious and worried at the same time.

Leo had offered Mike a beer and they'd gone off into the kitchen to chat. Mike, at last, was coming to terms with the imminent arrival of his grandchild and had tried to repress the resentment he felt towards Leo.

The death of Anna had changed everything.

Chapter 12

It was late and Rachel felt so devastated; the funeral had been an ordeal. Her hope (and need) for a good night's sleep was dashed, however – she'd slept for an hour and then woken up with a start, her heart racing. The night was black and the silence so loud and she felt utterly alone.

Anna's death came flooding back into her consciousness like a burst dam, her mind struggling to keep afloat ... and then there was Beth's involvement and how she must be feeling. Despite having never met Beth, she felt close to her: she was the girl George loved and she knew she too, would love her. She hoped the proposal debacle had been a temporary setback.

Demetris' imminent arrival tomorrow didn't help her emotional state either. It was the last thing she wanted to be doing. She wasn't in the mood to be a tourist guide and friend to someone who, to be frank, she hardly knew.

Why did I agree to this? But then ... she'd agreed before all this awful, awful news.

She turned on the bedside light and reached for her phone. She knew she shouldn't, that it wouldn't help her get to sleep with its blue light waking her brain up, but she went on her photos to remind herself of Cyprus and Demetris.

There he was, on that last night. So handsome ... so young. She really was stupid if she thought someone like him would ever want her. He probably just wanted a day trip to the sea. She scrolled past him and searched for Mike. She loved the photo of them sitting in that beach side taverna, his arm casually around her shoulders. She stared at it, trying to remember the feeling of warmth, the sun of her face, the smell of the sea and that arm, touching her.

She hated the way that Mike had this hold on her; she was a strong woman in every other aspect of her life but when it came to him, she was weak. He was someone else's husband, her best friend's husband, for God's sake. You'd think after so many years, she could have accepted the situation. But he felt like an extension of herself... and George was part of that extension; she *knew* he was. Mike would *never* be anything more than a friend to her and that was enough – as long as he was in her life.

Her mind swirled round and round. She got up and stared out of the moonlit window. Everything looked ghostly and pure, nothing moved. How small we are, she thought. We're tiny blips on the earth. Is Anna now somehow part of this vast universe or is she only a memory?

She shivered and went back to bed, snuggling down into the duvet, trying to block out her thoughts.

She must have fallen asleep soon after that, as the next time she was aware of anything, daylight was seeping in; her clock said 7.35.

She wasn't sure what time Demetris would call but she assumed it would be mid-morning. She got up, showered and spent longer than usual, trying to make herself look presentable. Some days she hated her appearance and this was one of them. Her eyes had lost any sparkle they had: Anna's death stared out of them.

Demetris texted to say he'd be on the train arriving at 11.35, so she hurried herself; she had to ring Millie about a funeral coming up in a few days and she needed to pop to the local shop for some basics.

She felt nervous as she parked at the back of the station; would they have enough to talk about or would it be awkward?

She'd told him where to exit the station and she got out and stood by the car, straining to see if she could see him walking amongst a sea of people traipsing out. Suddenly, she caught a glimpse of him; he hadn't seen her yet – he was looking around at, what to him, were unfamiliar surroundings.

She was shocked at how young and good-looking he was. His ingrained tan looked incongruous among the British whiteness; it was strange to see him with winter clothes on, a warm jacket and scarf. She waved and he caught sight of her, hurrying forward with a big smile on his face.

"Rachel, thank you for come to meet me," he said, as he flung his arms around her, holding her in a long, warm hug.

"Oh, that's no problem, lovely to see you, Demetris," enjoying the feeling of the embrace. He smelt wonderful – she tried to remember the aftershave he was wearing.

"How was your journey?"

"Good ... we have no trains in Cyprus so for me, it is fun," he said, laughing. "A lot of money for short journey," he added, with a raise of his dark eyebrows.

"*Everything* is expensive here," she said.

They got into the car and made their way slowly through the traffic. As they went along the sea front, she said, "This always reminds me a little bit of Limassol ... the busy road, the sea, right there ..."

LIFE'S COMPLICATED

"Yes, you are right ... but the sea looks a little greener – maybe not so warm?" he laughed. The sea, indeed, looked green-grey against the December sky. Waves were crashing onto the pebbles; there were only a few brave people walking on the beach, all muffled up against the wind.

"I thought we'd go back to the house to have lunch and then we'll leave the car and take buses into the centre and go exploring. Is that okay with you?"

"Of course," he said, grinning. "I am happy for anything."

Although she felt sad inside, his personality was infectious and she found his company was helping her to forget. She pointed out things as they drove and soon they were back home.

He stood looking up at the building. "You have beautiful house, Rachel. Do you live here all alone? It is big house for only you."

"Yes. Zach has left now. I don't like living alone, but sometimes it's better than living with someone," she said, realising she had contradicted her own previous thoughts. He didn't reply but he stared at her and touched her shoulder gently.

She showed him around and then they ate a simple lunch of soup, bread and cheese. She thought perhaps she should tell him about her recent news, as he knew Grace, but it seemed so momentous and not 'right' to share.

She did, however, explain that she had to make a phone call and left him with a newspaper, while she went into the sitting room. She wanted to just check on George.

He picked up straightaway. She asked him how Beth was today and he said she'd taken it all really badly; they were hardly speaking. He said he really didn't want to talk at the moment and he'd abruptly put the phone down. He hadn't sounded himself and she sat quietly for a moment, wondering what to do. Her son needed her but he was a grown up now. Maybe she should take a step back?

At that moment, Demetris came into the room.

"Eh ... Rachel ... I just wondered where the toilet ..." but he broke off when he saw her face and quickly came in and knelt in front of her. "What's the matter?"

She lost all resolve not to tell him ... she felt she needed to talk to *someone* about everything. "Oh, Demetris ... something so dreadful has happened."

She was now crying. It was as if she'd been holding back and having Demetris' sympathy gave her permission to let it all out.

He grabbed her hand. "What has happened? Tell me ..." and he raised himself up and sat down beside her on the couch. He put his arm around her and pulled her into him. Rachel tried to stop crying and eventually she felt calmer. With her head on his shoulder, she told him the whole story, including Beth's connection and he listened, not saying a word, just squeezing her shoulder now and again.

"Life is very *bad* sometimes," he said. "I'm so sorry for you, Rachel. When something like this happen, it is as if there is no God. How can he let this happen to innocent mothers and babies?"

Rachel had not even *thought* of God. She wasn't a religious person ... but all she knew was that it was all so unfair ... on Anna, on Grace, on Theadora and on Beth. She leant forward with both hands covering her eyes.

"I'm so sorry to burden you with this ... I wasn't going to say anything ..."

"But you *must* speak about it. You must not hide ..."

"But you're here on holiday ..."

"That is not important ... I am glad, I am *very* glad, that I am here to support you, Rachel." He rubbed her back, up and down, up and down.

She stood up quickly. She felt a connection to him but it felt wrong in the circumstances. He was being so kind.

"Let me go and wash my face ... we'll still go out ... I need to get some fresh air. Walking will be good."

"Okay, if you sure you okay? We will walk and walk, with the wind in our faces, and try to forget ..." he said.

"That would be good," she said, wiping her eyes. "I'll be five minutes."

THEY DID AS RACHEL had planned – they took the bus into town and walked along the sea front. The wind was strong and she felt its benefit; it was as if it was forcing all thoughts from her head as she battled to walk forward.

They ambled down the pier, absorbing all the lights and music as the wind got stronger. Then they walked away from the sea into the town itself and along the Lanes, with its quirky cafés, shops and Christmas decorations. They dawdled ... taking in the atmosphere, looking at things they weren't going to buy, stepping into a dark, toasty space to have a warming hot chocolate. It was as if they'd come to an agreement to forget the tragedy and just be 'in the moment', enjoying the surroundings, the anonymity and the unexpected closeness they felt.

He'd sometimes turn to her and smile and she could feel herself attracted to him again. His large, hazel eyes would crinkle, his mouth would widen to reveal perfect teeth and she'd feel her heart beating faster. Was she just grateful to him for being there at the right time?

She wondered whether she should know what his plans were; if he was planning to stay the night, it seemed fraught with difficulties now.

"So, are you catching the train back to London soon?" she asked, as they were walking back to the bus stop.

"Well ... I do not have to be back until tomorrow. My cousin, he is busy tonight. Why don't I take you out for a meal and I catch a late train?"

With relief, she realised he was saying he would leave tonight. "That would be lovely ... there's a little French Bistro I know near my house ... lovely food and reasonable prices."

"Perfect. Let's do that."

"I'll book for 7.30 – I can do it online."

The afternoon had made her feel better; he was good company and they didn't have any problems 'filling the spaces'. Conversation was easy, it flowed without any awkwardness and she had to admit to herself, the prospect of going out to a restaurant with him was so much more preferable than being home alone.

When they got back to the house, it was dark and as she let them in through the front door, it felt good to have someone with her as she turned on the hall lights; there was something so depressing about coming home to an empty house on her own.

She quickly booked their table and then went to the kettle to make a cup of tea. As she was standing by the cupboards, he came up behind her and touched her back. His hand rested there.

"Are you feeling better?" he said.

She turned slowly round, his hand keeping contact. He did not move backwards.

"I am."

"Can I kiss you, Rachel?"

She was surprised but at the same time, expecting it. He had a way of looking at her.

She didn't answer but she didn't need to. Their lips simply met, gently.

"Thank you," he said, taking both her hands. "You are a beautiful woman, Rachel. I think you know how I feel?"

"Demetris ... I'm not sure what to say ..."

"You don't need say something. I am happy here, with you." He squeezed both her hands and brought one up to his lips, looking into her eyes.

He really was a charming, gorgeous man. Rachel felt lost in the moment, mesmerised by those penetrating eyes but then the kettle switched itself off and she came back, back into her kitchen. She busied herself making them tea while he sat down at the table, casually leaning back on his chair.

The kiss now lay between them with its tenderness and sweetness. It was so long since she'd felt wanted. In truth, it had been years since Zach had kissed her with any kind of love. It was only Mike's kisses, all those years ago, she remembered so vividly.

They went into the sitting room with their mugs of tea and they sat together on the sofa. Rachel turned on the TV; it was nearly time for the news and it was a distraction.

"I never really asked if you like tea, Demetris. Do you? All English people assume everyone loves it."

"I do like it. I don't drink in Cyprus, only coffee, but ... with milk, is nice."

She thought he was probably being polite; she remembered most Europeans drank tea without milk. "I'm sorry," she said, "would you prefer coffee?"

"No, no problem Rachel. Relax," he smiled. "I am happy with tea. So English."

They watched the news, talking about the items that came up. At the end, she said, "I'm going to have a shower before we go out. Do you want one?" and then felt awkward, as if she was asking him to join her.

"No, I fine. You go ... I sit here and wait for you."

She felt relief when she left and went upstairs. They had started something and she didn't know where it was going. Did she want it to go in the direction he clearly wanted? He was so young.

It was crazy.

The meal at the Bistro was perfect: they both went for steak and chips, red wine and a light, fluffy meringue pudding. It was very dark in the restaurant with just a solitary candle lighting their faces. They sat opposite each other in the corner of the room; the waiter was efficient, the service quick, the food delicious. They finished a bottle of wine and ordered another small carafe, which they finished too. By the end of the meal, Rachel was feeling slightly drunk and the sadness returned.

How would Grace carry on? How could Leo and Amber cope with the situation? It was all so hopeless.

Demetris was quick to recognise that her mood had changed and as they put their coats back on, he hugged her and whispered, "It will be okay, you see, Rachel," and she was grateful to him for his empathy.

They walked back to the house; he took her hand in his and they strolled by lots of houses all shut up for the night, lights shining around drawn curtains, TV's flickering. Cosy, family homes, the kind of home she used to have.

All that was gone now; but here she was, getting depressed about her life when one of her best friends was facing the worst situation anyone could imagine.

Soon they arrived back to her house. She got out her key and turned it in the lock. Before she could turn on the lights, Demetris took her hand and led her to the stairs.

"Come with me to bed, my Rachel. We need no lights."

And they went slowly up the stairs, lit only by the street lights outside, to Rachel's bed.

Chapter 13

It was now early February and Amber was resting. That was all she did these days; three more weeks to go of this utter boredom, she thought.

How can time drag so much, yet fly terrifyingly towards the birth?

She was lying on the sofa; the doctor had said she needed to rest with her legs elevated to help her swollen ankles. She felt like an incubator, not a person – her only role was to produce this new human now. She missed work but acknowledged that she couldn't even heave herself around the home, never mind get to work.

Leo was relegated to an armchair and was looking through some papers. She was scrolling through the BBC news app, when something caught her eye:

A cluster of cases of a "mysterious viral pneumonia" in the city of Wuhan.

Anything to do with health was of interest to her these days.

She read the headline out to Leo, who mumbled something incoherent in reply.

"I wonder what it is … Leo, are you listening?"

"Yes, I am. Why are you interested in something happening thousands of miles away?"

"Well, it's just the way it says 'mysterious'. It makes me curious."

"I suppose they don't know what it is, that's all. There are loads of viruses everywhere, *all* the time. Don't worry about it. Concentrate on getting this baby out."

"Yes, you're right. That's my one purpose in life now ... baby producer extraordinaire. I'm so *bored* with being pregnant ... I'm not one of those women who 'bloom' and 'glow', am I? It's somehow rather dehumanising, I think. It'll be great when babies can be grown in a machine and let women get on with their lives."

"I don't think that'll be happening for a century or two, Amber. You're getting ahead of yourself. Anyway, in other news, I thought Grace looked a bit brighter today, by the way. Theadora is doing well – she's the right weight and making good progress. She's a brilliant mother ... and even though she's grieving, she's content when she's holding Thea. Maybe she will be able to come out of this long, dark tunnel, eventually. She's strong ..."

"I'm sure she will. Has she decided what she's going to do about work? They sound as if they're being very understanding, giving her all this time off."

"She says they've told her that her job is hers and that she can take as long as she needs ... but obviously she realises she's got to make some hard decisions. We were talking about nannies and nurseries today and whether she can start off going in part-time. She's going to make some enquires for good nurseries. She'd much rather stay at home, but she knows she can't."

"Will you mind if I go back full-time, Leo? I think I want to, at the moment. I can't imagine being a stay-at-home Mum, I just can't. I love work, I love being out and about, meeting people. I don't think I'm the right sort of person to stay at home with a baby all day. I think you can still love your child but want a *life*, can't you ... or am I being selfish?"

"Amber, it's your life ... I'll support you whatever you decide, you know I will, but I don't think you know how you'll feel until the baby actually arrives. Why don't you just wait and see? You never know, you might turn out to be the ultimate earth mother."

Amber looked down at her stomach and couldn't believe that soon this *thing* would appear and change her life forever. Who knew how she was going to feel? Right now, she felt like it was a disruption to her life, something to be endured; she hoped that her maternal instincts would kick in, with the onslaught of hormones.

She'd never been someone who drooled over babies – she didn't hate them or anything but they were just appendages of other people and to be fair, she hadn't had much experience of babies at all.

"But what if I'm a terrible mother? What if I haven't got what it takes? Apart from Thea, I've not had anything to do with babies ... what if the baby doesn't even *like* me?"

"Amber, don't be ridiculous. Of course the baby will like you – all babies *love* their mothers and are totally dependent on them for their existence. Of course, you'll be a good mother. Look how good you are with Thea? You look like a natural to me. Jen has been a wonderful mother to you – you'll inherit her ability, I'm sure. You're over-thinking it. Once it's born, everything will just slot into place. You'll have ages to decide whether you want to go back to work or not; you don't have to make a hasty decision.

Personally, I think you'll know what to do pretty quickly. I'll support you either way, you know I will."

He got up off the chair and came over to her, leant down and kissed her. She reached up and put her hands behind his head, pulling him down towards her.

"Will you still fancy me when I've got milk gushing from my boobs, stretch marks crawling all over me and a disgusting, flabby tummy?" she giggled, kissing him again.

"How could I resist such a wonderful description? Sounds like my kind of woman," he laughed.

Leo still couldn't believe he was going to be a father. He'd so wanted to be one when he was with Grace but when that hadn't happened, he'd grown to accept it and focussed on his career, which he loved. Part of him was terrified at the prospect. He'd been quick to reassure Amber that she would be a great parent, but he wanted someone to do the same for him. When he looked at Amber, she was so much younger than him, it seemed crazy that they were even together, never mind due to be parents.

How had he got himself into this strange life?

When he was with Grace, he felt like himself again; he felt comfortable. He'd missed her sensible, grown-up approach to life, her conversation, her ... familiarity. He found himself staring at her in the quietness of her sitting room, her beautiful hair falling round her shoulders; Thea, feeding contentedly, gazing in that intense, baby way at her and Grace's eyes fixed on hers. She dressed more informally these days; gone were the business suits, the high heels, the designer handbags ... and he liked her even more like this. He liked this 'toned down' version of her. If only they'd had their own baby ... he could see that they would have happily slotted into this image of themselves, the mother and father, devoted to their baby girl.

The more he visited Grace and Thea, the more Thea entered his consciousness and his very being. He loved holding her; he'd bend his head down and smell her little head, taking in the perfume. He'd even changed her nappy several times, laughing that he needed the practice. The first time Grace handed him her bottle, he was wary, but he loved the closeness he felt with her and became adept at putting her on his shoulder and rubbing her back until she burped.

Each time he left the flat, he felt as if he was leaving part of himself there, with them. The guilt that he was feeling this way, ate away at him: Amber didn't deserve this, she needed his undivided love and support. For all her bravado, she was vulnerable.

He felt torn between the two of them. It was a strange feeling – he couldn't work out how to deal with his emotions any more. Anna's death had brought Grace back into his life and ... he liked it.

His relationship with Amber was so different from the one he had with Grace; he sometimes felt like a father figure to her. She always wanted reassurance; for all her outward confidence, she lacked the ability to make decisions and constantly asked him for his opinion. If he was honest with himself, he found it irritating sometimes but ... she was young and beautiful and brought a lightness and fun into his world.

He just wanted the baby to come now. Surely with the birth of his *own* child, he'd be able to sort out his head and his heart?

LIFE'S COMPLICATED

THAT HEADLINE WAS, of course, the beginning of the global pandemic. Only two and half weeks later there had been a hundred deaths and infections in sixteen other countries.

Amber went into labour the day that it was reported that eight people had the virus in England, 10th February, 2020. She was scared enough of the birth but the added worry of this virus made the whole process frankly terrifying.

It was 2 am when her waters broke. She'd waddled to the loo and then it'd happened. She'd been having some Braxton Hicks contractions for a few days but had kept calm and decided they weren't the real thing. Her pre-natal classes had prepared her well and she thought she knew what to expect. She'd got a vague birth plan: to take any drugs that would help. She wasn't going to be a martyr to excruciating pain.

She called to Leo from the en-suite. He was a deep sleeper and didn't hear at first.

"LEO!" she shouted, as she stood there, helpless, leaning against the basin in the dark. "Leo, my waters have gone – call the hospital."

Through the mists of sleep, Leo roused himself, rubbed his eyes and swung his legs over the side of their bed. "Okay, I'm coming," he shouted, the realisation of what was about to happen hitting him in the stomach like a punch.

He stumbled into the bathroom, stepped onto the wet floor in his bare feet and nearly slipped.

"Oh God ... shall I ring for an ambulance or drive you in?" he said, putting his arm around her. "Come back and sit on the bed."

"Ring the hospital and tell them we're coming in, right now. We could be there in twenty-five minutes if we hurry. I'll change out of these things, I'm wet."

He grabbed his phone and rang the number they had stored and said what was happening.

As Amber was taking off her clothes, he was getting dressed as quickly as possible, swearing as he put on his jumper the wrong way round and then swearing again when he couldn't find his socks. In between, he asked, "Have you had any contractions yet?"

"Well," she said, as she put on the loosest things she could find, "I couldn't sleep and I was lying in bed, feeling strange. My stomach went rock hard, like the pretend contractions and so I didn't think much of them but I think they were real. Oh … it's happening *now*."

She leant against her dressing table, breathing slowly, as she'd been taught. When it had passed, she said, "Come on, Leo, we must get a move on. Get my bag …"

In the car, she texted Jen. *Hi Mum, I'm in labour. On way to hospital. Will text when it's all over. Oh God. A.*

There was very little traffic. "Drive smoothly, Leo. I don't want any sudden stops, thank you very much."

"I'll do my best, Honey. Why don't you try to time them?"

"I think they're coming every five-ish minutes. That's not too bad at the moment but I can feel them getting stronger. Oh God, Leo, I don't want to do this."

"You haven't got a choice, my love," he said, squeezing her leg.

His mind wouldn't stop going to Anna. His stomach was churning with the nervous tension.

At the hospital, he drew up right outside, rushed in and tried to find a wheelchair.

"My partner's in labour," he shouted to a passing nurse, who quickly found one and leaving the car where it was, they wheeled Amber to the labour ward.

At the reception desk, thankfully, they were expecting her and they were quickly taken to a room.

"Now, I'm just going to take a look, Amber. Lie back, try to relax ..."

"Hold my hand, Leo," she said. She looked pale and not her usual jokey self. "I'll be okay, won't I?"

"Of course you will. Relax ..." he said, feeling far more nervous than he was letting on.

After a while, the nurse said that she was progressing nicely.

"What does that mean?" said Amber, her face betraying her anxiety.

"Well, you're already 5cm dilated. Baby's in a great position. How are the contractions feeling now you're here and lying down?"

"I've got terrible pain in my back ..."

"That's perfectly normal. You're in the active labour stage now ... you just need to dilate to 10cm and then we'll be ready to push Baby out."

Amber was brave, very brave. Leo did everything to help but he felt useless. As the contractions got worse, he breathed with her, he massaged her, he rubbed her temples, but nothing seemed to help. She had some gas and air to help with the contractions and as she pushed the mask onto her face with ferocity, Leo was willing it to help.

Eventually, after what felt like forever, but what was, in fact, only four hours, she was ready to push and with much shouting, groaning and a couple of times, screaming, Amber pushed for an hour and then the miracle happened.

A beautiful baby boy, covered in blood, arrived into the world and cried almost immediately.

Joshua.

Leo stayed very much up at the head end, holding Amber as she pushed; he was giving so many instructions that, at one point, the midwife asked him to be quiet. When the baby cried for the first time, tears were flowing down his face. The relief was almost instant for Amber, of course. She sank back as the nurses fussed around the baby, a look of absolute exhaustion and happiness intertwined on her face. Leo leaned in to kiss her.

"You did it, Ams, you did it," he whispered in her ear. She was too tired to respond.

Neither of them had as yet seen the baby but within a minute, he was presented to them.

"Put him against your skin, Lovely," said a the midwife, "that way, he'll bond with you straightaway." Amber hadn't got the strength to sit up or take her top off so Leo put his arm round her shoulders and gently lifted her and she raised her arms like a child herself, to remove her tee shirt. The baby was slowly lowered onto her chest, his skin clean but red and purple, his face squashed and rounded. His misty, faraway eyes gazed unseeingly upwards into her face. Little snuffles could be heard. Leo and Amber stared at him, speechless.

"Let's see if he knows what he's doing," said the midwife. "Excuse me, Leo, can I just come and help Mum put him to the breast," and with that, Leo stepped away and the midwife, with much practised efficiency, placed the baby so that his face was near Amber's nipple. After a few seconds of burrowing, he began making his first attempts to feed. Amber did nothing at this stage; she simply held him. She felt as if she was having an out of body experience ... as if all this was happening to someone else.

"Have you got a name for your baby yet?' asked a nurse, bustling around the bed.

Leo and Amber answered almost simultaneously. "Joshua."

They smiled at each other, knowing how significant the name was.

"Awww ... I love that name," the nurse replied. Leo wondered if she said this to all the new parents.

"So, we need to get the placenta out now so, Dad, can you hold Joshua for a while and we'll sort out Mum. If you take your shirt off, you can do skin to skin too."

Leo quickly removed his shirt and soon Joshua was next to him. A nurse placed a warm blanket around them and Leo sat, not believing the overwhelming feeling of love that made every cell in his body sing. He'd dreamt about this moment for so long with Grace ... he'd longed for it, but it hadn't come. And now, it had happened. He could smell the newborn skin, he could feel the little wriggles. He stroked his head with his forefinger, feeling the softness of his skin, the boniness of the skull. His finger looked so large next to him. How could something so small survive? He moved his finger down to his left arm, tracing it down until magically, Joshua encircled it with his tiny hand.

Leo was lost in the moment. Poor Amber was going through the final phase of giving birth.

"All done," someone later announced. "No stitches needed. You've done brilliantly, Amber. Well done. A 7 lb 6 oz bouncing boy. Clever girl. Congratulations to you both."

Leo dragged his eyes away from his son to meet Amber's – she smiled wanly at him.

"I've done it, Leo. I've actually done it. I'm so tired …"

"Right," said the midwife. "Let me take Baby, Leo; we need to sort him out and Mum needs to be wheeled back to a room and cleaned up," and she reached forward to take Joshua. Leo felt immediately bereft. "I'm sure you've got lots of phone calls to make."

He'd forgotten everything and everyone else in the world. Who should he ring? He couldn't remember anything before this moment.

"Ok," he said, standing up. His legs felt weak, his mind had a blankness about it.

"See you in a bit," he said, as he walked out of the room, not sure where he was going.

AMBER ONLY HAD TO REMAIN in hospital for one day. Everything was straightforward … young mum, simple birth … no reason to stay in.

When Leo came to collect them, his stomach was churning, he felt so useless. All he could do was drive them home, keep them warm, watch over them. Everything about Joshua's survival was down to Amber and her alone. Her breast milk.

He knew he was being melodramatic, over sensitive … but he felt vulnerable for the first time in his life since the death of his brother. He was overwhelmed with the responsibility of caring for someone so small and fragile and now he absolutely understood what his parents had gone through, losing their son.

How did they carry on? How could life exist without your child?

They walked into the house with their precious cargo still in the car seat. It felt like a new house to them, as if they were seeing it with new eyes. So much had happened since they'd left it. Then, there were two of them. He'd been back once in between but it was as if he was in a dream.

Now there were three.

Leo had made all the phone calls and as they came through the front door there were several cards scattered on the mat.

"Do you want to go and have a shower, Amber? I'm sure you'd love to have a wash in your own bathroom?"

She put the baby down on the settee, took her coat off and said, "I'd love a coffee first, I'm dying for one. Then I'll go up."

She walked off into the kitchen, leaving Leo to wonder if he should say anything about a) the baby on the settee and b) drinking coffee when breastfeeding. He didn't want to criticise, but surely it was never a good idea to leave a baby on top of something it could fall off, even if it was secure in a seat. It was something that he thought they should establish now, rather than later. Maybe coffee was okay but surely caffeine would come out in the breastmilk and keep the baby awake?

Amber came back into the sitting room, carrying two mugs of steaming coffee and handed one to him. She sat down on the floor, which was one of her habits, warming her hands round the china. She glanced across at Joshua who was fast asleep.

"Well, that was all pretty straightforward, wasn't it?" she said. "Home without a peep from him. Long may it continue."

"Yes, indeed," said Leo, not being able to resist adding, "is coffee okay for you?"

"How do you mean?"

"Well, you know, caffeine and breastfeeding ..."

"They said something about cutting down, but I'm gasping ... the coffee in the hospital was disgusting. I've been dreaming about it."

"Maybe this should be it ..."

"Leo, don't fuss. It'll be me having to get up anyway, so I don't know what you're worrying about."

"I'm not worrying ... I just thought I'd mention it." He really didn't think he ought to talk about the settee now. He'd just quietly move him once she'd gone upstairs.

"Shall we open the cards?" she asked, not getting up.

"Yes, I'll get them for you," and he went back into the hall. He went outside into the garage where he'd hidden a beautiful arrangement he'd bought. He'd chosen a blue theme with iris and hydrangeas and they'd luckily maintained their freshness.

"This is for you, my love," he said, holding it with outstretched arms.

"Wow, Leo, amazing. Blue for a boy too. Put them on the table for me will you? Where are the cards?"

"Here," he said, turning to put the flowers down and dropping the cards on her lap.

"Aww ... there's one from Mum and Dad here," she said. "Cute," she added as she stared at the picture. There was another from his Mum and Dad, one from Rachel and a hand-delivered one from Grace.

Leo sat on the floor next to her and he read the cards too. He couldn't believe they were addressed to him. Me, a father? he thought.

"Thea and Joshua will be great buddies, I think," he said. "Kind of Grace to do this ..."

"Well, it's only a card."

"Yes, but it takes thought and effort ..."

"Yea, I suppose so."

After finishing her coffee, she slowly got up, peered at the sleeping baby and said, "All quiet on the western front. I think I'll go up," and with that she went upstairs.

Leo was left alone on the floor still. He looked at the cards again and decided to take a picture of Joshua asleep, to send to them all. He stood up and got his mobile out of his back pocket. He squatted down in front of the settee, rearranged the car seat and zoomed in on his son's face.

He really was perfect in every way. His lashes, long and dark, contrasted with his light brown skin. His apple cheeks, so round and juicy, you could almost bite them. His little snub nose ... his rosebud lips.

He clicked his camera's shutter and several identical photos appeared. He chose one and messaged them to all his contacts with the caption, *Joshua asleep. Home at last.*

He got several messages straight back, all along the lines of "Awww, he's gorgeous."

Several minutes went by and then he got another message. He opened it, it was from Grace.

It said, "*Oh Leo ... he's perfect. I'm so happy for you. At last the void has been filled. You must be so proud. With love from Grace and Theadora xx*

He stared at the words and wished he could put his arms around her.

Chapter 14

Beth was still very distant with him; they were living together but carrying on, with parallel lives: she'd go to the hospital, he'd go to the office and sometimes they'd have supper together if her shifts coincided with his day. He didn't try to force her into opening up to him, he knew he'd screwed up but he just hoped time and space would help.

Her work life was becoming more and more stressful with the onset of the pandemic; she'd come home exhausted and not want to talk about anything. He could only imagine what it was like to work in the NHS at this time – he watched the news like everyone else and saw the huge problems unfolding.

When lockdown was mooted, he felt a panic inside. He didn't want to be stuck in London, in a flat with no outside space ... the idea of being totally isolated all the time with the situation with Beth dominating their lives, appalled him. Rumours started spreading on social media that it was going to be imposed in two days and so he started to plan his escape. Could he go before it was too late?

Beth would be relieved – she would, of course, continue with her work as before, no working from home for her and it meant that she'd have the flat to herself and they wouldn't have to pretend that they were getting on. They'd had meetings at his office about this lockdown scenario and it was agreed that everyone would be able to do remote working with Zoom and Teams etc. He rather liked the idea, to be honest. His job was so computer-based that he'd often wondered why he bothered to go into work at all. He loved the thought of going 'home' to Brighton.

He texted Rachel.

Hey, Mum, how would you feel if I came and lived with you for a while during this lockdown thing? I'm sure it's going to happen any minute, so I need to come down tomorrow latest. Let me know, love George.

He got a text back almost immediately: *Yes, of course. That would be so nice. But what about Beth? Mum x*

He didn't want to go into detail, he'd talk to her about it when he was down there so he just said:

Ok, I'll get a train tomorrow lunchtime. Beth's fine about it. She's got to go into work as normal, of course. Don't worry, I'll wear a mask and I'll stay in my room for a few days to make sure I haven't got it. I don't want to pass it on to you. See you soon. Love George x

When he saw Beth later that day, in fact at 11 pm when he was already in bed, he explained what he was going to do.

"I thought it would give you some space ... from me," he said, quietly.

"Why do you think I want *space*?"

"Well, as far as I can see, you're still fed up with me ..."

"No, I'm not, George, I'm just *exhausted*. It's shitty at work ..."

"I'm sure it is, but things just don't seem to be the same between us, forget the pandemic. I feel you still blame me for putting you in that situation ..."

"George, that's ridiculous ..."

"Is it?"

"Yes, it is."

"Well, it doesn't *feel* like that to me. Anyway ... I thought you'd enjoy having the flat to yourself?"

"What, while you run home to Mummy?"

George didn't answer and they stared at each other. Beth continued to undress, throwing her uniform on a chair; George was sitting up, leaning against the pillows. The room was only lit by a small bedside table light.

"That's the sort of comment that makes me feel you don't even *like* me any more," said George. "You've never even made the effort to come and meet my mother. If you had done, you'd have realised what a lovely person she is and the least like a *Mummy figure* you could ever hope to meet."

He turned round, punched the pillows and lay down heavily.

"I'm sorry ... that was a mean thing to say, I know. I'm sure Rachel is lovely but ... anyway, you go if you want to."

She slipped on a pair of cotton pyjamas, brushed her hair and went into the bathroom; George could hear the electric toothbrush buzzing.

She came back into the bedroom, slid into bed and lay staring up at the ceiling. George turned off his bedside light and the room was plunged into darkness. A loud motorbike drove down the road outside their window, backfiring noisily.

George had his back to her; neither of them made any effort to touch the other one. The gap between them felt like a huge gorge.

"So is your work okay with this plan?" she said, quietly.

"Yes ... well, they don't care where I am, as long as I'm on the end of Zoom calls."

"When will you go?"

"Tomorrow. Any time soon, it'll be impossible to get out of London. I couldn't bear to be stuck here with no outside space."

"Mmmm."

Neither of them changed their position.

As George lay there, he wondered why he even bothered. She blatantly didn't love him as much as he loved her.

There comes a time when maybe you just give up.

"Goodnight."

"Night."

GEORGE DIDN'T WANT to let himself in with his key, as he was keeping his distance from his mother, so he knocked.

Rachel put on her mask and went to the door.

"Darling, it's so lovely to see you – come in. I suppose we shouldn't hug, but it seems all wrong." She stepped back to let him in.

He was already wearing his mask; he'd worn it all day. He hated the bloody thing, it made him feel claustrophobic. Did they really even work? He thought this every time he put it on.

"I think it's best, Mum, if we don't. I'd hate it if I gave it to you. What if you got really ill and it was all because of me?"

"George, I could easily catch it in the supermarket or in my shop. But I suppose it's sensible if we stay away from each other for a few days. At least the house is big enough."

"I'll go straight up to my room and sort myself out. I know it's gonna feel strange not being in the same room, but we must be sensible."

She looked at his back as he made his way up the stairs, wondering how she'd made such a sensible and sensitive individual. If he hadn't suggested this few days of isolation to start with, she wouldn't probably have even thought of it but ... he was right. She really wouldn't want to get ill. The news was scary.

After a while, she went upstairs and spoke to him through the door. "Would you like a cup of tea?" she said, leaning close in.

"Yes, please ... just leave it outside and I'll collect it."

"That's taking things a bit far, isn't it?"

"Well, not really. If we're going to do this, we have to start the way we mean to go on."

"Okay, then," said Rachel. "I'll bring you up an old spare kettle I've got and some tea bags. Anything else?"

"Um ... maybe a bowl and spoons, mugs and some cereal, then I won't have to bother you in the mornings, at least."

This whole thing was crazy. What a strange world we've stumbled into, she thought.

She went and got a tray and piled it with what he was asking for; she also found an old toaster. She left it all, including some bread, butter and marmalade, outside his door.

"Hey, your brother's just rung. It looks like his restaurant and every other bloody eatery and retail shop will close, so I suggested he came down here too. He's got tomorrow off anyway, so he's coming ... it'll be so lovely to have you both here. Even under these strange circumstances."

"That's cool. Bonding time with my little bro. Do you think you'll have to close your shop, then?"

"Yes, of course. They're talking about essential shops only. Flowers are hardly essential, are they?" she laughed.

"Oh God, Mum. What a nightmare for you. And Harry. And ... everyone. What on earth's going to happen?"

She leant against his closed door. She thought of all her closest friends. Amber and Leo, isolated with a small baby ... Jen and Mike, struggling with so much ... Grace, alone and also with a baby.

Demetris.

After he'd gone back to Cyprus, she'd tried to forget what she'd done. She'd loved feeling close to someone again ... the warmth, the intimacy and waking up to that gorgeous face ... but it hadn't felt right. She'd taken advantage of him, trying to forget who she really was.

When they'd parted the next day, he'd looked genuinely sad, but she had felt only relief and guilt. They'd promised all sorts of things: another visit to England, a holiday in Cyprus, FaceTime calls, but in reality, she knew she didn't want to do any of those things. What was she thinking? How was it ever going to work? He was young and carefree and perhaps most importantly, he lived two thousand miles away. Not a small problem. It wasn't right for either of them. He needed to find someone his own age, from his own culture, start a family.

"Darling, we're all living through something devastating. We're going to have to just do our best ... and cope. It's going to change us all, I think. Are you sure you want to be away from Beth? Don't you think she'll need your support through this? It must be awful for her and all NHS workers."

"No, she'll be relieved to be on her own. I think I annoy her at the moment."

"I'm sure you don't, Darling."

"She's very cold towards me now. I'm not sure our relationship will last, with all this going on too."

Rachel wasn't sure what to say to him. She didn't want to give him false hope; if Beth didn't want her gorgeous son, she was sure someone else would.

Lockdown was declared the next day, 23rd March. She had her two sons with her and despite the seriousness of the situation, she was relieved that they were all together and at that moment, safe.

Only three days later, the three of them stood, well apart, outside her front door, banging saucepans and clapping for the NHS. They smiled to each other through the amber darkness; Rachel was the only one who hadn't met Beth, but they all thought of her and silently praised her for risking her own life to help others. George was angry at her, but for that few minutes, he was proud ... and missed her terribly.

He texted her later and told her they'd all clapped on their doorstep. She wrote back, simply saying:

Thank you. It's really rough and there's no sign of it slowing down. It's nice to think people appreciate what we're doing.

Still no love shown to him, but at least she'd replied.

AMBER WAS GOING STIR crazy, stuck in the house with a small baby. Leo was a designated 'key worker' so sometimes went to court but the number of court proceedings that took place in person had decreased substantially and a lot of cases were now done remotely. Consequently, he had to find a quiet place to conduct his Zoom cases, away from the noise of everyday baby life. Their house wasn't big and this caused some problems; Amber would go out for her allowed exercise outside and stay out as long as possible but there were no coffee shops to go and sit in, no friends to meet, no 'normal' life to be outside for.

She would traipse around with the pushchair along pavements and sometimes she'd go up to Wanstead Flats, avoiding people as much as she could, watching the ducks who were swimming contentedly in the ponds, oblivious of this new world order. Physically, she was feeling almost normal again; her body had shrunk back to its original size quickly, leaving only a few stretch marks snaking across her stomach. She was always hungry but breastfeeding helped her regain her pre-baby weight. She was almost ready for some running.

She'd bonded well with Josh, as they now both called him. He was a contented baby and slept peacefully a lot of the time. A few other young mums she was in contact with over the internet talked of endless crying, colic, terrible nights, constant feeding, no rest – but she couldn't relate to that. She realised she was lucky, it wasn't anything she'd done or not done, it was just the way Josh was. Once he was fed, changed and cuddled, he'd happily go down and sleep for four hours and it wasn't long before he was having his last feed at eleven in the evening and only waking for the next feed at six in the morning. She had nothing to complain about.

"I must just be an amazing mother," she joked with Leo. "I've turned out to be the earth mother you predicted."

"Of course you are," he said, "I knew you would be."

He wasn't entirely convinced, to be honest. She *was* good with him and his contentment must be a reflection of her handling but ... Amber continued to be a little bit, to his eyes, 'scatty' – the putting of the chair on the settee was just the first of many incidents when he had to bite his lip. She'd lay him down on the floor to change him and then casually step over him, as if he was just an inanimate object. What if she tripped and fell on top of him? When Josh progressed into a bouncy chair, she'd put him on the kitchen table and turn away to wash up and Leo would notice the chair moving slightly.

The house became a bit of a tip, with everything strewn everywhere. Amber didn't see the point of tidying up as 'it just got messy again' and so, his cuddly toys, rattles, nappies, cloth books and all the other paraphernalia related to babies, migrated to every room. If it'd been up to Leo, they'd have had one room that ended up as the 'baby' room but that's not how Amber could operate.

She'd never been a tidy person. When she moved in with him, he'd had to get used to having her clothes spread all over the bedroom and bathroom, dirty dishes hanging around the kitchen (why didn't she put them straight in the dishwasher?) and shoes cluttering the hallway. He'd tell himself that she was young, funny ... a bit hare-brained and he could live with that.

But as lockdown continued and Amber tried to adapt to motherhood and isolation, the tensions in the house bubbled under. He felt she didn't understand the amount of stress he was under with work and she felt he didn't understand the stress she was under with Josh.

Early on, Leo had told Grace that she could have them as her 'support bubble' as she lived alone. He thought this might help in two ways: obviously, to give Grace some company but also he secretly hoped that Grace's influence might rub off on Amber. When she came round, they'd sit and chat about the two babies, swopping stories and advice and Grace would subtly pick things up and try to make order out of the chaos.

Grace was great with both babies, warm and kind. She was a natural and as time went by, the old Grace started emerging again after the grief that had consumed her. Leo would come into the sitting room and watch, amazed, as she sat on the floor, with a baby on each knee, laughing and jiggling them. Amber, despite the fact that she complained sometimes about the 'intrusion' of her visits, quite liked the fact that someone else was there to share the constant caring.

One day she asked Grace if she'd mind looking after both of them while she went out for a run.

"No, that's fine, Amber. You could probably do with some fresh air and exercise. That's the advantage of being an older mum, I'm quite content sitting here."

"Don't you miss 'life' out there? I feel as if the world has stopped."

"Do you know what? I don't miss work ... or shopping ... or any of the previous things I used to do. The only thing I miss is performing. I miss music but I can still listen to it, so that's okay."

They both thought of Anna ... the real thing Grace missed most of all.

"Wow, I wish I could feel like that. I feel as if I'm permanently waiting for something to happen and it *never* does."

"Well, you take advantage of me and get out, I'll be fine here. If they both start crying at the same moment, I'm sure I'll cope. When's he due his next feed?"

Amber looked at her watch, already standing by the door, anxious to get away. "Maybe ... in an hour? I should be okay if I leave now. I won't run far, I'm probably so unfit. If you're sure, I'll just nip up and change."

"Yea, go on ..."

Leo was in the spare room as usual, working remotely. He went downstairs about fifteen minutes later, to find Grace listening to music on her AirPods and the two babies fast asleep.

He walked in front of Grace so she could see him – she'd had her head back – and he said, "It's very peaceful in here. Where's Amber?"

Taking out her AirPods, she said, "She's gone out for a run."

"Really? Are you okay with that?"

"Yes, of course. Poor thing, she's getting a bit ... *down*, I think."

"Why do you say that?"

"Well, from certain things she's said to me ... and the state of the place. I think if she was happy, she'd want it to be tidy."

"I don't like to say anything in case she bites my head off ..."

"That's what I mean. I think it'll do her good to get out and run off some steam."

Leo shook his head. "What if Josh wakes up?"

"I'll cope ... she says he's not due to wake for an hour or so."

"Well, thank you, Grace. I don't want you to become Amber's unpaid servant, though."

"Honestly, Leo, I don't mind. I just said to Amber, I have no hankerings to be at work or in shops. I'm perfectly happy here, with these two." She looked across at the sleeping babies and smiled.

"Well, we love having you here," he said and went across to her, leant down and kissed the top of her head.

Chapter 15

It's true what they say about babies not bringing couples closer together. If there were problems before, they were only going to be exacerbated by a small person entering the dynamic.

Add in a global pandemic – and you have a bad situation.

Leo began to realise that the age gap was more of a problem than he'd first thought. He desperately wanted Amber to find Joshua all-consuming, to be the centre of her universe and indeed he *was* in her own way, but not in the way he wanted.

He knew now he wanted Amber to be a full-time mum, to devote her life to the upbringing of their son, but it became more and more apparent that this wasn't going to happen. Amber now talked openly about going back to work as soon as possible, of finding a nursery. Leo thought she took outrageous advantage of Grace's good nature too, asking her far too often to look after Josh while she went out for walks and runs. She'd also asked her to babysit when she began studying again, to help her prepare for her return to work.

When she'd first started talking about her future, he'd taken it with a pinch of salt, thinking that she was just simply thinking out loud, but it became obvious that motherhood on its own was not going to be enough for Amber. He tried not to sound disappointed or disapproving – he knew he'd said it was *her life* before Josh was born – but now he was here and so part of their lives, he understood how he'd hoped she'd change. His own mother had been at home until they were both at least five and he wanted this for his own son.

He talked about it to Grace, voicing his fears and concerns one day. Leo had pushed Josh round to Grace's flat one Saturday morning, leaving Amber to have a lie-in.

"Leo, you can't expect a young, highly intelligent girl with ambitions, to stay at home these days. Life for women has moved on – did you honestly think Amber would want to give up everything?"

"Well, I'd naively thought she'd want to be at home with Josh, yes. But I can see now I was wrong. She has every intention of going back to work."

They'd gone for a walk together with both babies in slings, on Wanstead Flats; the sun was shining and there was a feeling of new life thrusting through, with all the daffodils waving in the breeze. The April weather was magnificent, which made their allowed daily exercise a pleasure.

Josh was fast asleep and Leo tenderly stroked his hair, as he walked along.

"If that's what she wants to do, you've got to accept it. You knew the sort of girl she was when you got together. Josh'll be fine. Babies are very adaptable. Amber's a good mother, you know. I've seen how she operates at close quarters and she's very efficient; I do think Josh's contentment is partly down to Amber, not just his rather laid-back personality. She's very good with him. I think you should give her more credit than you do."

"I know I expect a lot from her. But when I see you and Thea ... I wish she was more like you," he said, linking his arm through hers and pulling her close. She smiled up at him.

"Well, I'm nearly twice her age for a start – I'm sure when I was her age, I would've been just the same: desperate to be back at work, desperate to be performing, desperate to be in the thick of things. I understand her, Leo. You've got to give her some slack."

"Will you help her when it comes to finding a nursery? Maybe Thea and Josh could go to the same one?"

"Of course, I'd already thought of that."

"Anyway, on another note, she's asked if she can go to Brighton to stay at Rachel's, as George and Harry are there. She'd be breaking the Covid rules ... but she seems so keen, I'm inclined to say 'yes'. She'd take the car, so the only people she'd come into contact with, would be Rachel and the boys. What do you think?"

Grace hesitated and then said, "I can really see it from her point of view – she wants to be with people her own age and just have a laugh. If Rachel's happy then ... maybe it'll be okay? I'm sure there are thousands of people breaking the rules *all* the time. She won't be endangering any old people or anything, will she?"

"No she won't, I'm glad you agree with me, I thought that. It might just give her a break and help her see life from a new perspective. She's always loved those boys."

So it was decided: Amber would drive with Josh to Brighton.

If Dominic Cummings could break the rules, then so could they.

Leo was going to miss Josh like mad but he knew he couldn't care for him and do his work at the same time. He'd okayed it with Rachel, who was looking forward to being a surrogate granny, she said and she thought how lovely it would be for the 'kids' to get together again. George was working a lot every day up in his room but Harry was hanging around with not a lot to do – he was spending much too much time playing computer games and sleeping, Rachel said, so Amber would be a welcome visitor.

Leo waved them both off early one morning, feeling a mixture or guilt and relief: guilt at breaking the rules and relief that Amber looked so happy. But ... it occurred to him that he also felt relief, that for a week or so, he'd have his peaceful house back; he'd be able to put all the toys and clutter in one place and they'd stay there.

And most importantly, he felt guilt, terrible guilt, when he acknowledged that his first thought when Amber disappeared down the road was that he could spend more time with Grace.

Just him and her (and Thea of course) but he so looked forward to being in the same room with her, without Amber.

It would almost seem like old times.

DUE TO THE PANDEMIC, Rachel and the boys had only seen pictures of Josh. It was hard to imagine Amber as a mother now.

By the time Amber arrived, George and Harry had stopped their self-imposed isolation and so far, so good: everyone one was Covid free. They'd decided they couldn't impose isolation on Amber ... and anyway, she hadn't been mixing with anyone.

As the car drew into the drive, the three of them went out to help her get all the requisite luggage inside. She got out and flung her arms around them all, one after the other.

"It's so lovely to see you – who cares if we all get Covid?" she laughed. "I just need some different human company. I feel starved of it."

The boys went to retrieve everything from the car.

"God, are you staying for a year?" laughed George, as he lugged yet another bag out of the boot.

"You need as much stuff for a few days as you do for a month, to be honest. Who knew that one tiny person could need so much *stuff*?" Amber laughed. Josh was still sleeping peacefully as they emptied the car.

Rachel was leaning in, letting the boys do all the hard work. "Oh my goodness, Amber," she whispered, "he's adorable. There's so much of Leo about him but he's got your mouth, I think."

The boys came and leant into the car too.

"Mum, all babies look the same. How can you possibly say that?" said Harry, laughing.

"Shh ... you'll wake him up," she said.

"Don't worry, Rach, he sleeps through anything, like his Dad," said Amber. "Let me grab him and go in. I'm in desperate need of a coffee."

Rachel noticed how briskly she got the car seat out; no nonsense there, she thought, just straight in and whisk him out. Still, he's a good sleeper, he doesn't mind being jiggled about.

"So, everything was okay on the journey, then?" asked Rachel as they moved into the kitchen and Amber put the car seat down on the kitchen table, as was her normal practice. "No Covid police about asking you why you were travelling?"

"No, nothing like that. I do feel just *a little bit* guilty but I'm not doing anyone any harm, am I?"

"No ... but I think we ought to keep a relatively low profile while you're here. I wouldn't want any of the neighbours to report us."

"Well, we'll all be inside most of the time," said George.

"Stop worrying, Ma," said Harry. "You're such a rule-follower normally though, I'm amazed you agreed to this."

"Sometimes, the rules can be broken ..." said Rachel. "So how's motherhood, Amber? You've certainly got your figure back already."

"Yea, it's fine. It's not easy being confined, though. It makes it a lot more difficult. I know I'm driving Leo a bit crazy ..."

"Really? Why do you say that?"

"Well, he's always quietly tidying up when he thinks I'm not looking. I've always been an untidy person but it's got truly out of hand since this little one came along." She put a finger on Josh's cheek and he snuffled and moved. "Oops," she said. "Don't wake up, mister ... anyway," she continued, "I can just tell ... he's always looking a bit stressed these days. I think that was why he agreed for me to come here; a chance to have his house back for a week."

"Whenever I speak to him, he's always saying how well you're doing and how good Josh is," said Rachel.

"Mmm, that's not the impression I get. Oh well, who knows? He's so busy at the moment, he's permanently on his computer."

"And do you see much of Grace?"

"All the bloody time ... sorry Rach ... I know she's your friend, but she's either round at ours or he's round at hers. We're her support bubble. But I shouldn't complain, she seems quite happy to babysit them both while I bugger off and go running. It's the one little bit of freedom I get."

"It must be hard for you. When I had these two, I was surrounded with other young mums with babies and toddlers. I'm sure you must miss the camaraderie and help. Just having a cup of coffee with other people going through the same things as you, really helps. But it was strange, I felt isolated too ... but in a completely different way. An RAF camp was a strange environment."

"God, yes, I would've hated that. Anyway, enough of me. How are you lot?"

"I'm enjoying working from home, to be honest," said George. "Well, not *home,* but you know what I mean. This has made people realise that actually going into the office for most people is a complete waste of time and money. I know I get much more done now. There's so much time wasted in an office."

"I'm enjoying doing sod all," laughed Harry. "Mum even cooks my meals ... I have literally *no* reason to get up in the morning."

Rachel swatted him on the head, affectionately.

"Nice for some. I have a good alarm clock that gets me up at six every day. To be fair, that's pretty good though, I do realise that."

At that moment, Josh started moving and crying. Amber stood up, clicked his straps to get him out and unceremoniously laid him on the table and peeled off his outer layer of clothing.

"God, he stinks," she said. "George, get that bag, can you? I'll take him somewhere else for this disgusting job. I fear it's a poonami. Where are we sleeping, Rachel?"

"I've put you in the blue room, George'll show you. I still had a travel cot that I've hung onto, in the vain hope that I'd get some grandchildren some day, so I've put it up for you."

"Oh thanks, Auntie Rach, that's amaze-balls. He was going to have to sleep in his carry cot. Come on then George, lead the way."

The two of them went upstairs, chatting.

"Well, this is going to be interesting," said Harry. "I'd love to see George changing a dirty nappy," he laughed.

"I don't think that'll happen," said Rachel, "but it's nice to see those two together again after such a long time."

Rachel secretly was astounded at how similar they were. Why didn't anyone else see it? Thank God they didn't.

"It's weird, isn't it?" said Harry. "How alike those two look? They could be brother and sister."

"Do you think so?" said Rachel, her heart hammering. "I can't really see it."

Oh God.

GEORGE WAS IN HIS OLD room, just along from the bathroom; he'd just finished for the day and closed his laptop with relief.

"Can you go and find the hairdryer in my room, George?" shouted Rachel. "It's somewhere in the cupboard; I think it's in the top, right-hand shelf. This one decided he was going to get his hair wet whether we wanted him to or not. I just want to make sure he doesn't have a damp head," she added; George could hear her laughing happily with Baby Josh.

He could picture the scene: Josh, on Mum's lap, wrapped in a towel, all snuggly and damp from the bath; Mum tickling him and blowing on his tummy. Josh really was an adorable child; he hadn't had much experience with young kids but he could honestly say he loved that child – he seemed to have inherited the best from both his parents. They were such a striking couple: Leo, with his older man ease and dark skin and Amber, with her long-legged athleticism and blondness. It was a bit of a mystery as to where Josh's hint of ginger hair came from (Jen had an aunt with red hair, so they all concluded that she carried the MC1R gene). Combined with his blue eyes and golden skin, he was something else.

They still all referred to the bedrooms as 'George's room' and 'Harry's room' despite the fact that they'd both left home years ago. It was comforting, though, to come back and find everything still the same: the photos on the walls, the bookshelf full of books he'd read when he was doing GCSE English and A level, the old posters of gigs he'd gone to, now faded and torn. He'd offered to help Rachel redecorate but she seemed to like it as it was, and so did he. Part of him was clinging to the past, when everything was normal.

Rachel's room was on the top floor and as he got off the bed to go upstairs, he decided to pop his head round the door of the bathroom.

"You're a little monkey, you are," he said, as he saw the scene, exactly how he'd imagined it. "Your Granny Rachel is far too soft on you! Where's your Mummy? Is she putting her feet up?" he laughed.

"I told her I'd do bedtime. I so remember how exhausting it can be after a long day; Amber looked peaky, I thought, when she arrived. She's gone running."

"Oh, that's nice of you. I'm sure she'll appreciate it; she doesn't get much chance to be on her own anymore. Mind you, it doesn't look like it's much of a sacrifice for you," he said, as Rachel kissed Josh's plump little belly.

"I love being a granny; I know I'm not his *real* granny, but ... I just love it when they're all clean and wrapped in a fluffy bath towel and smell so heavenly," she said, burying her nose in the bundle of soft skin and towel on her lap. "When are you two going to give me 'real' grandchildren?" she laughed.

George responded by raising his eyebrows. "It's not looking hopeful at the moment, Mum. Right, I'll go and get the hairdryer and bring it down to Amber's room."

He ran up the stairs and quickly scanned the room and then remembered where she'd said it would be. He grabbed the door of the cupboard roughly and the whole thing wobbled. He must take a look at it, in case it fell right over one day. He shuddered at a picture that came into his mind of this huge piece of furniture lying on top of Mum.

Rachel was never the most tidy person and the wardrobe was stuffed with far too many clothes and possessions; how she ever found anything was beyond him. He'd inherited his father's more military and spartan approach to possessions – everything had its place in his flat and minimalist was his style.

He spotted the hair dryer on the shelf she'd mentioned; it was behind a box full to the brim with what looked like her attempt at admin. He took both items out and put them on the bed.

He picked up the hairdryer and was just about to turn around and walk out when a photo at the top of the box caught his eye. He felt as if he was invading his mother's personal space but he picked it up anyway, intrigued.

It was a square photo of a group and on further inspection, he saw it was taken on the now infamous holiday to Cyprus, when his parents had split up. Thank God I wasn't there, he thought. He wasn't sure he would have been able to deal with his Dad, without physically attacking him.

How could he have done that to Mum?

He stared at the picture. It was so bright and colourful; stunning blue sky and sea forming the backdrop, with some sort of Mediterranean flowering bush bursting with bright pink petals, off to the side. It must have been taken before the big bust up and before Amber arrived and created another bombshell.

The six, Jen and Mike, Grace and Leo and Mum and Dad looked so happy and relaxed, smiling into the camera. They must have set it up so that they could all be in the photo.

Little did they know what secrets lay between them and what tragedies lay ahead. So much had changed since then: babies born ... a mother's death ... a global pandemic. Death had touched all their lives.

Tears stung his eyes as he continued to stare at the picture. It felt like a glance at a more innocent time, when friendships were still simple and marriages were in tact.

Life's complicated, he thought as he put the photo back on top of the pile of papers. He lifted the box off the bed and was just thinking to himself he must ask Mum if she needs any help with her accounts – a Nat West statement lay on the top of the pile and he couldn't help noticing the total in her account – when some letters on the piece of paper next in the pile, jumped out of the box.

D-N-A.

Why on earth did his mother have a piece of paper in a box with the letters DNA written on it?

His heart lurched and he sat down with the box on his lap, sweat breaking out, wetting his armpits, as if he had been heated from the inside. In the distance, downstairs, he heard Rachel laugh. The light in the room was fading and he wondered if he'd read it right. He couldn't bring himself to take it out of the box; he had a premonition that it was going to change everything.

He stood up slowly and put the box back on the bed; he went to the light switch, turned it on and stared at the box again.

Should he look?

He couldn't NOT look now.

He stumbled back to the bed, moved the photo and the statement, as if they were contaminated, laying them on the duvet.

There it was.

DNA Paternity Report, in bold type.

There were three columns: Mother, Child, Alleged Father. In two columns, not the one headed 'Mother', were lots of numbers he didn't understand.

His mind was racing as he scanned the page. What did it all mean? His brain was rushing ahead, trying to make some sense of it.

And then he saw it, at the bottom of the page.

Probability of Paternity: 0%

Calm down, he shouted inwardly. It's nothing to do with our family. There are no names, just child, mother, father. There would be a simple explanation.

What did it mean, anyway? *Whose* father has zero per cent paternity?

His legs felt weak and without even realising it, he slumped down, the paper in his hand. He folded his body forward, his arms around his stomach, trying to breathe, his hand still clutching the paper.

He could hear steps coming up the stairs, his mother singing 'Rock-a-bye Baby' as she walked. He'd heard her sing this a dozen times before.

When the bough breaks the cradle will fall, And down will come baby, cradle and all.

The steps continued down the corridor.

She pushed open the door.

"I thought I'd come up and get ..." she said, but stopped short.

It was if he was paralysed, he couldn't move or speak.

Rachel's face said it all.

"WHAT'S THIS?" HE SAID, holding out the incriminating piece of paper.

"I ... I ... need the hairdryer, George. Can you pass it to me?" her face ashen.

"Mum, I need to know why you've got this DNA document in your cupboard."

Joshua was cuddled into Rachel's shoulder and maybe feeling the tension that had suddenly erupted in the room, he began to cry.

"Shh ... shh ..." said Rachel, as she moved him away from her and lifted him up, so that he was looking down at her. "There you are, you're okay ..." she whispered. He stopped crying almost immediately.

"Mum ..."

"I'm going to get the hairdryer ... and then get him to bed. Amber expressed some milk. He's going to get hungry any minute and start yelling. When I've done that, I'll talk to you ..."

Her face was stoney and pinched. There was a look of a trapped animal about her eyes.

"Mum, you can't just walk away ..."

"I can, George, and I will. But I promise we *will* talk ... when he's down," and with that, she walked forward and picked up the hairdryer. Without another word, she walked out.

George was left stunned, sitting on the bed, holding the document, staring at the door. What the hell was going on? He knew that something had shifted, something huge.

DNA is only used for one thing; to determine the paternity of a child.

Who did '*Probability of Paternity: 0%*' refer to? There could only be one reason his mother had this hidden in cupboard: she wasn't sure who the father was, of either himself or Harry.

He now saw his mother in a whole new light: a woman who had buried a terrible secret for all these years.

But when had she decided to get this test? He quickly scanned the page; the date was *December, 2019,* so relatively recently.

Why now? What was she going to do with it? Did their father know? Or, should he say, who he *thought* was their father, until minutes ago.

He flopped back onto the bed, his feet still on the ground. He closed his eyes and could feel tears seep out of the corners and run down his face into his ears. In the distance, downstairs, he could hear his mother moving around. She was probably getting the plug out of the bath so that the water could drain away; finding Josh's nappy, putting on his baby gro, kissing him – as if her life hadn't changed in that split second.

How could she?

Where was Harry? He needed to speak to him before he talked to her again. He wanted to have a united front against her.

It could be either of them ... or even both?

Everything he thought about his life was suddenly being ripped away from him.

He sat up, rubbed his eyes with his sleeves and got up. He couldn't be bothered to put the boxes back – why should he? He'd leave them, as evidence of her betrayal. Why did she leave something so secret for someone to find anyway? Did she honestly think no one would ever go in her cupboard? What if she'd died suddenly? They'd have had to go through her things ... maybe in some sort of warped way, she wanted to be found out?

He was at a loss as to what was going on.

He left the room and went downstairs as quietly as possible; he had no desire to see her. He tiptoed down the corridor and without knocking, which he would normally have done, walked straight into his brother's bedroom.

He was sitting at his desk, playing computer games. His back was towards the him.

"Hey, Haz ..." he said, not realising that his brother had earphones in and couldn't hear him.

When he didn't respond, George slapped him on the back, maybe harder than he should have done. Harry responded with, "What the fuck?"

"I need to speak to you ..."

"I'm in the middle of a really important part of the game ..."

"Harry, for Christ's sake, I NEED to speak to you – NOW."

His brother looked a little askance at him, took out his AirPods and put them on the desk. "Hey, calm down, George. Chill ... what's so fucking vital that you need to interrupt me?"

"Look George ..." he said and sat down on the bed. "There's no easy way of telling you. Just *look* at this. I found it upstairs in Mum's cupboard."

He thrust the paper towards a bewildered Harry who scanned it, not understanding what he was looking at.

"What *is* this, man?"

"Just READ it ... it's not difficult."

There was a short silence as Harry, with a sigh, read the page.

"I don't understand ... what's it got to do with me?"

"It's a DNA test, Harry. Mum was hiding it ... it says 'zero per cent possibility of paternity'. Don't you *get* it?"

The colour drained from Harry's face. He looked at it again.

"Fucking hell. Does this refer to us?"

"I don't know, bro, that's the whole point. Mum came up with Josh and when she saw what I'd found, she went as white as a sheet. Something's very wrong, I know it is. She said she'll speak to me after she's put the baby down. I wanted to tell you first ..."

"What do you think ..."

"I have no fucking clue. Absolutely no fucking idea. We're going to have to confront her, find out."

"You found it, bro," said Harry. "Can't you have this argument with her?"

"No, Haz. It affects us both. We don't know what it means. You can help me out, surely?"

"If I have to, I suppose. Maybe it's nothing?"

"Maybe it is, but we need to find out. We can't just ignore it and the way Mum reacted was really odd. You should have seen her." George stood up. "I'll call you when she's ready to talk."

"Okay. But I can't say I'm looking forward to it much."

AN HOUR OR SO LATER, George was staring at the TV, trying to get his head round what was going on. He had the piece of paper in his pocket.

Amber was now back and had run upstairs to take a shower, oblivious to everything. Rachel had successfully put Josh down and was preparing supper.

They hadn't spoken.

George felt like the clock was ticking down to something big. He kept touching the paper that might change his world.

Suddenly, he'd had enough ... he grabbed the remote control and turned off the telly. He stood up and marched into the kitchen.

"Can you turn off the gas Mum, we need to talk. I'm calling Harry downstairs."

Rachel obediently turned off the cooker, washed her hands, dried them and sat at the kitchen table, waiting. She could hear George knocking on Harry's door, some unintelligible words and then they both banged down the stairs.

They sat down opposite her and waited.

"Well?" said George. "I've put Harry in the picture. We want answers."

"Yes, I'm sure you do," she said, awkwardly. "Shall I open a bottle of red?"

"No, I don't think that's a good idea. We need clear heads."

"Oh, okay. I thought it might help ..."

"No, I don't think so, Mum," said George. He was sitting formally on the chair – straight, his hands resting on the table.

"Could one of you go and get Amber?" said Rachel. "It affects her too."

"Don't you think it would be better to keep it amongst ourselves?" said Harry. "There's no point involving ..."

"No, I *said* – get Amber. I'm going to have a glass of wine, even if you two don't want one." She got up and went to the wine wrack that was to the left of the American fridge freezer.

"I'll go and get her," said Harry, jumping up, keen to have something to do.

Rachel and George didn't speak while he was gone. The silence was all-pervasive; the only thing that could be heard was the drip of the cold tap into the half-full washing-up bowl. There was a smell of cooking mince in the air. Rachel sloshed some red wine into a glass and slurped some, nervously.

"So, here I am," said Amber as she bounced through the door. "This all looks a bit serious? Thanks for sorting J by the way, Auntie Rach. He's sleeping like the proverbial baby, ha ha. Ooo, can I have a glass of that, Rach? I know I'm not meant to when I'm breastfeeding, but who cares? He won't wake up till eleven and it's only seven. It might even help him sleep, who knows? Anyway, Harry says you want to talk about something?" Amber threw herself down onto the sofa that was next to the table and put her head on the arm rest and her feet up on the sofa.

"Pass me the wine, and a glass, George darling, will you?"

He duly did and then stared at his mother. Amber attempted to pour a glass of wine from a lying position.

"Well?" he said. "Just to put you in the picture, Amber ... I found a DNA test upstairs and I want to know why it was there."

"That sounds exciting, Rach. Are you tracing your ancestors or something?"

"No," said George. "She's done a paternity test, haven't you, Mum?"

"What? Why?" said Amber. She swung her legs round and abruptly sat up. She took a long swig from the wine glass. "I get the feeling I'm going to need this."

All three stared at Rachel, waiting. She was sitting at the head of the table, sipping her wine. Amber stood up and joined them round the table.

It was as if Rachel was 'stuck'. She wanted to speak but couldn't get the words out. How could she possibly tell them?

"What I'm about to tell you will come as a shock. To all *three* of you," she said.

"Me, as well?" said Amber.

"Yes, Amber, you too. But before I say anything I want you all to swear NOT to tell anyone, not ANYONE. It's very important. Someone's health and well-being depends on it."

"We can't agree to that, until we know what it is," said George. His face was now red, as if his anger was burning its way to the surface.

"Well, you're going to have to, otherwise I won't tell you. You've got to swear ..."

"That's fine by me," said Harry.

"And me," said Amber, smiling across at Harry.

"Well, I'm not sure," said George.

"Oh come on, bro," said Harry. "She means what she says, you can tell."

George thought for a while; he got up and paced around the kitchen. He came back, slumped down and said, "Okay, but I'm not happy about it. At *all*."

"So ... all three of you promise, and I mean PROMISE, then, not to tell a soul?"

"Yes, we all do, Mum, we've just said it. Now, can you please get on and fucking tell us?"

Rachel stood up and taking her glass of wine with her, she went over to the sink and leant against it, looking diminished somehow, fragile even. She opened her mouth but nothing came out. She looked like a fish, gasping for air on dry land.

She opened her mouth again. "So, first of all, you must realise that I never meant to hurt anyone. I've lived with a situation since I was twenty ... that at times, has been unbearable." She looked as if she was near to tears and she took another large gulp of wine.

"I fell in love with someone at university. We met, then parted for a while and in the meantime, that person became attached to someone else. So I lost them."

"This is all very tragic, Mum, but I don't see how this affects *anything*," said George. "You met Dad after university ..."

"Let her *explain*, George," said Amber.

"Yea, shut up, George," said Harry.

"We still had feelings for each other but the situation was difficult and we both recognised that it was better to leave the past behind. So we did. He married the other girl and I met your father. But because of circumstances, we were still part of each other's lives and one night, just ONE night, I was unfaithful to your Dad, with this man."

She had decided not to mention the other time, before he was married.

The three of them looked at each other; Rachel had become someone different to them, in the space of a minute.

"What, so you had an affair?" said Harry. It was hard for him to think of Rachel in any other light, other than as his mother.

Mothers didn't have emotional lives outside their family, surely?

"No, Harry, I said, just *one* night. And that's all it was because we both felt so guilty. He loved his wife dearly and I still loved Zach at that stage ... but I must point out to you, that I was unhappy in *myself*. I was cut off from all my friends and family on the Air Force base. I never really felt part of that life and your Dad didn't, *couldn't*, understand. But ... I'm not making excuses for either of us. It happened and I had to live with it."

She went to the cupboard and removed a glass; she turned on the tap and filled it. She drank it down in one, as if she was trying to wash away her perceived sins.

"So, soon after this, I got pregnant with you, George," she said, turning to face him.

So, this was it, he thought. The moment when everything will change.

"It's me, then, right? It's *me* you were testing ..."

"Yes, George, it's you. It could have just as easily been your father, but I've always had this feeling ... this instinct ... that it was this man."

"So, I have *zero chance,* according to the DNA thing, of being Dad's son?"

George got up and came and stood in front of Rachel.

"Yes, my suspicions were confirmed. I can promise you, though, there were only *two* contenders. You can rest assured I know *exactly* who your biological father is."

"Oh-My-God," said Harry, "so we don't have the same father? I don't believe this, Mum. How come you've waited *all this time* to say or do anything?"

"Because I was in denial ... because I love you both to bits ... because ..." She turned away and started crying, bent over the sink, her hands over her eyes.

"Because you've been caught out, more like," said George, bitterly. "If I'd never gone into the cupboard to get that fucking hairdryer ..."

"But why did you get the DNA test *recently*? What made you finally confront your feeling?"

Rachel swung round, rubbing her eyes, trying to stop crying. "I just had to *know*, finally. Dad and I were divorcing ... I needed to know ... in my heart. I was never going to tell anyone ..."

"So ... wait a minute ... you were going to *lie* to me for the rest of my life?" George shouted. "You were going to let me go to my grave, thinking Dad was my biological father? I was never going to know about my *real* father?"

"What *good* would it have done, George? Zach is your father in every way. He's cared for you, he's been there for you. Maybe he's not been a particularly *good* father to you both, but he's *been* there," she said wearily and went and sat down at the table again, her chin cradled by her hands. "Zach *is* your *father*, George, in every possible way. You don't *need* another father. This is just a biological formality. It takes a lot more to be a father than to just donate his sperm."

"But Mum, surely you can see that you can't drop a fucking bombshell like this and expect George to just accept it? He needs to know who his real father is. Surely you understand that?"

"Yes, of course I do ... but ..."

"But hold on a minute," said Amber, "why does this affect *me*? You said I had to know too, but as far as I can see, this is a problem for your family. Not mine."

"So ... this is where you've all got to keep calm ... and just believe me when I say, the man involved has NO idea about all this. And he's NOT to find out, either."

"But what's it got to do with ME?" said Amber, but as she said it, it was as if something finally dropped into place. Her face betrayed what she'd finally understood.

She looked incredulously at the boys; her expression, a picture of confusion, anger and disbelief.

"Please don't tell me it's ..." she said.

"Yes, Amber ... it's your Dad ... Mike. Mike is George's father."

An arctic silence descended, as if the whole house had been covered in feet of ice and snow. No one moved; they were frozen, each person paralysed by their own thoughts.

"I don't ... I don't understand," said Amber, at last. "You mean ... you've loved my Dad since the nineties?"

"Yes."

"But how could you live like that? Your best friend married the man you loved ... how could you carry on being her friend?"

"Because, as you say, Jen was, and is, my best friend. She is innocent in all this. She is the reason you must *not* say anything,

Amber. She's been so ill, she's vulnerable. She adores your Dad and he adores her. Surely you can see that?"

"Yes, of course I can. But this, now ... you should have told her all those years ago, before she was ill."

"What good would it have done? Mike, your Dad, loved her; he wasn't going to hurt her by telling her. He wasn't going to leave her, for me. We discussed it and, whether it was right or wrong, we decided not to tell her. I have never, never told Mike about my thoughts about George. He knows *nothing* about it. Please don't judge him Amber, he's a good man. After that night, we agreed never to talk about it or to refer to it. We tried to avoid each other, but it wasn't always easy."

"So, Mike is my real Dad? Amber is my half-sister? I can't get my head round this. It's fucking mental," shouted George, marching across the room. He flung open the door, walked out and slammed it.

The remaining three stared at each other. "Am I definitely Dad's son, then? You haven't had any other one night stands then, Mum?" said Harry.

"Harry, don't be a dick. She said it was a one-off," said Amber, for some reason wanting to defend Rachel against an onslaught of abuse from her sons.

"With *your* Dad. Who knows how many others there have been?" said Harry, with an uncharacteristic nastiness.

"Please believe me, Harry. There has been no one else."

"Does Dad know?" said Harry.

"No, he doesn't yet but I will tell him when the time's right. And if we're comparing our behaviour, I think what Dad did to me is far worse ..."

"But maybe, now, we can see *his* side of the story ... maybe, just maybe, you've always treated him as *second best* and he finally got fed-up with it? Maybe he didn't know in reality, but subconsciously, he knew and decided he'd had enough. I've always blamed Dad for so many things wrong with this family, but now ..."

"Harry, I've buried my feelings for years, to *save* your Dad, to *save* Jen, to *save* Mike. It's been HARD."

She left the room, closing the door quietly behind her.

"Christ," said Harry. "What a bloody mess." He looked across at Amber who now looked pale, as if all the life had drained out of her.

"What do we do now? Should I follow one of them?"

"No, let them be. How am I meant to carry on, knowing what I do? I've always looked up to my Dad and now ..."

"In the grand scheme of things, Amber, this was one time, years ago," said Harry, being more like his positive self. "Don't change how you feel about him. He loves your Mum and ... he knows nothing about George."

He grinned, trying to lighten the mood, saying, "You two are very alike, you know, both looks-wise and personality. I feel a bit left out, to be honest."

He came round and sat right up close to Amber, putting his arm around her. "Look at it this way, you've gained a brother. You've never liked being an only child ... and now you're not," he smiled.

"Good old Harry, always looking on the bright side of life."

"Well, you've got to, haven't you? This kind of situation could break us, but we're not going to let it. The pandemic has brought us back together again ... don't let this news spoil it."

He kissed her cheek and she turned and put her arms around him. She snuggled right in and despite everything, she enjoyed a feeling of warmth. Maybe Rachel's predicament was making her think about her own situation, which felt, at this moment, almost as precarious.

She kissed Harry, without warning, full on the lips. She'd always been impulsive and this felt like one of those moments when she wanted to throw all caution to the wind.

He pushed her away with a look of surprise on his face.

"Amber, what on earth are you DOING?"

Her face was a study of regret, longing, surprise. "Sorry, Hazza, I don't know what came over me. My head is in a *complete* mess."

"Don't get me wrong, I enjoyed it, Ams, but, perhaps your timing could have been better?" he grinned.

"At least we're not committing incest," he added, grinning.

"Harry, don't ... that's an awful thing to say. What the hell was I thinking? I love Leo, don't I?"

"Well, yes, I think you do ... but who knows?"

"Life is a bloody nightmare. What's love anyway? It turns out that Auntie Rach has been in love with my Dad forever and has had to bury it. I can't help but feel sorry for her. I need to know more about the past. How did they meet? Why did they have a break? Why did my Dad end up marrying Mum instead? It's a mystery. God, I'm going to find it so hard, acting normally when I go home."

"Well, you're going to *have* to, for the sake of both your parents."

They were still sitting, arms around each other. "And by the way, I've always rather fancied you, if you must know. I know I'm younger than you, but ..."

"Really? You kept that quiet."

Amber was quietly flattered.

"Well, it's not something you want to go on about when you're kind of the 'younger brother' but thank God that's not the case. Can I kiss you back, now?"

"Oh, go on then, for old time's sake. But don't get any ideas."

He leant in, gently and their lips met, softly.

It's strange how a shock can make people totally act out of character. Harry hadn't had many girlfriends and was shy around girls, but for some reason, this felt as natural as if they'd done it thousands of times before.

They drew apart, neither of them sure what to say.

"We better go and find the other two," said Amber.

"Yes, before they kill each other."

Chapter 16

"I'm just not sure how to go on from here. Everything I thought I was, everything I thought I knew about myself, about Dad, has been proven to be lie. What am I meant to do now?"

George was sitting on his childhood bed, feeling like the child who used to live there. Harry was standing by the door, Amber was sitting on the floor with her back against the wall. Some music was playing quietly through a portable speaker. Rachel had gone to bed and Joshua was still asleep; Amber was expecting him to wake soon.

"You don't do anything, bro," said Harry. "You take it in, you deal with it. Yes, it changes things, but you're still *you*, you're still *George*, the prat who embarrassed himself in my restaurant."

"Yea, thanks for reminding me of that, Harry. Just what I needed at this juncture. I know I'm still fundamentally the same person, but ... it still changes everything. And this added complication of not being able to even *talk* to my new biological father is terrible. I don't want to hurt anyone, particularly your mother, Amber, but, you can see it from my point of view, surely?"

"Course we can ... we're all struggling here. As far as I can see it, we've just got to sit on this information, live with it, don't act on it. Imagine if your mum had said this same story ... but that your real father was a stranger. How would you feel, then? Would that have made it better or worse? Maybe you can't find him, maybe he rejects you if you do; maybe he's dead, even? There are so many other scenarios that could have been even worse. At least *this* way, you know who he is, you've spent loads of time with him – hopefully, you even like him already? And on top of all that, you've got me as a half-sister. That's surely an added bonus?" she laughs.

"I suppose when you put it like that ..." said George. "It's weird ... when Mum was talking about Zach, how I didn't need another father ... how even though he hasn't been the best father in the world, he was at least there for me ... I was thinking, I've *never* really felt close to him. There's always been something missing. It kind of made sense ..."

"But don't forget, George, it's not Dad's fault ..."

"I didn't say it was, but, I was just saying, I've always felt distant from him. She said he was always there for us, but I kind of dispute that. He was distant, both emotionally and often physically. It was always Mum who was really there for us."

"So, you've got to be careful how you are with her now, George. As you say, her whole life has been dedicated to us; she's really upset right now. You've got to see it from her point of view."

"I know, Harry ... I don't want to upset her any more than she is already, but she does have to take some responsibility. It was a choice she made, all those years ago, and it's been a choice, ever since, not to tell me. Anyway, I'm fed up of talking about it ... can you two fuck off now, I need to go to sleep. What was that?"

"What?"

"That noise ... oh, I think it's Josh, Amber, isn't it?"

She looked at her watch. "Yes, 11.05 – he's beginning to wake around this time, like clockwork." She stood up slowly. "Come on Haz, leave your brother alone and come and help me."

"Well, there's not a lot I can do ... I think breastfeeding is really your domain."

"Come and talk to me, anyway," she giggled. Harry opened the door and the crying from Joshua got louder. "Hurry up," she said, dragging Harry out.

"Night," said George, as the door closed and he was at last left alone with his thoughts.

AMBER FOUND HERSELF rather dreading going home.

Rachel's revelations had made her realise just how complicated life could be and when she analysed her own life, she wasn't at all sure it was how she'd foreseen it turning out. She'd always envisaged her life as a career woman, a hot-shot barrister; before she'd got herself pregnant, she'd loved the freedom, the intellectual challenge. But then Leo, with his glamour, his good looks and court presence had turned her head and she'd forgotten what she'd set out to do. She realised now that down the line, she felt lost.

Here she was, stuck in a small house with a baby, with a man old enough to be her father, who blatantly still had feelings for his ex-wife, whom he hadn't even divorced.

She adored Josh, she really did; she loved being his mum ... but she didn't feel fulfilled, she needed something *else*. She loved Leo, she always would, but was it the passion she'd first thought it was, or something more like a celebrity crush? She knew she didn't feel like Rachel, loving her Dad from afar, her whole life.

She loved this house in Brighton – the rooms were large – squarer and lighter than theirs. People could get lost in it, it was uncluttered. She liked the company of the boys. Despite everything, they'd had laughs; it had almost made her feel normal again, being with them. And the bond that had somehow crept up on her and Harry had taken her completely by surprise. They were so different, but somehow they'd just clicked during this week, and the pair of them had felt as natural as gin and tonic. There was a frisson that hadn't existed before. She was going to miss him.

She was also going to miss Rachel's extra pair of hands; she was only too willing to share the care of Josh. Sometimes, it felt as if Rachel was the one in charge. She loved the sense of freedom she felt when Josh was being looked after by her; she had absolute faith that he was happy and it left her to get on with doing what she wanted, whether it was running, reading or just watching TV.

Now, it was the day she was driving home. Yes, she would have Grace to help her, but it wasn't the same. Every time Grace came over, she felt as if *she* was the 'extra' one, the 'young' one, the 'silly' one. It was nothing Grace did as such, it was Leo and her history that crept through the house, making her feel like a spare part, like a young babysitter who happened to live there.

She'd packed the car; Rachel was cuddling Josh, the boys were milling around, carrying bits to the car. She felt conflicted – she didn't have to go but felt she *ought* to. She needed to go back and re-establish herself. But she'd enjoyed this time away, enjoyed being with the boys. Or one particular boy.

She could sense Harry's disappointment as her belongings finally filled the car. They hadn't kissed again but somehow their relationship had transmogrified into something else, without either of them knowing what it was.

She was collecting the last few bits from her bedroom, when Harry slipped through the door and closed it. Leaning against the door (in his mind, to make sure they weren't interrupted) he said, "Ams ... I know this is completely out of order, but ... I just wanted to say ..." He stopped awkwardly, scratching his head and smiling nervously. "I just wanted to say ... if you ever need me, I'll always be there for you."

She turned round, closed the wardrobe door, and said, "Aww ... thanks Harry. I've really enjoyed this time ... it was great to spend time with you. This bloody pandemic at least brought us together again. I know technically I shouldn't have come here and I broke the rules, but we didn't do any harm, did we? I can't remember when we spent more than a few hours together. It's weird, isn't it? I've always regarded you two as my surrogate brothers ... and now one of you really *is* my brother."

"Thank God you're *not* my sister," said Harry, grinning.

"It's going to be so difficult to keep this to myself," she said. "I'm meant to be Face Timing with the parents tomorrow. How can I do that and act normal?"

"I don't know, but you've got to try, Amber, you really have."

She came over to him, clutching a few nappies, some items of clothing and a cloth book. "Come on, open up, I need to hit the road. Timing is everything when you're travelling alone with a baby."

He reached out and put his hand on her arm. They stood, inches apart, facing each other. "I'm going to say my goodbye here," he said and gently leaned forward and rested his lips on hers.

For a few seconds, everything fell into place, for both of them, but then the moment was gone and they had to face the reality of lockdown. No work for him and the tedium of being stuck in this house without her – and an uncertain future for her: frustration and a feeling of being an outsider in her own home.

They pulled apart, the softness of the kiss still vibrating on their lips. "Right, this is crazy … open that door, Haz, I must go."

He turned and pulled the door open,

"Ok, folks, I'm all done and dusted," she called down the stairs. "Let's get Josh in the car."

They all trooped outside and after five minutes of strapping Josh in and checking everything, turning on the sat nav and setting the destination set to "home", she was off down the drive, with the other three waving until she disappeared.

"Well, that was so nice to see her properly, wasn't it? And Josh is an absolute poppet. I'm going to really miss him," said Rachel, her face betraying her sadness.

"I must go upstairs and carry on working," said George and turned away, back into the house. He and Rachel hadn't really spoken since the revelation; they'd just exchanged formalities.

"Yes, I'm going to miss them, too," said Harry to Rachel. "I'm so bored … I really need to start a hobby or something. No work is bad for me."

"Have you heard from your boss at all?"

"There's not much to say, is there? Until we come out of this lockdown I'm here with nothing to do. It's making me question whether I really want to be a chef, Mum. But what else could I do?"

"You'll be all right, Harry. At least you're getting some money for doing nothing," she said. "And you'll be ready and waiting when things get going again. If this hadn't happened, would you be questioning your career choice?"

"No, but it has ..."

"So, don't over-think everything. Just sit it out. That's what I've got to do with the shop. I've just got to hope that when I can open it again, people will be queuing up to buy flowers from me. Everything's a risk, Harry. Don't just give up."

"No, you're right. I *do* love cooking."

"Why don't you spend your time here creating some new recipes or even writing a recipe book, with a unique slant or something? I'll be your guinea pig."

"Actually, that's not a bad idea, Mum. I don't want to work for someone else all my life. Maybe I should start planning now."

"There you go, Harry. You don't need to spend all this spare time doing nothing, or as you call it, playing computer games. At least you'll be able to concentrate now."

"What do you mean?"

"I saw the way you look at Amber, H."

"Huh?"

"I saw it ... I wasn't imagining things, was I?"

There was a long pause.

"You always could read me like a book, Mum."

She laughed and went and put her arms around him. "Come on chef, let's create some recipes."

JEN SOMETIMES REGRETTED her decision not to continue with radiation therapy but as the pandemic progressed, it became increasingly obvious that the worst place to be was in hospital, so she was glad that she'd declined the treatment. Mike wasn't happy with her but he respected her views. It was her body, after all.

She'd adapted to lockdown with ease; she'd surprised herself that she was so content to be at home. She didn't miss going into the office and she could work from home with no issues.

Mike, on the other hand, was like a caged animal. Since the collapse of his company, he'd felt a failure and no one could persuade him otherwise.

He'd eventually taken a job in London just before the first lockdown, despite his misgivings about the awful commute. The company was within walking distance of Paddington so at least he didn't have to get on the Tube. He'd justified his decision by looking at the positives: a regular salary, stability and a new, upcoming company. Once he'd got over the shock of getting up at 6 am during the week, he began to enjoy the enforced quiet 'sit' in the mornings. He'd thought he'd work on the train but often he'd daydream or listen to his favourite music on his headphones.

He'd just got used to his new lifestyle when the pandemic struck and he was forced to stay at home, working on Zoom. He was a sociable person and enjoyed the water cooler moments and the banter of the office; being alone in his study was not his idea of fun at all.

They had to adapt, like everyone else though and they got into a routine. He and Jen would have lunch together in front of the BBC News at One, depressing themselves with the horrific numbers of global deaths.

"I think we should stop watching the news, Jen," he said one day. "This is just so awful ... and knowing all the statistics really doesn't help."

"I know what you mean, but I like watching the news. Don't you think we should know exactly what's going on?"

On the TV, Matt Hancock and Boris were droning on at their news conference. Mike had finished his lunch and stood up, taking his plate to the kitchen. "You can watch if you like, but I've had enough. Life is so bloody depressing at the moment. There doesn't seem to be any end in sight. I'm going back to the study, I think. Do you fancy a walk at 4.30?"

"Yea, okay. Come and find me when you're ready."

When Jen wasn't working, she'd taken up a couple of new hobbies to fill the hours. She was doing an online creative writing course, which she was thoroughly enjoying. She'd always enjoyed writing, hence why she'd become a journalist, but working for the local rag was hardly creative. She wanted to challenge herself, to do something right out of her comfort zone.

She'd opted to study the writing of short stories on this course; her online tutor was good and had set her several tasks to do, one of which was reading some of the best short stories ever written and to analyse why they were so perfect. She also had creative writing exercises to do, which she found challenging. She'd never had to use her own imagination before at work; the blank page sometimes taunted her with its lack of words. But it certainly kept her occupied during these long, empty August days.

The other hobby she took up was gardening. She'd never shown much interest in it before – Mike had mown the lawn and done the absolute minimum in the garden to keep it looking nice. But with so much time on her hands, she started growing herbs and vegetables, enjoying the opportunity to get outside in the fresh air and get her hands dirty. She made a new veg patch, a herb garden and enjoyed filling colourful pots with flowering plants. She'd often think how lucky she was; she couldn't imagine being stuck inside, at the top of a high-rise block of flats, with no outside space.

These contrasting hobbies, one mental and one physical, completely satisfied her and she found herself actually enjoying lockdown. The only thing she missed was seeing Amber and her friends in person.

She tried to FaceTime with Amber at least three times a week; she loved to see Joshua, even if it was only online. She could see him changing and developing, before her eyes.

When Amber got back from her stay at Rachel's, Jen made a point of ringing her; they hadn't spoken when she was in Brighton as Amber had plenty of company and things to do and Jen didn't want to disturb her fun. Jen wasn't sure she should have broken the rules, but Amber was a grown-up and she had to make her own decisions.

Once the News at One had finished, Jen washed up and went to sit in front of her computer. She was meant to be writing the opening paragraph of a short story entitled "Escape" and she stared at the screen with absolutely no inspiration. The trouble with computers is there are always other things that you can do to divert yourself from the job in hand, so Jen was quick to find the FaceTime icon; she pressed Amber's number and waited for her to answer.

Her face appeared on the screen within three rings.

"Hi Mum. Long time no see! Josh is here, say hello to your Grandma," she said, thrusting his face into the camera.

"Aww, hello Joshy ... oh he's so gorgeous. I hate the fact that we can't just come and see you whenever we want. Bloody pandemic. How are you, anyway? How was your stay at Rachel's?"

There was a moment's hesitation and then Amber answered, "Oh, it was so nice to see them all."

Jen noted the slight pause and wondered why, but said, "How are they? I haven't spoken to Rach for a while. How's she coping?"

"Okay, I think. It's very difficult for her with the shop being closed but she's putting a lot of effort into her website and social media accounts and it's beginning to pay off. She's selling a lot more gifts, books and greetings cards online, which I think is a really good idea. With weddings and funerals as they are, there's no real need for flowers. She's also selling more indoor plants than she used to. Anything that can be sent via a courier or online, basically. We all tried to help – Harry's a bit of a whizz with technology, it turns out so, and he's been helping her a lot. He's got sod-all else to do as he's been laid off."

"That must be so hard for him. What about George? Is his job okay?"

"Yea, he was working 9 to 5 when I was there but we went running together a bit in the evenings and had some great meals ... not sure what's happening with Beth, though."

"How do you mean?"

"Well, they're quite happy living apart, it seems. They chat online etc but I'm not sure if it's a long-term commitment or not. Ever since the 'proposal' incident she's been very distant apparently."

"And how are *you*, my love? How are you coping? Are you pleased to be home?"

Again, another pause. Not like Amber, she normally jumps in, Jen thought.

"Yea ... I'm okay ... but having been away for a while, I realise how lonely I am. Leo's always working and there's only so much conversation you can have with Josh. Don't get me wrong, I love being a mum but I *need* something else. How did you cope with the boredom, Mum? When I was a baby, was that enough for you?"

"Well, for a start I didn't have a pandemic to deal with. That's making being a first-time mum *so* much harder. And I didn't have the ambition you have, Amber. You've always been so focussed, so dynamic. I wasn't the same, so I was content. You were such a good baby and I spent my life going to coffee with other mums, which you can't do."

"Yea, you're right I suppose. The isolation is definitely exaggerated now. I'd definitely be out there joining every conceivable group: baby yoga, baby sensory, baby *anything*... but I'm stuck here. Bored. Am I a terrible person?"

"No, of course not, Ams. You should think about going back to work when he reaches a year. It would be good for you ... and him. Good nurseries provide stimulation, routine and playmates. He'd be happy and so would you. It would be hard, don't get me wrong, but it would be right for *you*."

"Oh, thanks Mum. I thought you wouldn't approve of me going back. Rach said the same, actually and so did Harry."

Jen noted the mention of Harry several times and said, "What about Leo? What does *he* think?"

"Well, he used to say, '*do what you think is right, it's your life*' but recently I've got the distinct impression he'd rather I stayed at home."

"Why's that?"

"I'm not sure ... it's just a feeling I get. I've talked to Grace about it. She's obviously going back soon, as she's the sole provider. She's started looking for nurseries. I'm thinking we could send them to the same one, maybe."

Josh started to cry. "Actually Mum, I'm going to have to go. His nappy's full and he's due a sleep. I'll call you in a couple of days."

"Okay. Love you."

As the screen froze and then went blank, Jen sat, staring out of the window. Amber seemed different. She'd lost her spark. And, she realised, she didn't ask to speak to her Dad or didn't even mention his name.

That was unusual for her. She adored her Dad.

AS THE PANDEMIC DRAGGED on, Jen secretly began to have doubts about the state of her health. She found her energy levels were so low that after only twenty minutes of gardening, she felt washed out.

Her creative writing still intrigued her and she *wanted* to do it, but gradually found her inspiration just wasn't there and the motivation to sit in front of a computer simply dissipated. She found herself getting up later and later, having naps in the afternoon and going to bed at 9 pm. She wondered if it was just a general malaise to do with pandemic – she'd heard a lot on the radio about people suffering from depression and levels of drinking going up – but in her heart, she knew that wasn't the case. She began to believe the worst had happened.

It got to a point when she decided to speak to her doctor. Mike was so involved with his work that he hadn't really noticed the change in her but he did comment when she declined his offer of an evening walk or when she fell asleep in front of the TV. She'd make excuses, saying things like, "All this gardening's wearing me out," or "all this creativity is taking its toll" and he just accepted it.

She arranged to have a Zoom call with her GP and because of her history, he was sufficiently worried to get her to come in to see him. It was like getting into Fort Knox entering the surgery and when the doctor appeared, she could hardly recognise him behind his mask, visor and PPE. Seeing him was like a surgical procedure in itself. He listened while she explained her symptoms and tapped away on his computer.

"I see you opted not to have radiation therapy?"

"Yes, I didn't want it." She looked down and then bit the nails on her left hand.

"Mmm. I think we'll take some blood and see what's going on."

She left the surgery feeling more worried, if possible, than before. She wanted to speak to someone but there was no way she was going to worry Mike or Amber. Or Grace. Maybe she'd ring Rachel? But was it fair to burden her with it all?

She put it off for a day but then gave in. She *had* to speak to someone. Mike was ensconced upstairs and she took her phone and went and sat on the garden bench under the oak tree in the garden. It wasn't that warm but the sun was out and the sky was blue. A robin hopped on the grass near her feet, diverting her momentarily.

Rachel picked up straightaway. Jen had opted for an audio call; she didn't think she could cope with seeing Rachel's concerned face. She wasn't sure she could control her own emotions either.

"Hey, Rach. How's it going?"

"I'm good, thanks. How are you? Your voice sounds strange, what's going on?" Rachel was always so quick to pick up on things.

"Well, I hope you don't mind me burdening you with this ..."

"Don't be daft, Jen ... you know you can always talk to me about *anything*."

"I know, Rachel, but this is so hard. I haven't told anyone else. No one. I think I'm ill again."

"What do you mean? The lump?"

"Well, yes ... I've been feeling so unutterably worn out. It's been going on for a few weeks now. I put it down to this strange world we're living in now but ... it's been getting worse so I went to my GP."

"Did you actually manage to *see* someone?"

"Yes. I could just tell he was concerned when I told him my situation. He's doing a blood test to see if anything's changed."

"Well, that's good. At least he's doing something. When will you hear?"

"Not sure but I hope I hear soon. I don't want it dragging on, this uncertainty."

"Try not to worry, Jen. I know that's easy for me to say but ..." she didn't finish her sentence. It felt like she was spouting platitudes.

Jen could feel tears welling. She was frightened.

She shook her head, relieved that Rachel couldn't see her. She wanted to say something to Rachel, something important and she knew she would have to be strong to get the words out.

"Rach, I rang ... to talk to you about how I was feeling but ... I want to ask you something too."

"You know you can ask my anything, Jen."

"I know ... but this is a big ask. So ... if anything should happen to me ..."

"Jen, you're going to be okay, I know you are."

"Rach, please listen to me. If anything should happen to me ... can you ... look after Mike and Amber for me?"

"Jen ..."

"No, don't say anything ... I mean it. Please will you *promise* to look after them for me? I know Amber regards you as her second Mum and Mike ... I know you two ... have always been very fond of each other. I've always been aware ... of that bond between the two of you, Rach."

There was a silence that pulsed over the airwaves like a heartbeat. Rachel's stomach dropped, leaving her legs shaking. She sat down with a bump onto the nearest kitchen chair. Did she know how Rachel felt about Mike? Had she known all this time?

She ran her hand through her hair, then rubbed her eyes, wondering what she could possibly say. She thought that whatever she said would be inadequate. Her mind crashed back to the discussions she'd had with the boys and Amber ... it felt like her world was imploding.

"Of course I'll always be here, for you all, Jen ... but nothing is going to happen ..."

"But we don't know that. I'd be ... I'd be relieved, happy even, if I knew that you and Mike would look after each other, if I wasn't here. Mike, for all his macho-man outside, is such a soft, gentle man inside. He'll be lost if ever ..."

"Jen, please don't talk like this. You're frightening me. *I'd* be lost without you. This isn't like you ... why are you being so pessimistic? Maybe you're rundown ... lacking in iron ... please don't jump the gun like this."

Rachel got up quickly from the chair and went to gaze through the window. There was a blustery wind and clouds were scudding across the sky. She couldn't bear this conversation ... the guilt she felt was biting at her guts, the sorrow was weighing her down. She held onto the sink.

"Mike will need you, Rach. He won't be able to cope on his own, please just say you'll look after him?"

"Okay, okay ... I'll look after him ... but you're not going anywhere, Jen; stop talking like this."

"That's all I wanted to hear ... Rach ... thank you. And thank you for having Amber and Josh over. You are family, you do realise that, don't you?"

"You're my family too, Jen."

"So, I'm going to go now. I need to go and have a lie down."

"Okay. You must take a rest whenever you feel the need. Just give in to it, that's the best thing. Will you please ring me when you hear from the doctor."

"I will. Bye Jen. I love you." The phone clicked and she was gone.

Rachel looked at her phone, frightened by Jen's call.

She put the kettle on, made a large pot of coffee and sat back down at the kitchen table. Jen's words were swirling round and round in her head.

It felt like Jen was giving her permission for something, giving her blessing, even.

JEN DIED JUST ONE MONTH after that phone call.

It happened so quickly, so tragically, that it was hard for anyone to comprehend. The blood test had indeed revealed the extent of problem. The cancer had spread and she was told that she must go into hospital immediately.

Her instincts had been correct; it had felt like an inevitable outcome to her. Maybe the decision she'd made earlier, about not having radiation therapy had been a stupid one, a reckless one ... who knows? Maybe she was destined to die at that time, maybe her time was well and truly up.

But the strange and incontrovertible truth was ... that the cancer didn't kill her ... Covid did.

She was admitted to hospital in a pandemic; people were dying at frightening rates at the time, both inside and outside hospital. In her weakened state, with her immune system compromised, she succumbed to Covid within a week of arriving on the ward.

She became part of the grim statistics.

And the most agonising aspect of it all was that she was alone. No one could visit her, no one was allowed near. The restrictions were so tight that each case was judged on a case by case basis and Mike had been allowed in once, but was told at the time that he probably wouldn't be allowed in again. They provided an iPad so that he could see Jen but she was totally unaware of him; she was in an induced coma on a ventilator.

She wasn't technically alone ... she was surrounded by nurses and doctors doing their best for her, but in her final few days her body was too weak and she finally passed away with no loved ones holding her hand, no loving words whispered to her.

She was one of the many who died alone.

Chapter 17

The weeks following Jen's death took their toll.

Nobody escaped the feeling that they had somehow failed her.

Mike had been in denial from the moment she told him about her imminent hospital admission. He had been so absorbed in his work, he genuinely hadn't noticed the level of her fatigue. The fact that she didn't want to go for walks or that the garden was beginning to look a bit neglected, didn't penetrate his consciousness.

How could I have been so unobservant and selfish? he thought.

He wanted to go back in time, to re-boot. Even when she went into hospital, he was convinced they'd cure her. She wasn't going to actually die, was she?

Rachel harangued herself – why didn't she tell Mike, or *someone,* how desperate she'd sounded on the phone that day? Why did she let Jen talk about a future without her in it? Was she so selfish that she secretly *wanted* to be Mike's saviour? Why hadn't she jumped in the car and rushed to the Cotswolds to reassure her? Bugger the restrictions, she should have gone to be with her best friend.

Amber couldn't believe she'd allowed her mother to go through this. Was she so self-absorbed, so suffering from baby-brain, that she didn't see what was happening to her own mother? Why had she gone to stay with Rachel and the boys and not her Jen, who needed her so desperately? Why didn't she question her more? She looked awful on her FaceTime calls – why didn't she *say* something to her or to her Dad? Was she so pig-headed because of what Rachel had revealed?

Leo didn't forgive himself for the fact that he'd been neglecting all his friends since the arrival of Josh and his mixed-up feelings for Amber and Grace. Jen, the *one* person in their close-knit group who was so straightforward, so beautiful, both inside and out, who never demanded anything, needed him and he'd failed her. Not once had he rung her for a chat. Why?

Grace'd had to cope with so much since Anna died; she'd been so wound up with Thea ... surviving ... re-orientating herself to this new world of babies ... the pandemic ... that she'd disappeared from the world, her friends, herself. She had been a truly terrible friend. Anna's death had been the worst thing that had ever happened to her and now Jen, wonderful Jen, had gone too.

All of them were traumatised by her death. Their own mortality stared at them in the face. If Jen could die, so could *they*.

Life could be snuffed out like a candle; one minute you were there, the next, you were just a memory in other people's brains.

Rachel kept going back to the night in Cyprus when Jen had stripped off all her clothes and gone swimming in the warm, moonlit pool. Had she foreseen her demise and thrown caution to the wind, to swim naked under the starlit sky? To immerse herself in the moment ... to forget her normal, cautious self? It had been such a memorable night, to see Jen so free, so at one with the world. If only they could do that again together.

But she was gone. Forever.

Grace's persistent memory of Jen went further back, to that very first day they'd met at uni. Grace had gone through the door to their room, to find this lovely, innocent young girl, as fresh as a pure white snowdrop popping up through the earth in spring. She'd been lying on the bed asleep with a huge novel on her stomach ... she could still see her now. Jen had helped her unpack and then together, they'd found Rachel in the kitchen and they'd drunk some wine.

The three of them had formed such a wonderful bond; Jen had been like a blank canvas, waiting to be filled in with colour. Mike had come along and made her complete.

Mike's memories were muddled and sullied with grief and guilt. He had loved her from the moment he met her. He knew he was her first proper boyfriend and he'd loved her innocence ... but he'd been deceitful from the start. Why hadn't he come clean at that rugby party and told her he already knew Rachel? It would have been so much easier, so much more *honest,* but he chose to hide their past and as a result had complicated everything, made their whole life bound together by a lie.

Jen would have understood, he knew she would, and she would have forgiven him. At that point, there was nothing to be forgiven for; his and Rachel meeting in that nightclub was just part of life. But he'd chosen to keep it all a secret; the unfinished business between them had crept up on them both and made them behave so badly.

As a consequence, he was now being punished.

He'd lost his wife, his best friend, the mother of their only child.

He would never be able to forgive himself.

He would never get over it.

THE FACT THAT THEY couldn't give Jen a proper funeral made everything worse. They had to endure a cold, heartless event, relayed on Zoom to the others, with only Mike and Amber present. It was too sad to even contemplate – Jen, beautiful Jen, so uncelebrated, so alone.

Mike's life crumbled around him.

Unable to work, he went to bed and stayed there. His company were understanding about the situation but everyone was so worried about him; the more he withdrew, the more he drank. His days started and finished with alcohol, with sleep in between.

People tried to FaceTime him, but he often ignored their calls. If they did get through, he looked so dreadful: dishevelled, unwashed and glassy-eyed and he frightened them all. They talked to each other about what to do, but no one could see a solution.

Amber had gone to the Cotswolds to be with her father. Josh was the only lightness in the house; even he seemed to pick up on the emotion and was particularly difficult. Mike couldn't cope with him and would go up to his bedroom, leaving Amber and Josh to look after themselves.

Amber had all but forgotten the revelation about her father's past misdemeanours; the current crisis had put everything into perspective. What was the point of worrying about something that happened years ago?

She was rapidly realising that life wasn't as black and white as she'd thought.

She missed Jen with so much force, it took her breath away. The house had lost its love, its warmth, its reason for being. Her father was a shell.

It felt like life would always be like this.

Knowing the story now about the long-term affection between Rachel and her Mike, she asked Rachel for support.

"Rach, could you possibly come up here and help with Dad? I know it's a lot to ask, but I just don't know what to do. He's going to drink himself to death, if something doesn't happen. He won't listen to me, I don't think he wants to hear anything I've got to say. It's bad enough being here surrounded by the absence of Mum, but I feel so useless."

"Oh God, Amber, it's such a difficult situation for you. If it wasn't for the pandemic, I'd have been up like a shot but with all these restrictions ... there's rumours they're going to ease them soon. I tried to ring him yesterday but he didn't pick up again. I texted him but I doubt he read it. Look, I'll come up next week, whatever happens. If they haven't lifted the lockdown measures by then, I'll come anyway, but it's looking hopeful. Harry's hoping that this Eat Out To Help Out thing will mean he can get back to work; he's going stir crazy here. Have you two been in touch? He mentioned you'd been texting each other ..."

"Yea, he's been so sweet ... he's been constantly texting to check up on me since Mum ..." She wanted to change the subject so said, "How's George? What's going on with him?"

"He's planning to go home to Beth next week. They seem to be getting on better recently, thank goodness; he told me she said she misses him. He certainly seems to love *her* a lot; he's prepared to do anything as far as I can see, to save their relationship. I do hope it works out for them in the end. I actually FaceTimed with them both the other day and I thought she was lovely. She's promised to come down to Brighton when this lockdown is all over."

"That's good. How are *you* getting on with him?"

"Okay ... things aren't the same as they were; there's still a barrier between us but hopefully, we'll be able to get over it."

"How's the shop?"

"Well, it's been good for me in some ways, as I've had to concentrate on our online presence. Orders have picked up over the past few weeks. Funny how some good things have come from the pandemic." As she said this, she realised she shouldn't have. How could Jen's death *ever* be anything but the worst result of the pandemic? "... I'm so sorry, Amber, that was so thoughtless of me."

"No ... don't worry ... I knew what you meant ... I've got to get used to her not being here."

Rachel could hear the catch in her throat as she tried not to cry. "Ams, I'll be up very soon. Hang on for a bit longer."

"I will ... hopefully see you soon."

THE MOMENT LOCKDOWN measures eased, Rachel, as promised, drove to the Cotswolds. In truth, she should have stayed and concentrated on the shop, but she desperately wanted to see if she could somehow drag Mike back into the world.

She left Millie in charge and set off one morning at 10 am. It was strange to be going so far afield after so long; the M25 was busy and she wondered where everyone was going. Staying at home had made her insular and although she wasn't looking forward to confronting Mike, she enjoyed the freedom the motorway gave her.

When she drew into their drive, the reality of Jen's death pierced her. It was only now, weeks after her actual death, as she stared at their house, that she finally understood – she'd never see her again. She felt sick as she undid her seatbelt and reluctantly opened the door.

Amber must have been waiting for her; she emerged through the front door, holding Josh. They didn't speak, they simply hugged and smiled at each other. Rachel went to the boot, retrieved her case, lugging it into the house. She was so aware of Jen not being there, it hurt. She caught site of a black and white photo of her and Mike on their wedding day on the wall in the hallway; her stomach lurched.

"It's hard, isn't it?" said Amber, understanding.

"Mmm. I ... can't believe she's gone. It's so ..."

"Come through and I'll get you a coffee. Journey okay?"

"Yea."

Rachel couldn't speak. The kitchen was Jen's domain: her cookery books were still on the shelves. Notes in her handwriting were on the notice board; there were even a pair of old shoes Rachel recognised as hers, sitting in the corner.

She sat down wearily at the kitchen table, looking around, tears flowing down her cheeks.

"Why has it taken me *all* this time to *actually* connect her death with never seeing her again?" she said, sniffing. "It's as if I was able to con my mind, pretending that she was still here. But she's gone, hasn't she?"

Amber, put Josh in his chair and came and put her arms around her.

"Yes, she's gone. It's just so unfair. She was too young to die and had so much more to give. Let me go and get you your coffee. I'm sure you need it."

As Amber busied herself, getting out cups and pouring water into the cafetière, Rachel tried to pull herself together.

There was no sign of Mike.

"Where's your Dad?" she asked, already knowing the answer.

"In bed. He never emerges before 2."

Amber bought the two mugs of steaming coffee over, Rachel picked up hers and wrapped her hands around it. "When I've finished this, do you want me to go up and see him?"

"Well, you can try … but I don't think you'll get much response."

"I'm going to have a go at talking to him. He can't go on like this. I'm going to have to be tough on him. Tough love. That's what he needs."

The word *love* hung in the air. Amber had tried tough love too. On one occasion she'd ended up shouting at him which made things worse, but it was so frustrating to watch someone you love self-destruct. Maybe Rachel's lifetime of loving him would somehow get through.

Josh was playing with a loud rattle, banging it against the side of his chair. The coffee had soothed Rachel's nerves and she said, "Can I have a cuddle with him before I go up?" as she got up to go towards Josh.

"Of course, get him out."

The familiar weight and smell of him filled her with love. She sat him on her lap, jiggling him up and down on her knees, pretending to let him fall, much to his amusement. She brought him up to her face and she kissed his rosy cheeks loudly.

"Oh, I've missed you," she said, hugging him to her.

"He's missed you too. You'll be his granny now," she said, as Jen's ghost flitted through both their minds.

"Right," she said after a while, "so here goes. You take him and I'll go upstairs. Wish me luck."

She handed over Josh and walked out of the kitchen to the stairs. She ascended slowly, stopping three times, hanging onto the banister rail, thinking about what to say.

She stood outside their bedroom, dreading going in. Seeing Mike in their double bed, on his own, would be so painful. The last time she was here, she and Jen had sat on that very same bed together, deciding what to wear, laughing and drinking wine before a night out.

She knocked, quietly, once, then twice. There was no answer, so she tentatively opened the door slightly, just peering in, but staying outside.

"Mike," she whispered, "it's me ... Rachel."

No reply. Just a shuffling further down into the duvet.

"Mike, I'm coming in."

She entered the room, closing the door softly behind her. She looked around. Through the low light, she could see clothes strewn everywhere, on the chairs and on the floor. Standing on the bedside table was an empty bottle of red wine and a glass. On the floor, on its side, was another empty bottle. The room smelt musty, of unwashed man.

She walked over to the curtains and pulled them open softly, half-way, to let some light in and quietly opened the window, just a little. She looked around but he hadn't stirred.

"Mike, it's 2.30. It's time to get up." She stood, looking down at his outline, not knowing what to do next.

"Mike ..."

"Leave me alone."

"No, Mike, I'm not going to leave you alone."

She sat down on the bed and felt him turn over, away from her. She waited a few minutes more, looking around; she noticed Jen's bottles and cosmetics were still on the dressing table. She felt tears welling up but fought them; she needed to be strong for Mike. Why hadn't Amber removed some of her things? Maybe Mike wouldn't let her ... maybe she herself couldn't face it?

She thought back to the phone call with Jen. She'd promised she'd look after him, hadn't she?

"Mike, Amber says you sometimes get up around now. Come on, you need to get up. You can't lie here all day."

"Why not?" he said. "What is there to get up for?"

"Mike, I know it's hard ..."

"You *don't* know, Rachel. You know *nothing*."

He started to move, heaving himself up into a sitting position. Rachel was shocked at his appearance. He'd lost weight, his face was gaunt and grey, his hair long. His facial hair had grown into a dishevelled beard, peppered heavily with grey.

"Tell me, tell me what you're feeling, Mike ... so that I can understand."

He looked so defeated, she wanted to cry for him. She reached forward and took his hand.

"My life has no meaning ... I can't see a future ... I don't want to live any more ... but I'm too much of a coward to kill myself."

He said this with quiet intensity. She squeezed his hand. She didn't want to lecture him or talk *at* him, but she had to say something that might get through. She took a deep breath and said,

"Mike ... at the moment, you are facing huge grief and anger at what's happened. But you know ... Jen wouldn't want you to be like this, would she? She'd hate seeing you like this ... she'd be in here, dragging you out of bed, throwing away the alcohol, making you tidy up. You *know* she would. But she'd do it with such love and care, because that's the sort of person she was. You must *try* ... I know it's hard ... to see the positives that are still here. You have a beautiful daughter, a gorgeous grandson. You need to be here for *them*. They need you now, more than ever. You have so many people who love you ..."

He took his hand away and rubbed his eyes. Despite how old he looked, he had a childish vulnerability about him.

"I know all that, Rach. I know Jen would be furious with me for giving up so easily. I know I need to be here for Amber and Josh ... but I just haven't got the strength to fight. I want to hide, here, and never face the world again."

"Look, Mike, *I'm* here to support you. First of all, I think you need to see a doctor to get some help. You are depressed, you need some anti-depressants to get you over this terrible time. It's not a failure to admit you need help, you know."

"I don't want to take pills ... I've never taken any in my life."

"But you've never had to face something so terrible as losing your wife, Mike."

"She was my best friend."

"I know, I know ... she was my best friend too and I want to be here for you, to give you the strength to face life. I know Jen would want me to do that."

She took his hand again, held it hard and said, "We can do this together, Mike. We can."

He looked at her, for the first time, directly.

"Do you know, Rach, one of my biggest regrets? I wish I'd told her everything. About how I'd met you before I met her. About how I felt ... about what we did. I think she would have understood and maybe even forgiven us. Now she's gone and I'll *never* be able to tell her the truth."

Silence embraced them. Guilt was torturing him, she saw that now. Out of somewhere an idea formed in her head.

"Do you know what you could do? You could write her a letter. Tell her everything. I know she'll never be able to read it, but maybe, just maybe, it will help you."

He didn't say anything for a while and then said, "How can I live with myself after a lifetime of betrayal?"

"Mike ... it wasn't a lifetime of betrayal. You were a brilliant husband to her. You made a mistake with me. *I* was to blame, not *you*. Don't beat yourself up about something that happened so many years ago. You had a wonderful marriage. You're a human being, Mike. Humans make mistakes, they are attracted to people they shouldn't be ... these things happen. Jen knew you were an honest, kind man. I think you could write down all the things you wished you'd said to her when she was alive."

"Maybe ..."

"I think it would help," she said, her mind flying to George. She must never tell Mike now, it would kill him.

But didn't he have a right to know that he has a son?

"So, come on ... I'm going to run you a bath. I'm going to sort out your clothes and find you something nice and clean for you to wear and then you're going to go downstairs and have something to eat. Come on, Mike, get up," she said, pulling his hand as she stood up.

"Okay," he whispered and slid his feet to the floor. Rachel pulled the curtains right back and went into the en-suite. The bath water could be heard tumbling into the bath.

"So, you go in there, have a shave, do your teeth and have a long soak in the bath. When you're ready, come down and I'll make you some eggs."

He shuffled into the bathroom while she opened the window further, collected up the bottles and gathered up all the dirty clothes. She stripped the bed, threw all the linen down the stairs and then went into the airing cupboard to find some clean sheets. Having made the bed, she went downstairs and loaded the washing machine.

Three quarters of an hour later, he emerged. He *had* shaved, he was in clean clothes and he'd brushed his hair. His loss of weight made his clothes hang loosely and his hair needed cutting but he looked better than he had since Jen had died, Amber whispered to her, behind his back.

"You're looking a bit more like your old self," said Rachel.

"Yes, Dad, you look good," Amber said, coming up to him and kissing his cheek.

"I've got you an appointment tomorrow, Mike," said Rachel. "Two-fifteen."

"But ..."

"No buts, Mike. You're going."

"Yes, Dad. You've been through so much ... and I know men don't like going to the doctor but Rachel's right. You know she is."

He sat down with his elbows on the table, linking his hands behind his head.

Amber mouthed "thank you" to Rachel. They smiled at each other, hoping that today might be the start of his recovery.

RACHEL COULD ONLY STAY seven days; she had to get back to the shop but she was determined to clear out at least some of Jen's things before she went.

She drove Mike to the doctor's; she didn't want him to have any excuse for not going. They sat together in the waiting room, everyone hidden behind their masks. Normally, there would be conversation in these places but today, there was no talk from anybody. The atmosphere was subdued.

When the doctor walked in and called Mike's name, he rose from his seat slowly and Rachel whispered, "Good luck." She felt responsible for him and hoped she'd made the right decision to insist on him going. She waited, looking around at the notices on the walls about HIV, anxiety, Dementia and every other sort of illness she hoped she'd never have and when she'd had enough, she scrolled through her phone.

After twenty minutes, he came back; she couldn't see his expression behind the mask and he said nothing. He just stood at the entrance of the waiting room and moved his eyes towards the exit.

They walked in silence back along the corridor and out into the fresh air, where they took off their masks with relief. There was a pharmacy attached to the surgery, so Rachel said, before she got into the car, "Do we need to collect a prescription at all?"

"He said it would be ready later today," and he got into the car.

As they drove off, she said, "How was it?"

"Okay."

"Was he nice?"

"Yes."

"What did he say?"

"He said roughly what you did. He's giving me something 'to smooth the edge' of my grief, whatever the hell that means."

"That's good. I'm glad he was okay. Are you going to see him again?"

"In four weeks. He suggested some grief counselling."

"And how do you feel about that?"

"He said I'd have to wait for ages with the NHS and suggested I go private. I'm not sure I want to talk about it."

"I know it's weird to talk to a stranger but they're trained and know what to say and how to help you. Sometimes, just talking helps to get it out, Mike. Amber and I are too close to you. Someone you don't know can be objective. Why don't you give it a try? Because of the pandemic, a lot of this type of thing has gone online, you won't even have to leave the house."

"Mmm ... I'll think about it."

Rachel, forever trying to fix him, spent the rest of the day doing research on the internet about grief counselling and looking for a suitable person. She wanted to present him with somebody who he might be prepared to go to.

She also managed to get him to eat more and each day, they went for a walk. She thought fresh air and exercise might clear his head of negative thoughts, even if it was only temporarily.

She admitted to herself that she was indeed terrified that he might do something 'stupid'. She'd read about the rise of male suicide and how often there's no warning. She felt frantic when she thought of him being alone here; both Amber and she were going to have to go home, they couldn't be here forever.

She hatched a plan to take him back to Brighton with her, so that she could keep an eye on him. He could have some lovely, windy sea walks, breathe in the salty air ... but she didn't mention the idea. She wanted to leave it until she was imminently leaving.

But the thing that she wanted to achieve before she left was ... beginning the terrible task of removing Jen's clothes and belongings. She didn't know how to address this with Mike. When she and Amber were alone the day after the doctor's appointment, she asked Amber if she'd talked about it with her dad.

"I tried to, but he said he wasn't ready. I didn't want to press it, he was so upset when I mentioned it ..."

"You know we've got to make a start, Amber. Being surrounded by her things is just too upsetting. The process will be very difficult, but it's something that's just got to be done. It's a good moment to do it as I'm here to help. Shall we say that's what we're going to do and don't give him an option? Will you back me up, if we say something when he gets up?"

"Yes, I'll back you up. But Rachel, I'd like to keep something of hers ... maybe one of her jumpers?"

"Of course you can. Keep whatever you want. I'll suggest that he does the same. I just think having her dressing gown hanging on the back of the bathroom door, their wardrobe full of her things, her slippers by the bed ... it can't be right. It's a constant reminder."

When they broached the subject, he was acquiescent. It was as if he'd given up the fight, as if he'd given in to the inevitable.

Rachel speculated that the pills were already working but then thought that couldn't be the case; the doctor had said it would take at least three weeks for the pills to 'kick in'. She concluded that, for whatever reason, he now felt ready and decided not to question it.

The next day, when he got up and had eaten something, he was about to go on the computer when Rachel asked him if he felt okay to make a start.

"Yes, I suppose so."

"Do you want me to do it or do you want to oversee? You may want to keep something ..."

"No, I don't think I could bear to put Jen's life into black plastic bags. You and Amber do it."

"Are you sure?"

"Yes."

He walked out.

Rachel, Amber and Josh went up to their room; Josh was put into his chair and he watched as they opened the wardrobe door. They stood for a few minutes, staring at the dresses, tops and trousers that were so *Jen* ... and couldn't bring themselves to touch them.

"Come on, let's make a start," said Amber, tearing off a black plastic bag from the roll. She grabbed some clothes, threw them on the bed and started taking the clothes off their hangers and shoving them in the bag, with no ceremony. It was as if she couldn't spend any time on the task of folding them – what was the point, she said to Rachel, who questioned her method. They were all going to get crumpled in the bag, anyway.

Suddenly, she sat on the bed, tears flooding her face. She buried her head in her arms. Rachel came over and comforted her.

"You've been so strong, Amber. This is a horrible thing to have to do, to pack up your Mum's things. Would you like me to do it, on my own?"

Amber sniffed, got up and went to find some loo paper in the en-suite. She came back and blew her nose, wiped her eyes and said, "No, I'll be okay in a minute. It was just that I could smell Mum on her clothes. It was like she was here."

"I know, I can smell the perfume she used to wear, *Diorella*, I think it was. So lemony, so Jen."

They hugged and then proceeded to fill as many bags as they could. The dressing gown came off the door, the slippers were taken away and they threw her cosmetics from the dressing table into the bin. It was a waste, but neither of them could face using them.

When they'd finished, they took all the bags downstairs and put them in the garage, away from Mike so that he wouldn't have to see them. Rachel would take them to a charity shop tomorrow.

"What about something for you to keep?" said Rachel to Amber later.

"I'd already taken the jumper I wanted. It was one of her favourites and I loved it. We used to 'share' it whenever I was home."

"What do you think your Dad would want to keep?"

"I'm not sure ... maybe it would be too difficult for him. He would smell her, like we can."

"I know it sounds odd, but I'm going outside to the garage to rescue her tracksuit. She always loved putting it on and it's so *her*. I won't ask him now but I'll keep it for him and when he's stronger, I'll tell him I kept it. He's got framed photos, albums ... her books ... maybe that's all he needs."

The time to leave was looming and having discussed the idea of Mike coming to Brighton with Amber, who thought it was a great idea, she put it to Mike.

"Oh, I don't know, Rach. I feel 'safe' here."

"I'm sure ... but it would do you good to get away, even for a few days. Why don't you think about it? You don't have to tell me now."

"Okay, thank you for offering. I don't want to seem ungrateful. You've been so kind. But I'm not the best company and I don't want to be a burden to you."

"Don't be silly, Mike. You'll never be a burden to me, you know that. I think Jen would want you to come, if that helps at all. And you can start your online counselling there."

"Mmm ... let me think."

The next day, he said, "I'm very grateful to you, Rach, I really am, but I'm not ready to come right now. I need to spend some time in the house, alone. Amber's been with me for weeks and I need to know what it feels like to be here, without Jen, without anyone. But I will come, maybe in a month?"

"I'm not sure it's a good thing for you to be alone at the moment, Mike."

"Well, I'm sorry, but that's the best I can do."

She didn't want to press him but she thought that she could pop up for the weekend to check up on him. She was determined to get him to Brighton, though.

The day she left, it was raining and the weather reflected her mood. She didn't want to leave him like this but she had to go. She had responsibilities. Amber would be there for two more days.

He came out to wave her off.

Before she got into the car, she turned to him. He looked so thin, so old and fragile. Grief came out of him, like an aura.

She hugged him, wrapping her arms around him as tightly as she could.

"You hang in there …"

"I will, Rach. Don't worry about me, I won't do anything stupid. I'm too pathetic."

"Ring me ANY time, day or night, if you need to talk. I'll always be there. And I'm going to hold you to your month's delay – I'll nag you until you come down to stay."

She squeezed him again and then turned to get into the driver's seat.

As she drove away, she looked back at him, standing alone in the drive and tears rolled down her cheeks. She could see his son, George, so clearly in him. They stood in the same way … the way he raised his arm and waved.

What should she do?

Chapter 18

Amber felt like Rachel when she left; she hated leaving him like this, but she couldn't stay in the Cotswolds forever. Maybe in the future, she could persuade him to come and live in London so she could see him frequently but she knew what he'd say. He loved living in the country and when Jen was alive, they'd only visit London now and again. He'd often text her when they'd got back home to thank her for whatever they'd done together but then add how glad they were to be home 'amongst fields and hills'.

While she'd been away, she'd been in daily contact with Leo who was missing them both, although she was convinced he was missing Josh more than her.

Life had moved on since she'd left. Leo often went to work – he still worked a lot from home but there was more opportunity to get out of the house.

When she arrived home, she opened the front door, wondering if Leo would be there; she called his name but there was no reply. As Josh was asleep, she left him in his car seat while she unloaded the car – she'd been lucky to find a parking spot right outside the house. She then went back and gently got the chair out with a sleeping Josh; he didn't stir, so she put him down in the sitting room and tiptoed out.

She felt as if she'd been away a lifetime. She walked upstairs, checked Leo wasn't in his study then went into the bedroom and began to unpack her clothes. She took out Jen's jumper and held it to her face. She stayed like that for a minute or so, breathing in the very essence of her mother. The clearing out of Jen's things came back with full force; she lay back on the bed, her legs dangling over the edge, holding the jumper. Staring up at the ceiling, she felt utterly lost.

So much had happened over the last few months: the birth of her gorgeous son; lockdowns; the revelation that her Dad was George's biological father; her mother's sudden demise. How was one individual meant to cope with such life-changing things, coming one after the other? She'd tried to be strong for her Dad and she thought she'd at least *acted* strong, but now she was home again, she felt as if everything she'd been suppressing for weeks was coming to the surface.

Her feelings for Leo were changing, she knew they were. They'd lost that closeness and he was no longer that god-like figure she saw in court. He was just a man, an older man, with an ex-wife.

Her phone vibrated by her side; she grabbed it and saw a text from Harry. Could she face reading it now? His name kept leaping out at her – she couldn't resist opening his message.

Hey – Just thought I'd text to see how you are? I know you'll probably be home by now. Does it feel strange after all this time? Was your Dad okay when you left?

I'm working really hard at the moment, doing loads of shifts. It's actually great to be back in the thick of it.

George is getting on better with Beth I gather. Maybe they'll be okay. I don't really know her at all but she seemed nice, I think you'd like her. I wonder when it's right to tell Mike? He has a right to know, doesn't he, that he's got a son?

Anyway, can we meet up sometime?

Love from Hazza, your friend and dare I say it, Admirer?!

She read the message through twice. Josh still hadn't woken up (she assumed he hadn't anyway, she certainly hadn't heard anything).

She sat up and replied:

Hey Hazza - Is that what I'm meant to call you now?!

Dad is just so sad, it's like he's broken, but your Mum managed to get him up and about and to the doctor, which is more than I could do.

Yea, it's such a tricky one – Dad definitely has a right to know. I haven't said anything to your Mum but if she doesn't tell him, I will. It's only fair. But I agree with her that now's not the time. He's too depressed. I'm just not sure what his reaction will be. Will he feel cheated for all these years or will he be happy to 'find' a son?

Glad you like work, you always were a glutton for punishment! Yea, let's meet up, you old flatterer, you.

Ambs xxx

She felt so at ease with Harry and she wanted to see him. He always seemed to sense when she was down – he'd texted too often now when she was at particularly low point. It was almost as if they were telepathic or something. When she was with him or talking to him or texting him, it only served to emphasise the age gap between her and Leo.

She scrolled through her photos on her phone of when she was with him down at Rachel's. They were laughing in every one. In this one, she was sitting at the kitchen table; she remembers that Rachel sent her the photo, as she'd taken it. She, Harry and

George were all holding up glasses of wine – they were shouting 'Brighton' and laughing at something (she couldn't remember what). In another one, she and Harry were dressed, ready for a run; George had taken it – they were pretending to be ready for a fictional starting pistol. Just after this photo, he'd set off at a fast pace and she remembers she had to sprint to catch up.

She was in a world of memory when she was bought back to reality by a loud cry coming from Josh downstairs.

She jumped off the bed and ran down the stairs, calling, "I'm coming, I'm coming. Mummy's here."

Harry, however, was still in her head.

LEO GOT HOME THAT NIGHT at about 7.30. He called out as he hung up his coat and Amber, holding Josh, came out to greet him.

"Oh, there's my boy ... my beautiful boy," he said, as he extracted Josh from Amber's grip. He kissed her on the cheek and then turned his full attention to his son.

"I'm sure you've grown, you big boy," he said, walking with him towards the sitting room. "Oh, I can see your Mummy's back, she's such a naughty Mummy, isn't she? She doesn't know how to keep things tidy, does she?"

All this was said as if it was 'funny' but Amber felt chastised. She'd only got back a few hours ago and she hadn't had time to clear away things. Didn't he understand how busy you are with a child around all the time? Saying it to Josh like that, was really *fucking annoying*.

"Well, Mummy has been a little busy since she got home, actually," she said, staring at him.

"I'm sure ... let's get him set up with some of these toys, then you can tell me how it's been. Is your Dad coping?"

She noted that he wanted to change the subject and she knelt down on the floor with Josh, giving him a xylophone and a little drum to bash, which he duly did. Over the noise she said, "Well, he's no different from when I spoke to you yesterday. Very quiet, very sad."

"At least he's been to the doctor now. When's he going back to work?"

"They've said he can stay on compassionate leave for a few more weeks but I do wonder if it would be better for him to be working. To have some routine, some friendly chat. That's what I miss."

"Talking of which, Grace has been round quite a few nurseries and she's found one that can take Thea from the beginning of next month. She's going to ease herself back into it with three days to start with, but she's going to increase it to five after three months."

"Where is it?"

"Not far, five minutes in the car. She seems very happy with it. She's getting much better ... she's beginning to look her old self and I even found her practising her singing the other day – Thea loves it when she sings."

"Oh, I'm glad. Rachel was trying to persuade Dad to go to Brighton with her but he says he's not ready at the moment."

"Poor man. How are you bearing up? I'm still finding it hard to grasp the idea that we'll never see Jen again. God, that holiday in Cyprus seems like yesterday and look what's happened since? Unbelievable."

He reached down and picked Josh up – he had a picture book which he held for him and Josh pressed various buttons which made animal sounds.

"I know it's a cliché, but life is too short."

Amber was so tempted to tell him about George being Mike's son but she'd promised Rachel she wouldn't tell anyone and she wasn't going to break her promise. But what would Leo's advice be, she wondered?

"Yes, it is ... while I was away I thought a lot about what I want to do with mine. I've made a decision, Leo. I'm *definitely* going back to work, full-time. I love being a mother but it's not enough for me. Mum said she thought it would be good for me before she died and Rachel agrees too."

"Oh ..."

"If I was older, if I'd planned this pregnancy, maybe it would be different ... but it was thrust on me ..."

"Hang on ... you make that sound as if it was all my fault or something."

"No, I didn't mean that ..."

"When you came to Cyprus, you seemed thrilled with the pregnancy."

"I was ... but it's not reality is it? When you're pregnant you are in a dream world of fluffy teddy bears, sleeping, angelic babies – all brought on by your raging hormones. You see life through a haze of unrealistic, perfect scenarios where you can carry on your life as before ... but have a beautiful baby tagging along. The reality is *so* different, Leo. It's days filled with drudgery, boredom, crying, nappies and night after night of being sleep-deprived (although I know I've got been lucky there). If I was the type of girl who'd always dreamt of having babies, I'd find all this wonderful, but I've *always* wanted a career, I've *always* had ambitions. I've never desired to stay at home with a little person. I've decided the best thing for *me,* is to work. It will also be good for Josh to be with other little people."

"I'd hoped this wouldn't be your decision."

"Well, I'm sorry if I'm a disappointment to you."

"I feel it's a shame for Josh. He'll be small for such a short time and it's always better to be with your mum."

"How do you know that, though? You don't think that having a miserable, bored mother might be the worst kind of child care? Don't you think that being with loads of other children to play and interact with, might be *better* for him? And why are you happy for Grace to go back full-time and not *me*?"

"It's a completely different situation for Grace. She is the sole breadwinner, she has no choice. She'd *love* to be at home full-time, in fact. And with regard to what you said, I don't have any data to back up my views, but surely it's logical that a child is better off with its mother?"

"I disagree. Anyway, I've made up my mind. This whole pandemic thing has changed things. The lockdowns have been torture for me; they've made the whole thing a lot worse. I want to get back into the outside world again."

"Yes, I'm sure the pandemic has made it all a lot worse for you, Ams, I do see that."

"Right, well, that's settled."

"Is it?" he said, sadly.

"Yes, it is."

A FEW MONTHS HAD PASSED and Amber had gone back to work, as she said she would.

She'd been able to get Josh into the same nursery as Thea, which was a blessing. She secretly felt incredibly guilty about putting him into a nursery every day, but the fact that Thea was at the same one, made her feel better about it. She had to keep telling herself that this was the right decision for both her and Josh.

Leo had come round to accept it in the end, but it had put a wedge between them. He'd wanted to be the traditional father, whose partner stayed at home with the child, while he looked after them both financially; he couldn't understand why Amber didn't want to wait 'just a few years' until Josh went to school. They were never going to see eye to eye and soon it became one of many topics they didn't talk about. Others included: her untidiness, her lateness (for everything), her poor housekeeping, his increasing closeness with Grace – the list was getting longer by the day.

Now that she worked, the house came even further down her list of priorities; it was all she could do to get Josh to the nursery on time, work, get him into bed and cook a basic meal. Leo *did* help when he could, but his job was so full on that he was rarely at home during the week. He complained that Josh was always in bed when he got home, but what did he expect? Most nights he didn't walk back through the door until 8 pm. He never seemed to hear him when he woke up at night.

The fact that they worked in the same building was an odd one. They had very different schedules, so, they didn't travel together to and from work. Leo often had to be in far earlier than her and she had to leave work, earlier than him, in order to get to the nursery.

When she went back initially, they'd meet up for coffee if they could, but this became less and less frequent. Gone were the days when they used to run together after work, pre-Josh. Amber looked back on those days and wondered how she'd had the energy or the motivation to run so far. (Most of the motivation and energy came from her burgeoning attraction to Leo, she admitted to herself). She still went jogging, but only at weekends and only for a mile or so. She could only go out if Josh was asleep and Leo was free to look after him.

Their weekends typically were a time when they lived in the same house but lived parallel lives. They both enjoyed spending time with Josh but it was usually without the other one, so that they could each get on and catch up with life admin.

Leo would stay at home when Amber went shopping, Amber would stay at home when Leo went to visit Grace. They rarely went out at night; in fact, most evenings, they'd watch separate TV programmes. Amber wanted to relax by watching what Leo called 'crap' ('Love Island' and the like) and Leo wanted to relax by watching sport and political or spy dramas. She'd lie on their bed watching on her laptop, he'd stay downstairs in the sitting room.

Their age difference was certainly reflected in their choice of TV programmes.

At least when she was at work, she got the opportunity to meet up with Harry, if he happened to have a day off. They'd met up several times and this particular day, she'd arranged with Grace that she'd collect Josh for her from nursery and take them both back to Leo's house for tea, bath and bed. She'd never asked before, but Grace had been quite happy to oblige. She'd told both Grace and Leo the truth about having an early meal with Harry – but ... it wasn't the *whole* truth.

The whole truth was that they'd got increasingly close and that she lived for these meetings.

Ever since that time at Rachel's, there had been something binding them together. For a start, their friendship went way back to childhood and they already knew each other's ways. They'd always 'got on' but somehow that week had changed everything. The huge secret that they'd all shared was one factor of course, but also they'd kissed and suddenly their relationship had tipped over into a different zone. For Harry, he'd 'fancied' Amber for years but for Amber, her physical attraction to Harry had come out of nowhere ... or at least that's how it felt to her.

They now texted each other every day and Harry would trek across town (involving three tube changes) just to have a quick lunch with Amber.

This evening meal was the first 'proper' date they'd been on. They were meeting at a pub round the corner from Amber's work at 5.30. She rushed to the ladies loo before leaving, to re-do her make-up.

As she was staring into the mirror applying some foundation, she realised she felt a bit like she had as a teenager. Her stomach was fluttering and her heart was beating just a little bit too fast. She was enjoying the prospect of a bit of child-free evening time, she admitted to herself, but she was excited about spending time with Harry. If she thought about it too hard, she felt guilty about what she was doing but, for now, she was just looking forward to the next hour or two. Her personality didn't lend itself to looking too far ahead and the consequences of her actions.

Last time they'd met for lunch, there had been a tension bubbling up between them and when he'd leant in to kiss her goodbye on the cheek, she'd deliberately moved her head and they'd kissed on the lips. It was just a brush, not a passionate snog, but it had been electric – she'd kept touching her lips all afternoon.

She now got out some lipstick and glossed them with a cherry red shine. She had golden brown eye shadow on her eyelids and a hint of blusher on her cheeks. She wasn't a great one for wearing lots of makeup usually, but she was pleased with what stared back at her. She didn't look like the rather unkempt vision of motherhood she normally saw in the mirror.

Checking her watch, she realised she was already five minutes late (as always) and she ran down the steps onto the pavement and jogged along to the pub. She burst through the door, panting, and headed to the bar, looking around for Harry.

He had seen her come in like a whirlwind and was smiling at her from a corner seat.

"Hey," she said, "sorry I'm late," walking quickly over to him.

"No worries – I wouldn't expect anything less," he laughed, standing up to greet her. He leant in and kissed her cheek, squeezing her arm at the same time. She kissed him back, savouring the feeling of his skin on her lips. She left a faint red outline on his cheek and she rubbed at it with her forefinger.

"Lipstick kisses, ha ha," she said, with affection dripping from her voice. "Anyway, I'm not *always* late … it's just that I'm not a clock-watcher and time runs away with me."

"Yea, yea, heard it all before. Come on, sit down next to me, I'm only joking." He pulled out the chair and she plonked herself down, took off her jacket and chucked it on the floor.

"Would madam like me to hang that up for her?" he added, reaching for the abandoned jacket.

"No, don't worry about it. Life's too short to hang up jackets ... or to stuff a mushroom. It'll be fine down there," she laughed, kicking it backwards with her foot.

"So, what do you fancy eating and drinking? I had a look at the menu while I was waiting: they've got a curry and I know you love curries or ... some fish ... or fillet steak?"

"Do you know what, I'd love good old-fashioned fish and chips. Have they got it?"

"Yea, I think so," he said, running his finger down through the choices. "Yup, battered cod. Not very gourmet ... "

"Well, we're not all super-interested in fancy food, you know."

"No, that's fine by me ... what a cheap date you are. I'll join you, actually. My life revolves around making food into works of art, so having a bit of battered cod will be a light relief. Red or white?"

"White, please ... even I know it's better with fish, even if it's covered with oily batter," she laughed.

He went up to the bar to order, she watched him go, loving the look of him. When did he suddenly become someone she fancied, she thought? She couldn't remember the exact moment. Was it when he'd kissed her that first time? Or did it slowly creep up on her? They felt so 'in tune' with each other, in every way. When she reflected on her attraction to Leo, it was so bound up with her job; he'd been so unattainable at first, so heroic, so perfect. Harry had never been any of those things, he was just ... Harry.

LIFE'S COMPLICATED

He came over clutching an already-opened bottle of wine and two glasses. He gave her a small amount and asked her to taste it.

"It's fine, I know nothing about wine but it tastes all right to me," she said, draining the glass and holding it out for him to pour in some more. "Don't go all upper-class wine snob on me," she laughed. "I can't stand it when people sniff it and roll it round the glass and start talking about it having hints of gooseberry and rhubarb. It's made of fucking grapes, for God's sake ..."

"Ha ha, I know ... we get a lot of those types at the restaurant. It's almost compulsory to be a twat with wine if you can afford to eat at our place. To be fair, though, I'm actually interested in wine myself – I wouldn't mind doing one of those courses, you know, where you end up being a Master of Wine, in the future. You never know, I might one day fit right in with all the twats."

"Well, if that's something you want to do, then *do* it. Despite what I've just said, I think it would be great to be an expert like that. And it would tie in so well with all your chef experience. Maybe one day, you could open your own Michelin starred restaurant."

"I wish ... it's a nice dream, I suppose. During lockdown, Mum and I talked about the exact same thing."

At that moment, the waiter delivered their meals to the table and they started eating.

"It's good to have dreams," she continued, looking at him intensely, smiling. "Since Mum died, I've realised how important it is to do *exactly* what you want to do with your life. I'm not sure whether Mum fulfilled *her* dreams. I don't even know what her dreams were ... I wish I'd talked to her more. It's only when someone's gone forever that you realise how little you actually *knew* about them. You just accept your parents as how they are, you don't think of them as people with a past, people with dreams. They're just there in the background all your life until suddenly, without much warning, they're gone ... forever."

"Yea ... Dad was never much of a father to us I suppose, but he was always there in the background. When it came out about Mike, I saw Dad in a different light, if I'm honest. Maybe my mum always had him as second best and he'd sensed it. Now that he's finally gone and is living and working abroad, I miss him – I never used to miss him when I was younger. He was always away, but Mum was enough. Now – I think about him a lot. He's never been a great communicator and neither am I, so we hardly ever speak. It's me who usually instigates it by texting. I'm not sure he'd ever just ring for a chat, like normal fathers. When Mum finally bit the bullet and told him about George, she said his reaction was strange. He'd always known that George was different, he said. She explained that Mike had never known anything about George and that now, under the circumstances of Jen's death, she didn't want to tell him. She had to make Zach promise not to contact Mike and he *finally* agreed, after a lot of persuading."

"Wow ... I feel sorry for him in a way. I know he's never been a great father to you two but ... how can you simply move on from that sort of secret? Does he ever mention anything about it to you?"

"No, not really. I feel sorry for him too. He's a very closed-down person. Any emotions he has aren't talked about. He's joked with me about having a half-brother and how George, with all his love of rugby in the past, should have been an indicator, but I don't know what he truly thinks and I probably never will."

"It's sad, isn't it? Do you think you'll ever go and visit him?"

"Probably not. I don't know this woman he's with and I've never spent long periods of time alone with my dad, so it would be odd. Anyway, I don't get much holiday and I never have any money for travel."

"Maybe, one day, you should make the effort. You don't want to be like me and realise too late that you've only got one parent left."

"Well, on that cheery note," he laughed, "… let's change the subject. Families are depressing. You can't choose you family but you can choose your friends. A very true saying."

"Yea, I'm glad we've chosen to be friends," she said, watching him out of the side of her eyes, as she finished the last chip on her plate.

"Me too. Ams, can I ask you something?"

"Yes, of course, you can ask me anything."

"Are you happy with Leo?"

"Wow, straight to the jugular."

"Well … I don't want to be too presumptuous, but … I feel, and I think you feel it too, that there's something happening between us. I wasn't going to say anything tonight, but somehow all this talk has made me … take the plunge."

He took her hand and she turned towards him. "Well … *are* you happy with him?"

She looked away, reached for the remains of her wine and drank it down in one gulp.

"I … and I'm being honest here … I don't know how I feel about him. I will always love him for giving me Josh; we'll always be bound by that beautiful boy ... but as time's gone by, I've come to understand that what I felt for him at the beginning wasn't true love. It was more like a crush ... I admired his skills in the court ... I worshipped the ground he walked on, at work. I wanted to *be* him – he was what I aspired to be. Then ... we got close and I was flattered that someone so mature, so out of reach, could feel anything for little old me. Then ... I got pregnant. Looking back, I wonder if we'd still be together if I hadn't got pregnant. There was never any question about abortion or anything. I knew I wasn't that person, who could 'get rid' of a baby because it wasn't convenient. I think what would have happened ... we'd have slowly come to realise the age gap was a huge barrier. After Anna died, he would have gone back to be with Grace and become Thea's dad and I would have continued as a single person, with a passion for the law, not for a lawyer."

"Wow. I ... don't know what to say."

"Yup ... it's a bit of a facer, Haz. I've got myself into a situation I don't know how to get out of. Don't get me wrong, I'm not unhappy, in the sense that I want to kill myself or something – nothing so dramatic – but I know this situation isn't right for me and I don't think it's right for Leo either. I know I annoy him ..."

"Does he annoy you?"

"Sometimes ... he's very critical of my housekeeping skills but then I'm pretty useless, I know I am. I wasn't designed to look after houses and cook. I've always been ambitious. I don't think he's ever understood how ambitious I am, to be frank. To him, me staying at home until Josh was old enough to go to school was a perfectly logical 'ask'. To me, it was like being asked to be locked in a cage for four years."

"I think I'm beginning to see how determined you are."

"I love Josh, I *adore* him ... but if I wanted to be looking after small children all day, I would have trained to be a nursery nurse."

"But isn't it different with your own child?"

"No, not really. You can love your child but still want other things. I do seriously think the pandemic made it much worse for me. If I'd been out and about with other mums, maybe I'd have enjoyed it more. But there is a limit as to how long I can discuss feeding regimes and sleep patterns."

They were both silent for a while. The waiter came over and collected their plates and they ordered a coffee.

"So ... where does that leave us, Ams?"

His comment fell on the table and lay there. Amber took a deep breath, took both his hands in hers and said, "As you can tell, I'm a fucking mess right now ... but, I do know this ... I love being with you. Your texts always brighten my day. I feel I can say anything to you. I've known you all my life and ..." she said with a giggle, "we're roughly the same age."

He squeezed her hands and leant forward to kiss her. This time it *was* a passionate 'snog' (although that word rather belittles the feelings stirred in both of them).

She pulled away and said, "Harry, do you like children?"

"Yes, I'm a big kid myself, so I always feel I've got a lot in common with them."

"Good," she whispered.

Chapter 19

When a month had elapsed from the time of Rachel's visit to Mike and he still had shown no interest in coming to Brighton, she rang him one day and said she was coming up to visit. Her intention was to persuade him to come back with her. She didn't say that on the phone.

When she arrived, she was shocked to see him. He'd lost even more weight and he was back to looking unkempt. She'd had to ring the doorbell repeatedly to get him to come to the door.

"I thought you weren't here, I've been ringing for ages."

"Sorry ... I was in the study. I think I might be going a bit deaf."

"Never mind. I'm here now," she said and kissed him on the cheek. "I'll just get my things from the car."

She reached for the bunch of flowers she'd got Millie to make. "These are for you," she said, handing over the beautiful arrangement of roses, delphiniums, carnations, irises and greenery.

He looked a little taken aback – maybe he'd never been given flowers before?

"Oh, thank you, Rachel – what a kind gesture."

"Well, who said men can't receive flowers, anyway?" she laughed.

After entering the house, she took her things to her 'normal' bedroom and then came back downstairs. She couldn't help looking around to see if the house was messy. It certainly seemed as if it could do with a good clean and hoover.

Mike was making her a coffee as she came into the kitchen.

"How have you been, Mike?" she asked, knowing that she wouldn't get a straight answer.

"I'm okay," he said, without turning round.

"It must be incredibly hard."

"Yes."

"Are you sleeping?"

"Not very well, no."

"Do you think the pills are working?"

"Maybe ... although it's hard to tell. Maybe I do feel a little less ... a little less distraught."

Rachel didn't have much experience, so felt she couldn't comment except to say, "Did you contact that counsellor I found for you?"

"I did. We've scheduled a session on Zoom for next week."

"That's great."

The conversation was stilted and she thought she ought to stop interrogating him, it didn't feel right. So she changed tack.

"Shall we go out for a walk after this? I'd love to stretch my legs after that long drive."

"Okay, if you'd like to."

And that's how her visit continued. She would instigate the chat, he'd respond but there was nothing else coming from him. She made a point of getting him out to exercise each day, cooked him nutritious meals and cleaned the house from top to bottom.

He made a vague attempt to say she shouldn't, but his heart wasn't in it and she insisted.

On the third day of her visit, she managed to persuade him to come to Brighton with her. He didn't cave in immediately but maybe, in the end, even he could see it would be good to have a change of scene. He took his laptop so that he could do his Zoom counselling session; his compassionate leave was coming to an end and Rachel was keen to try to get him back to work.

As they got in the car for the journey, he turned and looked at the house; the house where he and Jen had lived and was now a symbol of his loneliness. He sighed and Rachel noticed how he wiped his eyes once he'd sat down.

They set off and very soon into the journey, he fell asleep. He was so heavily comatose that his head fell forward for at least half an hour and Rachel was concerned about his neck but then his head came up again, he settled back and continued his sleep. She had to brake heavily at one point and he still didn't wake. It was almost as if he'd at last relaxed and succumbed to being looked after.

He only woke as they entered Brighton and were stop-starting in traffic.

"Oh my God, Rachel, I'm so sorry. I don't know what happened there …"

"Don't worry about it, Mike. It was lovely to see you so peaceful. You obviously needed it."

"Mmm," he said, peering out of the window. There were people, cars, bikes, dogs – everywhere. So different from his sleepy village. They were going along the front, the blustery sea looking as grey as ever. Passing the pier, they carried on slowly making progress. At a traffic light, Rachel opened the window and even above the traffic fumes, the smell of the sea wafted in.

"This is going to be great for you, Mike, it really is. To be amongst people, to breathe in the sea air, to be somewhere totally different. This is the tonic you need. I think Jen would approve of me dragging you here."

"You didn't drag me, Rach. I think I wanted to escape that house. It isn't the same without Jen in it."

"No, I know."

They drove on and soon they drew up at Rachel's. He got out and looked around. "I can't remember the last time I was here, can you?"

"No ... was it Jen's birthday?"

"Yes, maybe."

She showed him to his room and left him to unpack.

They hadn't discussed how long he was staying.

As far as Rachel was concerned, he could stay forever.

SINCE GEORGE HAD RETURNED to the flat all those months ago, he and Beth had slowly found each other again. It had been a long process; George was worried about alienating her and constantly agonised about what to say.

He wanted to let her know how he felt about her, without frightening her off again. So instead of words, he chose actions ... he'd bring flowers home for her, hoping that, in a small way, they'd brighten up her day. He'd invite her out for date nights formally – organising theatre tickets and tickets to see her favourite bands.

On two occasions, he'd arranged a weekend away as a surprise. Once he'd discovered when her next weekend off was, he'd get on the internet and look for a romantic hotel in a beautiful setting.

The first trip had been to the Lake District; it had been a great success and they'd walked for miles. For the second one, he'd taken her to Paris, on the train and they'd stayed near the Eiffel Tower. Neither of them had been before, so they'd done as much of the touristy things as they could, the highlight being a dinner by candlelight in a boat, drifting down the Seine.

Beth had responded to all these gestures with what he now believed was love; she'd smile at him differently, grab his hand when they were walking along and send him little texts during the day, saying things like, *Can't wait to see you later. Won't be home til midnight. Hope you'll still be awake, if you know what I mean xx*

Things were going so well, that he even began dreaming of a second proposal. Did he dare or was it madness?

He simply didn't know.

It was about two weeks into Mike's stay at Rachel's and although he knew about his stay, he hadn't interfered at all. To be frank, he wanted to leave them to get on with it. The last thing he wanted right now was another family drama.

He'd arranged with Beth to meet her at 6pm at a new restaurant near his work. They were going to eat early and then they were going to a comic play at a theatre around the corner. The show started at 7.30 so they had about an hour to eat.

He was already seated and saw her come in; he still got a buzz every time he saw her; she looked so chic, her hair so shiny and bouncy. He stood up and waved and she came across. They kissed warmly and he held both her hands.

"You look stunning," he said.

"Well, thank you kind sir."

She laughed as she took off her jacket and gave it to the waiter who was standing patiently by the table.

They didn't spend too long deciding on their food as they were tight for time. He chose a fillet steak and she had fish pie. When it arrived it was very artistically plated up and it tasted delicious. They each had a glass of wine to accompany the food.

After some every day chat about their days (Beth had had a free day and had done nothing except read, she said, and his day had been fraught with 'a million meetings') she put down her knife and fork, wiped her mouth with her pristine white linen serviette and said, "George, I want to say something."

He put down his glass and looked at her curiously, hoping that it wasn't going to be bad news. But she was smiling ...

"George, I've wanted to say this for *so* long. I need to apologise for how I behaved that day." She reached across the table and took his hand. "I behaved like a spoilt brat, I really did. I don't know what came over me. I've thought about it so much, particularly recently ... you tried to do something so lovely, so romantic and I threw it back in your face. I'm so sorry." She lifted his hand to her lips.

George felt tears spring to his eyes and he tried to blink them away.

"Don't worry, Beth. It was a long time ago, all forgotten," he whispered, even though he knew he'd thought about that terrible moment every day, ever since.

"Well, I haven't forgotten it, George. I haven't treated you well, I know I haven't. I had this fear of 'settling' for the first person who said they loved me. I had this fear of being committed, of being trapped. I think my parents' relationship may have influenced me but that's no excuse. I can see now, George, that you're perfect for me. We're good together and ... far from being trapped, I feel safe, I feel secure with you."

"I don't know what to say ..."

"You don't need to say anything. I've seen all the wonderful gestures you've made recently. I know you were making an incredible effort but you know, you don't need to any more, George. I love you, totally, and I *know* that now."

She stared at him, smiling and said, "... In fact, am I too late to say ...'yes'?"

George couldn't believe what he was hearing. After all this time, was she really saying what he *thought* she was? He was tongue-tied, he had no idea what to say.

"Perhaps I should put it another way ... George, would you do me the honour of marrying me?" She smiled and took his other hand. "I'm not going to get down on one knee, though," she laughed.

His smile was so huge, it was as Rachel used to say, hooked over both ears. "Beth, I would *love* to marry you ... I can't believe this. No and don't, please, make any grand gestures. This is perfect, exactly how it is."

At that exact moment, the waiter came over and said, "Was everything okay with the meal?"

They both burst out laughing, leaving the poor boy looking rather bewildered. "Everything's absolutely *perfect*. Thank you," said George. He was tempted to tell him what had just happened, but he stopped himself. This was between the two of them. They didn't need to make a song and dance about it.

"Would you like desserts?" asked the waiter.

"No, thank you," said George, making sure Beth agreed with him. "Just the bill, please."

As he walked away, leaving them alone, Beth said, "I hardly dare ask, but what happened to the gorgeous ring you bought me?"

"I've still got it. I didn't want to take it back. I was hoping ... one day, you'd say yes, but I never thought it would be me who said 'yes'."

"Also, George, now that I've finally seen the light, I'd like to get married soon. I don't want a long engagement ... do you? What's the point in waiting?"

"No ... oh my goodness, are we really doing this?"

"Yes," she laughed. "Let's get married. Just a small ceremony ... in a register office, with a few friends and family. No fuss. We could even come here, to this restaurant, for the dinner afterwards, the place where at last, I stopped being an idiot."

"You're not an idiot, Beth ..."

"Well, I think I am. I met the right man ... and now it's the right time."

They paid the bill and walked hand in hand to the theatre. They joined the throng of people outside, waiting to get in. To everyone else, they looked like an ordinary couple ... but to George, they were the perfect couple, the soul-mate couple, the till-death-do-us-part couple.

They laughed at all the jokes in the play, holding hands and looking at each other. At the end, when the audience stood up to applaud, he turned to her and said through the noise of the clapping, "This is the best day of my life."

"Mine too. I love you, George."

"WOULD YOU MIND IF I ring my Mum and tell her our news?" said George, a few days later. They'd wanted a couple of days, just the two of them, to enjoy being engaged. Beth kept looking at her left hand, admiring the ring, which had fitted perfectly.

George kept looking at Beth, admiring his future wife.

"Of course ... go for it. Perhaps we could go down to Brighton on Friday and take her out for meal?"

"That would be so nice. She's got Mike staying, you know, the friend she's been looking after since his wife, Jen, died."

They were sitting, cuddled up on the sofa, not really watching a drama on the TV. George reached for the remote control and turned down the volume.

He put it back on the coffee table and then turned to her and said, "I need to tell you something, Beth. It doesn't affect us or anything, but I want to be absolutely honest with you."

"God, what is it?" she said, looking anxious.

"I found out something that is pretty fundamental ... about who I am. I found out during the first lockdown."

"What on earth do you mean?"

"I didn't tell you *then* because we weren't getting on so well and also, it was meant to be a secret ... but I don't want any secrets any more. They're corrosive and I don't want anything to come between us, ever."

"So, what is it?"

"Well, unbelievably, it turns out I'm not my father, Zach's, son. My biological father is ... Mike, who's staying with Mum now."

She sat up and turned to face him.

"What? So, you're telling me, you found this out ages ago and you never *told* me?"

"I'm so sorry Beth, I didn't want to lie to you ..."

"No, I don't mean that I'm angry or anything ... I mean that you've had to live with this enormous piece of information all this time and you didn't think you could tell me? I'm so sorry, George. That must have been *awful* for you. I wish you'd felt able to share it with me. What a shock to find out something like that out, after thinking all your life you were Zach's son. How do you feel about it now?"

"Well, I was in bits about it, as you can imagine. But when Mum told me, she'd only just relatively recently found out herself, by doing a DNA test. She'd always thought it might be a possibility. Harry and Amber were there at the time but because Jen had had cancer, we didn't want to say anything ... and then she died and Mike hasn't coped at all well. I'm glad we haven't told him now, it just wasn't the right time. The four of us decided to keep it between us ... but maybe now ... maybe now is the right time?"

"Maybe ... only *you* can make that decision. It would be lovely to have your 'real' father at the wedding, wouldn't it?"

Beth, as always, had said exactly the right thing. He stood up and went into the kitchen to phone his mum. He told her that they'd both like to come down to Brighton this weekend. He could hear the hesitation in her voice, when she said, yes, of course they could come – she knew that George and Mike would finally be together in the same room and she wasn't sure how things would play out ... but she wanted to meet Beth at last and she could tell from his voice that he had some news. She was hoping that at last things had worked out for them both.

"So, we're going," he said, coming back into the room. "It turns out you're going to meet *both* my parents."

"Do you want to tell him the truth?"

"I do, yes. But I'm going to see how he is ... he's been through so much. He really loved Jen and to lose your wife to cancer and coronavirus must have been horrific. He was so absolutely powerless. He couldn't even be with her when she died."

"That's so tragic, poor man. Maybe it will give him a boost. Who wouldn't be proud and happy to have such a gorgeous man as his son?" and she reached forward and kissed him. "I'm so pleased you've told me. I'm just sorry you didn't tell me before. No more secrets.

"Yes ... no more secrets."

THEY GOT THE 7.05 TRAIN from London the following Friday evening. It was as crowded as ever ... full of people on their way for a fun-filled weekend by the sea. George felt both excited and nervous. He was excited to show Beth his home city – apparently she'd never been before, which he couldn't understand (why wouldn't you want to go to Brighton, for goodness sake, he laughed with her) and he was nervous about seeing Mike. He'd always liked him but had never really given him much thought. He was just his mum's friend, Amber's father, one of the close group of friends that hung out together.

Now, he'd become someone else completely; the person who'd given him his genes.

It made him compare Zach and Mike – one who'd brought him up, one who'd given him life. Fathers were confusing people ... it took so little effort for a man to become a father, unlike the mother who spent nine whole months carrying and nurturing a child. Once his sperm was inside the woman, that was it ... he could choose to walk away or stay. Mike, of course, never knew ... George wondered what would have happened if he'd learnt about him earlier. Would he have left Jen or would she have chucked him out? Would he have helped with bringing him up? Would he have contributed financially?

The more he thought about it, the more he realised that, despite his first thoughts, his mother had probably done the right thing. It would have disrupted Jen's life and she was totally blameless in all this. He was no longer angry with Rachel ... he was, when he found out, but it was *he* who'd pried into her private box, *he* who'd forced her into confessing. If he'd never found that box, he'd never have known.

And that made him sad.

He realised that he was glad he'd found out who his real father was; he felt an affection towards Mike that came from deep within him. He'd never got on with Zach; he'd always felt different from him and distant and now he'd got over the shock, he was glad that he didn't have his genes. He didn't feel proud of that thought and he decided he would never say it out loud, to anyone.

They hopped on a bus outside the station and as they went on their twenty minute journey, George pointed out landmarks and talked about things from his past. He still loved that feeling of 'coming home' and that was all to do with his *mother*, not his father.

They walked, arms linked, up the driveway.

"So, this is it. Here we are."

"What a beautiful house, George. You must have had a great time living here."

He looked up at it, now silhouetted against the night sky, the odd light shining brightly from a couple of windows, and said, "I did ... yes, I truly did."

He put his key in the front door lock, turned it and shouted, "We're here," and Rachel and Mike, his parents, came into the hall to greet them.

GEORGE'S FIRST REACTION to Mike, was a combination of love and shock. He looked so different from when he'd seen him before. He'd always thought of Mike as a large man, with his rugby player's physique, as a man full of life and fun – but the person in front of him was smaller, diminished.

He felt an overwhelming feeling of sorrow for him and he hugged him hard when they greeted each other; before, they would have probably, in the past, have just banged each other on the back in a matey way.

Rachel looked on with a smile.

Beth also hugged Rachel. Despite the fact that they'd never met in 'real' life before, they felt like they knew each other and immediately recognised a bond – they knew they both loved George with their entire being.

George was taken aback at how similar they looked, seeing them side by side. It was almost as if he'd tried to find a clone of his mother.

Rachel had been so excited to hear their news; she'd insisted on breaking open a bottle of champagne that she'd had for two years in a rack and they'd had a celebration supper.

They told them their plans for a small, intimate wedding which would take place as soon as possible and they talked about possible venues. Rachel put forward the idea of Brighton and the reception at home, with caterers – and suddenly that seemed *perfect*. Beth was up for it – she said she was easy where it took place, she just wanted to get married.

On the Saturday, when they'd all gone for a walk along the Undercliff towards Saltdean, Mike and Beth were way ahead and George, his arm linked through Rachel's said, "How would you feel if we told Mike, Mum? He seems stronger, even though he still looks thin but ... do you think he'd cope? Doesn't he have a right to know?"

"I'm not sure ... I'm so torn. It does feel like the right time to tell him, while we're all here together. If that's what you want, then, yes ... but we'll have to handle it carefully. Shall we do it tonight?"

"Yes ... I just want to get it over with. It might be selfish on my part, but I do think he has the right to know."

They'd built up a healthy appetite; they'd been out for a couple of hours and the sea air had invigorated all of them.

Rachel had wanted to continue the celebration of their engagement with a trip to a restaurant that was getting amazing reviews on Facebook. "My treat," she said to them all on their way back home.

They duly all showered and dressed a little bit smarter, gathering in the sitting room for pre-dinner drinks. Before George and Beth came down, Rachel said to Mike, "Are you all right with this, Mike? Do you feel up to it?"

"Yes, of course. I want to say something ... Rach. Thank you for having me to stay. You were right, as always, it's done me good. And you were right about the counsellor ... he's really helping. I've never been one to talk about my feelings but he somehow knows the right triggers and responses. He even thinks your idea of a letter to Jen, is a good one." He took her hand, "I'm truly grateful to you, Rach."

"I've loved having you here, Mike."

They set out, walking again, as it was only ten minutes by foot.

It turned out the food was excellent and the conversation flowed.

After the main course, George looked across the table at Mike and decided it was now or never. He looked at Rachel, widened his eyes and raised his eyebrows and she nodded in answer.

At the next short lull, George, holding Beth's hand tightly under the table said, "Mike ... Mum and I need to tell you something ... we're not sure whether it's the right time to tell you, but it's something very important."

Mike froze ... he looked towards Rachel and back to George. He was confused.

"Tell me ... the worst possible thing has happened to me, losing Jen ... nothing can be worse than that."

George froze too; his hands were clammy and sweaty but Beth squeezed his hand, encouraging him.

"Mike ... not so very long ago, Mum found out ..." and he looked across at Rachel, willing her to join in, "that ... I ... am ... your ... biological son."

Mike stared ahead, as if he hadn't heard.

"What ..."

"Yes, Mike you're my father. My real father."

Rachel came in. "Mike, I'd always wondered ... but I didn't want to upset the status quo, I didn't want to upset Jen. So ... I let the idea bury itself below the surface of my life but when Zach left me, I knew I had to know ... so, with Zach's hair and George's ... I was able to do a test and it came back that Zach wasn't his father. *You're his father*, Mike."

Tears were falling down her cheeks as she was talking.

He was silent for what felt like an eternity and then said, "This is a lot for me to take in ... would you mind if I went for a walk outside, on my own?"

"No, no ... we'll order some coffee. You take all the time you need."

He pushed his chair back and walked slowly across the restaurant and out of the door.

"Do you think I should go with him?" said George.

"No, leave him. Let him absorb it on his own," said Rachel.

They stared at each other, not sure what to say or how to react.

"It's not every day that you get news like that," said Beth, squeezing George's arm. "He's going to need a lot of time to digest it."

The waiter came over and cleared the table. They ordered coffees and wondered when he'd come back in.

What if he didn't come back?

What if he was so shocked, he decided to leave Brighton?

"Maybe I should go and find him now," said Rachel, looking at her watch.

"He went at least fifteen minutes ago. Do you think he's all right?" said George.

Rachel stood up and said, "I'll just pop outside and see if I can see him," and she was gone.

When she got outside, she looked around and couldn't see anyone resembling Mike. It was a crowded street – she walked along it, praying she'd find him.

But, suddenly, there he was ... sitting on a bench, under a street light.

She didn't say anything to him, she simply sat down next to him, their shoulders touching.

"Are you angry with me?" she whispered.

There was a long silence but the noise of the city wrapped itself around them. Laughing groups of young people walked by, a motorbike roared, cars revved.

"No, Rachel ... how can I be angry with you? You've carried this with you for so long. If I'm honest ... I too have often wondered. When you got pregnant so soon after me coming to the camp, it went through my mind ... I would see likenesses between Amber and George but then I'd put it down to my imagination. When he took up rugby, again, I thought ... but loads of boys play rugby, what would that prove? Over the years, I've tried to rationalise it. All I can say is that I'm so pleased Jen never knew. What good would it have done? She would have been heartbroken. She wanted to have more children and we couldn't."

His hands were resting on his knees. Rachel took one ... she'd avoided all physical contact with him since Jen's death. She wanted only to be his friend but now, she had to touch him. She had to feel the warmth of his skin against hers.

"I hope you feel I've done you proud? George is such a beautiful man ... kind-hearted, loving ... and a wonderful son. And now it's *your* time to get to know him. I can see how alike you are."

"It's funny ... I feel like I've known all along, even though I haven't. It seems so logical, so inevitable, so ... right."

"Let's go back; he'll be wondering if you're okay. Let's go back, so that you can meet your son properly," said Rachel and they stood up and walked back to the restaurant.

The Epilogue

Many years later, the island of Cyprus, was set out beneath them as the plane descended. They were flying over the sea, as blue as a sapphire, a chalk, white line feathering the edge. The land got nearer and she could see white buildings with red roofs, wind turbines and a smattering of swimming pools scattered around like blue material on the red soil.

She looked ahead at the stewardesses sitting and strapped in, waiting to land. In truth, she wasn't that keen on this part of a flight, the strange lurching drops, the loud bang of the wheels being released beneath, the anticipation of the land rushing up to meet you. She turned to him and gently took his hand. He smiled, that wonderful smile that had always reassured her.

They hadn't been back since that fateful holiday, nearly twenty years ago but her heart was racing at the thought of walking into the Cypriot sunshine again. She'd thought about this place so much since then, she couldn't wait to revisit her memories.

So much had changed since then. Now, at 74, she was officially old. She didn't feel it, but when she looked in the mirror she could see the wrinkles etched into her skin, the saggy arms and the unmistakable excess round her middle. She'd come to accept it.

Poor Jen had never got the chance to get old.

She'd never been happier. Yes, she was what a lot of people would call an old woman, but she was fit, she was content, she was active and above all, she was with the love of her life.

As the wheels screeched and bounced along the runway, she squeezed his hand. However many times she experienced landing, she couldn't stop her body reacting to it. He reached over and kissed her cheek.

"We're down," he said, "you can relax."

The speed began to ease, the scenery passing the window slowed and finally they came to walking speed, pulled into their space and the engines stopped. She could hear the sound of seatbelts clicking, mobile phone notifications pinging, lots of chatter and people standing, opening the overhead lockers. She picked up her bag from the floor and began to pack her things away. They, however, sat still. They had a row of three to themselves; there was no hurry to get out, they were content to let everyone else stand in the aisle, leaning on the chair backs.

Let the younger ones hurry out.

Soon, the doors opened and everyone started filing out; they continued to wait until the aisle was almost empty.

"Okay, time to move," she said, standing stiffly.

"Right," he said. "You go ahead and I'll get the case down."

She waited for him at the top of the steps and as he joined her, they both looked around, remembering. The familiar smell ... the piercing light ... everything came flooding back to them in that moment.

"It's good to be back," he said.

Last time, he'd been with Jen, his darling Jen. He could feel his stomach turn over at the memory of her. It was all so long ago but yet so familiar. He felt her by his side, as he began to follow Rachel down the steps.

Once they were on the tarmac, they walked shoulder to shoulder towards the arrivals building, Jen's presence flitting effortlessly from one to the other.

Rachel's best friend, Mike's wife, forever with them, wishing them well in their journey through old age.

THIS TIME, THEY WERE staying in a luxury hotel; gone were the days of self-catering holidays. They both wanted the comfort of room service, buffet breakfasts and evening meals provided. They laughed that they'd earned the right to a bit of pampering at 'their age'.

They hired a car at the airport, though; they weren't *that* old that they didn't want to be independent and go exploring, that would be a step too far.

They found the hotel easily, checked in, unpacked and were lounging by the pool in the golden, evening sun within half an hour of their arrival.

After ten minutes on the lounger, she got up and dipped her toes into the pool. It felt as warm as a bath and without further thought, she walked down the steps and floated forward.

"Come on in," she said, as she hung onto the side near where Mike was lying. "It's heavenly. It feels amazing after the journey."

"Okay, I'll be in, in a minute," he answered and she swam off.

After a few minutes of no movement from him, she swam up to the edge again and flicked some water in his direction, which made a direct hit.

"Hey!" he said, sitting up slowly. "Okay, I'm coming."

He stood up, struggling slightly to get off the lounger. He put his hands in the small of his back, moving his hips to loosen them. His body was much the same as it had been (slowly the weight had gone back on) but with a few extra aches and pains.

Rachel looked up at him, filled with love.

He walked down the steps and sank into the water like a sea lion. He swam to her and put his arms round her waist.

"Heaven, isn't it?" she said.

"It is."

She twisted herself around so that she was facing him. "We're so lucky ... to have each other. So many people at our age are on their own and desperately lonely. Yet here we are, friends since God knows when ... and together. I think Jen would be happy for us, don't you?"

He moved his hands around her back and pulled her in. Their stomachs squashed together; he placed his cheek on hers.

"I think she'd be pleased that we'd eventually found each other, after all."

"Can you remember when she swam naked that night in the villa's pool?"

"She looked so beautiful that night," he said, "I can still see her ..."

They hugged each other hard, remembering.

THEY WERE DETERMINED not to spend too much of their holiday going down memory lane ... they wanted to visit *new* places too but they couldn't resist returning to the village where the villa was.

They set out one morning after a late, lazy breakfast. It was only a twenty-five minute journey and they remembered the way so well. Rachel was secretly a little worried about seeing Demetris after all these years. She couldn't help but feel guilty; she hadn't treated him well, she knew she hadn't. And she'd never told Mike about her relationship with someone so much younger than herself. He'd found it bad enough when Amber and Leo got together; she thought he'd find her dalliance with the young Cypriot, faintly ridiculous.

They drove around the village to get their bearings.

Nothing had changed; it was still the sleepy, dusty, quiet haven of Cypriot charm it always had been. They reckoned there were a couple of new houses on the outskirts, but the rest of the village seemed to be stuck in a time warp. The next generation of cats and kittens wandered languidly in the shade, a dog barked at them as they drove past, from the end of his chain on a front patio which was covered with pots of geraniums.

"Shall we pull up here and have a coffee?" said Mike, as they drove near the square.

Not wanting to show any reluctance, she said, "Yes, good idea; we could have a drink and then walk from here to the villa."

They left the car and walked to the taverna; it hadn't changed much, except for the fact that there were newer, smarter tables and chairs and white cloths on every table, with delicate glass vases holding real flowers – but it still had that timeless quality. The village shop was there too, with its array of huge water melons, avocados, nectarines and grapes.

No one was about; they sat down at one of the tables, wondering if they would be noticed by anyone, except the local cat which had appeared from nowhere and sat expectantly by

Rachel's side. Mike looked at the menu, which was largely the same as he remembered but with a more modern-looking design.

"Would you like a coffee ... or something cold?" he asked.

"Oh, fresh orange, please." She looked around, waiting for the embarrassment of Demetris appearing. What on earth would she say to him?

Suddenly there was a familiar voice.

"Kalimera, my friends!"

They both turned, to see the outline of Andreas in shadow against the sun; as he approached they saw he was, of course, older, a little bulkier, a lot slower, but with the same baked-in smile.

"Kalimera, Andreas. Do you remember us? I'm Mike ... and this is Rachel. We came here for a holiday many, many years ago," said Mike, standing up and extending his hand.

His smile broadened and his eyes twinkled. "Of course, my friends. You came to my farm, I remember it well," he said, grasping Mike's hand. "Your party had some difficulties, I think ... you, my dear ... your husband ..." and he looked between the two of them, waiting for someone to help him out.

"Yes, my husband ... we broke up, do you remember? And Mike's daughter, Amber ... do you remember her? She arrived and everything was turned upside down?"

"How can I forget? Your lives were very complicated to me," he laughed. "Is it just you two, this time? Where is your wife, Mr Mike?"

Andreas realised his mistake and started making a fumbling apology.

"... Is none of my business, I sorry."

"No ... don't worry, my friend ... Jen died many years ago, I'm afraid. It was cancer." He looked at Rachel, wondering how to continue.

"And now we are together, Andreas," she said, smiling. "And together we have lots of grandchildren. One of my sons, Harry, is married to Mike's daughter, Amber, now and they have three children. My other son, George, has two ... Let me show you some pictures on my phone," and she got out her mobile and proudly showed off her beautiful grandchildren.

"That is so good for you both," he said, "... my wife is dead. Her heart. I miss her every day ..."

"I'm so sorry, Andreas," said Rachel, taking his hand. "How long ago?"

"It was five years ... but it feels yesterday. I am lonely on the farm ... but I have my animals."

There was no sign of Demetris. She wanted to ask a leading question but was saved by Mike.

"And what about Demetris? Is *he* still here in the village?"

"No ... after all his life, he has moved, to another place. He is married now, he too has three beautiful children."

Rachel was relieved not to have to face him. She was so pleased that he'd found happiness. Andreas had implied he'd moved far away with his 'another place' and she was sad for him.

"Oh, that's lovely. Do you see him at all – has he gone far?"

"Not far. He lives in the next village, with the parents of his wife."

Cyprus villages were such close-knit communities; sometimes it was as if the next village was a million miles away.

"And what about the other couple?" said Andreas, "Mr Leo, was it? And the lady with beautiful red hair, she go home early?"

"Yes, they are very happy together. They have a daughter, Thea."

"But ... Mr Leo ... he was with the young girl, I remember."

"Yes," said Rachel, "you have *such* a good memory, Andreas ... but it didn't work out and Leo went back to Grace. Their son, Josh, sees Leo all the time as they all live close to each other. It all turned out perfectly in the end."

"My goodness. Cyprus is a very sleepy place, not like England," he laughed.

They ordered their drinks, Andreas sitting at their table, chatting as he used to do. At least he had his taverna for company, Rachel thought.

"And what has happened to the gorgeous villa we rented, Andreas?" she asked.

"Well, it is no longer a holiday place. An English couple bought it, maybe since two years. They live here now. They are very nice, they sometimes come to my taverna."

"We're going to walk round there now, just to take a look," said Mike. "How much do we owe you?"

"No ... it is, how you say, on the house?" he laughed. "It is good to see my old friends again."

They didn't argue and thanked him, shaking his hand and saying they would be back, but knowing they probably wouldn't be.

They walked down the hill and along the drowsy streets. Rachel remembered all the pictures she'd taken on her mobile phone when they were here before, but somehow she didn't feel the need this time. It was all so seared into her memory, it was as if she'd never been away.

Eventually, they came to the house. The blue painted shutters looked a little less tired than when they'd been here before; the pots of lavender and geraniums, each side of the door, were still there, proudly inviting visitors in.

The big blue door was firmly shut, however, and there was no sign of life.

Both Rachel and Mike were somehow pleased not to go in; it was enough to just *be* there, to stand and gaze.

The memories came pouring out of the windows, spilling through the shutters, filling their hearts and minds.

"What a holiday that was," said Rachel, squeezing Mike's hand.

He turned to her, kissed her gently on the cheek, and said, "It certainly was."

THE END

Also by Sarah Catherine Knights

The Aphrodite Trilogy:
Aphrodite's Child
Now Is All There Is
Shadows in the Rock
The Life Series:
Life Happens
Love is a State of Mind

About the Author

Sarah Catherine Knights is a British novelist and lives in the beautiful town of Malmesbury and has done since 1985. She came to Wiltshire, like so many others, because her husband was in the Royal Air Force. The family have now settled there and so she spends hours walking through the surrounding fields with her black labrador, Mabel and as she walks, she thinks about her next writing project.

Sarah studied English Literature at Birmingham University and went on to do a Creative Writing MA at Bath Spa University where she started to write her debut novel, "Aphrodite's Child" which was published at the beginning of 2014.

"Aphrodite's Child" grew out of the family's posting to Cyprus with the RAF in the early nineties. While there, Sarah realised it would make a great setting for a novel. With its microcosm of English life, the camp was a strange place to live. At that time, there was little or no communication with the UK and being somewhat cut off from the island too, life inside the camp became intensified and sometimes like a prolonged Mediterranean holiday. It was easy to dream up a dramatic storyline.

Having been an English teacher of both secondary level children and foreign business people, Sarah retired to concentrate of photography and writing.

Her three children have now all flown the nest but often come home for chaotic weekends of dog walks, laughter and noisy meals around the large kitchen table. The whole family, including Peter her husband, have been very supportive and patient with Sarah's late career change as a novelist, always willing to help with the plot or read a draft.

Read more at www.sarahcatherineknights.com.

Printed in Dunstable, United Kingdom